Into the Wilderness

THE LONG HUNTERS

**Center Point
Large Print**

**This Large Print Book carries the
Seal of Approval of N.A.V.H.**

Into the Wilderness

THE LONG HUNTERS

Rosanne Bittner

CENTER POINT PUBLISHING
THORNDIKE, MAINE

This Center Point Large Print edition
is published in the year 2006 by arrangement with
Tom Doherty Associates, LLC.

Copyright © 2002 by Rosanne Bittner.

All rights reserved.

The text of this Large Print edition is unabridged. In other
aspects, this book may vary from the original edition. Printed in
Thailand. Set in 16-point Times New Roman type.

ISBN: 1-58547-862-8
ISBN 13: 978-1-58547-862-0

Library of Congress Cataloging-in-Publication Data

Bittner, Rosanne, 1945-
    Into the wilderness : the long hunters / Rosanne Bittner.--Center Point large print ed.
        p. cm.
    ISBN 1-58547-862-8 (lib. bdg. : alk. paper)
    1. United States--History--Colonial period, ca. 1600-1775--Fiction. 2. United
States--History--French and Indian War, 1755-1763--Fiction. 3. Indians of North
America--Wars--1750-1815--Fiction. 4. Iroquois Indians--Wars--Fiction. 5. Large
type books. I. Title.

PS3552.I77396I58 2006
813'.54--dc22

2006016298

Dedicated to the great Iroquois Nation and to the brave settlers who faced the incredible power, cleverness and brutality of such a formidable enemy during the French and Indian War.

I have written about many western Native American tribes in previous books, but I don't believe I have ever encountered any who could be as dreaded an enemy in times of war as the eastern tribes, especially the Iroquois. Studying some of the accounts of their war tactics in preparation for this book was not easy reading. I have incorporated some of this stark reality into my story. It can't be helped, so be prepared.

Perhaps upon reading this book, you will develop a whole new respect for the bravery and determination of our early settlers, as well as for the dominance and fierceness of the eastern Native Americans. I know that I did.

ACKNOWLEDGMENTS

I could not have written this book without the aid of a book called *Wilderness Empire*, by Allan W. Eckert (Little, Brown & Company, Toronto, Canada)—a must-read for anyone interested in the early history of the United States. For nearly twenty years I have written about America's West of the 1800s and western Native Americans. That is my first love; but I must say that *Wilderness Empire* and other books about early America by Mr. Eckert have stirred in me a great interest to write more books set in the East and involving the eastern tribes. There are few moments in history as exciting as the early years of the formation of this nation.

I also garnered a great deal of information from the *Atlas of the North American Indian*, by Carl Waldman (illustrations by Molly Braun; Checkmark Books, New York City).

The biggest problem in writing this story was sorting out which Natives were involved in which area and on which side during the French and Indian uprisings against the English. As an example, tribes living from Michigan east to the Atlantic comprised Ottawa, Potawatomi, Kickapoo, Miami, Shawnee, Susquehannock, Lenni Lenape, Huron, Seneca, Cayuga, Onondaga, Oneida, Mohawk, Mahican, Pequot, Nipmuck, Penacook, Narragansett, Penobscot, Abenaki,

Algonkin, Nanticoke, Powhatan, Tuscarora, Passamaquoddy and Maliseet. Many of these tribes made up the whole of the Iroquois Nation. Some were deeply involved in the French and Indian War, such as Chief Pontiac of the Ottawas; others had very little to do with that war. Most, except for the Mohawk, favored the French.

Sorting all this out and deciding which tribes to use in this story while keeping my facts straight was a formidable task, and if I have misrepresented anything, my apologies. I followed actual history as closely as possible. Forts/locations mentioned here really existed, and major battles really did happen, as in the slaughter at Pickawillany. I have depicted real characters, such as George Washington and Governor Robert Dinwiddie of Virginia, as best I could, based on their roles in the history of this story.

The major characters in this book and their personal stories are fictitious.

One last thank-you—to my sister, Linda Henke, for helping me with some frantic, last-minute proofreading.

Into the Wilderness

THE LONG HUNTERS

1

June 1752

Noah charged through the cornfield, bending low to stay hidden in the half-grown stalks. He'd left his buckskin shirt behind in the canoe hidden downstream with twenty other canoes, and the edges of the corn leaves cut at his face and bare arms.

The weather was hot, damn hot. Besides that, what lay ahead meant he'd need complete freedom of movement. His musket already primed, he carried it in one hand as he batted at the corn leaves with the other. At his waist hung his large hunting knife in its sheath, and a tomahawk.

For the moment he felt as much an Indian as the Miami, Huron and Ottawa who ran with him, beside him, ahead of him, behind him. French soldiers, mostly infantrymen in blue and white, were also part of this war party, all on a mission: to attack the English trading post of Pickawillany in Ohio Territory. The French were determined to seal their hold on all land west of the Ohio River, which meant destroying Pickawillany.

He skimmed over the packed earth in moccasined feet. Most of the Indians with him were barefoot and nearly naked, as was the custom among most Iroquois in summer's heat. Soon the sounds of men panting as they ran grew into the sounds of women and children screaming as they fled the cornfields, heading for the trading post as the French and Iroquois routed them from the fields. The attacking Iroquois began slaying as many as they could catch, as did the French soldiers.

How he hated being a part of this! He couldn't do a damn thing to help the women and children falling to this cruel enemy. He could have warned them, but the words of his good friend, Miami Chief Cold Foot, nudged at his conscience: *Do not warn them, my friend. If you do, it will be very bad for me and my people. You know what Chief Pontiac will do.*

Cold Foot had saved his life three years ago, when Noah was attacked by a bear. For weeks he'd lain in Cold Foot's village being cared for by the Miami. He owed them. But the people Chief Pontiac and his French cohorts attacked today were also Miami— those who'd chosen to side with the English. The man who led these people was Chief Unemakemi, who'd become unpopular with the Detroit-area Miami. It was those Miami, led by Pontiac, who now warred against their own people.

Already bodies lay strewn about as Noah exited the cornfield. Those women still alive hoisted their babies under their arms and tried to reach the wooden stockade ahead of them. Their men poured from the fort to protect them, and in minutes cries of horror filled the air as one-on-one fighting took place.

The attack came as a complete surprise: more than two hundred primed warriors led by a bloodthirsty Chief Pontiac eager to take scalps. Noah had spied for the English for years, ever since his precious wife was killed by the French and Indian attack on Albany seven years ago. Hate was all he'd felt since then, and a desire for revenge against the French. As a spy, he'd ended up a part of this horrendous mission, hired by the unwitting French to scout for their French soldiers. If somehow he could have warned these people, and they had appeared prepared for this attack, Pontiac would have blamed it on Cold Foot, thinking the old chief had managed to get word to them after promising not to do so. Among the Iroquois, to betray one's word meant death, and not an easy one.

They reached the main village, and sickening fear permeated Noah as he dodged arrows and musket fire. This was only one of the sad results of the English and French vying for land and trading rights. Here at Pick-awillany, Miami were fighting Miami, the tribes of the Iroquois becoming split over loyalties. It took a man of considerable experience hunting in the wilds and dealing with the numerous tribes to even know which man was enemy and which was not. Noah had no idea how many English traders might be here, and he had no desire to kill any of them, but kill he must to make his French sympathies appear genuine.

Two Miami warriors headed for him, and he raised his musket, opening a hole in the chest of one man. He tossed the musket aside then and dove headfirst into the midsection of the second man, wrestling him to the ground as he growled with determination. He grasped the man's wrist, twisting viciously until the warrior dropped the knife he carried. Quickly, Noah grabbed the knife and slashed it across the man's throat, grimacing at the blood that spewed forth, hitting him in the face.

There was no time now to feel sympathy for any of them. Still holding the knife, he leapt over the man he'd shot and rammed the knife into the heart of yet a third attacking warrior. Now it was each man for himself. With his left hand he pulled his tomahawk from the loop at his waist and turned to land it into yet another attacker. His own war cries mixed with the others, the air reverberating with screams, war whoops, children crying, men shouting, muskets firing, grunts and blows.

Noah turned and yanked his knife from the dead warrior, and for the next several minutes he fought with knife and tomahawk as the battle progressed toward the wooden stockade, over which Indians and French soldiers swarmed. Noah expected to feel a slash or a blow to his body, but he remained unscathed. Bloody, dismembered bodies lay everywhere, and as the fighting outside the stockade finally eased, Noah turned to see Charles Langlade, a French and Indian long hunter, straddling the mangled body of a Miami warrior.

Noah ran back to pick up his long gun, still surprised he'd not been harmed. When he looked back at

Langlade, he realized the warrior the man had pinned down was Chief Unemakemi himself, a man for whom Langlade carried a deep hatred. The main reason Langlade had agreed to help lead the French here was because Langlade knew he'd find Unemakemi. He wished to kill the chief, simply because Unemakemi had insulted him a year earlier. Now, true to his Indian side, Langlade literally carved the heart out of a still-living Unemakemi. He yanked it out of the man's chest and cut the vessels and tendons holding it, then took a bite out of the still-beating muscle!

There was a time when such behavior would have made Noah vomit. No more. He'd learned the ways of the warrior, as had Langlade. To cut out and eat a man's heart was to gain great strength. He simply turned away for a moment. He could not stop the hideous act. His job was to infiltrate these forces and see what the French were up to. He would have to march back to Quebec with them, which meant he'd probably be forced to spend the winter in Canada before returning to Virginia to report on the things he'd learned and seen: an English trading post, occupied by English-sympathizing Miami Indians, had been attacked by surprise and destroyed; the occupants, including a Miami chief who'd allied himself with the English, brutally slain. He certainly had considerable news for Virginia's Governor Dinwiddie when he returned east.

He looked down at the blood on his own hands,

hardly able to believe he'd been a part of this hell. Besides the bodies of dead Miami Indians, he recognized a few Shawnee. Several of the attacking warriors were also dead and wounded, but the rest were already rejoicing.

Everything had happened so quickly. Noah scanned the hideous scene as the air came alive with screams of victory and death. Sporadic gunfire came from inside the fort, and Pontiac himself headed toward the gates, his body covered in blood, four scalps hanging from his waistband. When the shooting inside died down, Pontiac held up his hands and shouted to those remaining inside.

"Hear me, you warriors who betray we who love the French! You will be let go if you take your families and return to your villages and no longer bring harm to the French. It is your chief, Unemakemi, whom we came here to kill, for he killed and ate the flesh of ten French traders and their slaves! Now you can see he is dead, and you must pledge to no longer call the English your friends! We want only the English traders you now protect! Send them out and the rest of you will not be harmed!"

Langlade proceeded to chop off Unemakemi's head, as a demonstration of what could happen to the others, who were outnumbered. He shouted a warning to them, declaring he'd eaten of Unemakemi's heart, and so had become stronger. Quickly, those inside the fort made an exit, several Miami warriors shoving four English traders ahead of them. Terror showed in their eyes, and to Noah's horror, one of them was young Johnny Peidt!

Johnny glanced at him, and in that moment Noah saw a young man of great courage. Johnny said nothing, even though he knew Noah was an English spy. Revealing that fact might save the young man's life, but both knew it could also spoil Noah's efforts at learning the strength of the French, and what their plans were against the English. Old Cold Foot knew it, too. That was why he'd asked Noah not to warn these Miami. He knew Noah would be mighty tempted to do so. Cold Foot was a good friend. He, too, had kept quiet.

Now it was Noah's turn to keep quiet, to force back the deep urge to run up to Johnny and beg Pontiac not to harm him. He could only pray that would not be necessary. Perhaps they would only take him prisoner. After all, the wealthy William Fairfax was good friends with Johnny's father. He would pay any reward necessary to get Johnny back.

Now Langlade marched in front of the prisoners with Unemakemi's head held high, warning that this was what would happen to other Iroquois who dared call the English friend. Chief Pontiac proceeded to ram his knife into the heart of one of the traders, then yanked it out and turned to slash open the chest of another. He bare-handedly ripped out the man's heart and took a bite from it. Noah's blood ran cold as the chief passed the heart on to other warriors, who proceeded to eat of it before tossing it to the ground for dogs to fight over.

Johnny! Noah screamed inside as Pontiac walked up to the young man. Johnny's eyes grew wide with horror, and Noah was forced to look away. He heard a hideous grunt, and he knew Pontiac's knife had found its mark. There came another grunt and a ripping sound. He closed his eyes when he heard Johnny fall, and when he finally looked back, Johnny's eyes were still open as he stared blindly into nothingness. Noah knew the sight would haunt him the rest of his life; yet he had no choice but to swallow his horror.

He was, after all, supposed to be a part of this. Besides that, he had his father to think about, a Frenchman living in Albany among English. Because of him, Noah spoke French. He even had a little Mohawk blood through his fraternal grandmother, who was a Mohawk married to a Frenchman.

All of that made his job easy. Many said he looked Indian, as he wore his dark hair long now, and had learned the Indian ways. He dressed in buckskins because they were more comfortable for living and hunting in the wild. He fit right in with these Indians, and with the French trappers. With every act like this one, he learned to hate the French, and men like Chief Pontiac and Charles Langlade, even more fiercely.

To his relief, Pontiac had killed Johnny quickly rather than by slow torture. Langlade ordered the five remaining English traders be held as captives and taken to Montreal as a prize. If only he'd done the same for poor Johnny. Noah supposed that on their trek back to Canada, they would stop along the way at Detroit and tell Captain Pierre Joseph Celeron de Bienville of their great victory here. It was Celeron who'd ordered the attack.

Still holding Unemakemi's head, Langlade marched the five prisoners ahead of him, joined by Pontiac, a small-built and heavily tattooed warrior whose size belied his brutality. Noah was ordered to fall behind and look around for any who might have escaped. In doing so, he glimpsed two figures running off in the opposite direction. They did not look Indian.

Giving no indication of what he'd seen, he dove into the underbrush after them, tomahawk still in hand, his musket slung over his shoulder. He jumped over fallen branches, tore through undergrowth that cut across his face, gaining on the two escapees, most likely English traders afraid their hearts, too, would be ripped out and eaten, then tossed to the ground like so much bad meat.

Finally, he came close enough to see they were indeed white men. One of them whirled to face him, and for a quiet moment both just stared at each other, panting and sweating. Noah guessed the man was out of black powder, or he would have shot at him. He straightened from a defensive posture.

"Tell the English what happened here today," he shouted to the man. "Tell them they've got to bring soldiers from England and be ready for war. Build up the colonist militia! They think they have nothing to worry about, but what you saw today proves other-wise!"

The trader frowned, watching him warily. "Who the hell are you?"

"It doesn't matter. Just do what I say. Go to Albany or Alexandria and let them know!" Noah turned and headed back to join Pontiac and Langlade. He couldn't help wondering how William Fairfax would react when he learned what had happened to poor Johnny. The man would probably think Noah should somehow have been able to save him. Men like Governor Dinwiddie and William Fairfax had no idea what life was like out here in the wilderness, especially for a man who was playing both sides in this hellish war. And this *was* war! The English didn't think so. Maybe after this they would wake up to the gruesome reality.

2

April 1753

Jess turned up the collar of her coat, still proud that she'd made the wonderfully warm garment herself from several raccoon skins her brother had given her for her sixteenth birthday. Sonny's hound dog, Gabe, loved to tree coons so Sonny could bring them down with his long gun. Times like that, Gabe's howling would echo all over the surrounding hills.

Sometimes Jess felt sorry for the playful, masked raccoons, but here in the Alleghenies, survival came first. A person could hardly make it through cold, damp winters without real fur for warmth, both on his feet and around his shoulders; and God put animals on earth to serve man's needs, anyway. Beaver was the best fur, but its skin was worth a lot to English traders. Pa preferred not to use the valuable skins for personal clothing. Rabbit and coon would do. Bear and wolf skins were even warmer, but those animals were more difficult and dangerous to hunt.

She pulled her hood over her head, hoping she didn't run into either animal today. This time of year, just coming out of hibernation, bears were extra dangerous, mean and hungry, the females ferocious in guarding their cubs.

She grumbled to herself about the weather. At least the harsh winds of winter had caused hundreds of small branches to fall. With most of the snow melted, kindling was easy to find. It wouldn't take her long to load her sled with starter wood for the fireplace, the chore she'd been assigned for the day. Her father believed that young people should never have "idle hands." To him, working hard was the most important lesson he could teach his children.

She tread almost soundlessly over a thin coating of snow with moccasins she'd made herself, the fur turned inside to keep her feet warm, like the local Indians made theirs. She didn't really mind her chores. After all, she was sixteen—"of marriageable age," her father had announced on her birthday. She needed to know how to fend for herself and a family. Trouble was, she couldn't imagine how or when she would have the opportunity to marry. Out here in the wilderness, a young woman didn't often meet young men, let alone have much time for courting. Maybe she would meet someone this year at the annual gathering.

Every year she and her family journeyed three days to reach the fork of the Allegheny and Monongahela rivers, where settlers, trading companies and Indians dickered over everything from buttons to canoes. That was just about the only time her family saw other people, except for rare visits from distant neighbors, usually because they needed supplies or help.

She stopped to place an armful of dead branches on the sled, made from a deerskin stretched over two solid but light branches. Sometimes she used it to pull her baby brother around in the snow. Little Billy was two now. Her mother often referred to him as her "miracle" baby, claiming she never thought after Jess's difficult birthing that she could ever have another child. The story always made Jess feel happy for her mother.

Her thoughts quickly jumped to the coming summer trading, since the event was always a bustle of exciting activity: ax-throwing and shooting contests, and judging for the best stitching, the best quilting, the best pies. It was the grandest event of the year, and certainly a nice break from the quiet, lonely life here in the mountains.

Her heart quickened at the thought of the colorful spectacle, Iroquois coming up the Monongahela and down the Allegheny by the hundreds, bringing with them all kinds of furs for bargaining with the English trading companies for tobacco, beads, cloth, whiskey and guns. The trading companies in turn struck deals with settlers, trading farm implements, axes, guns, cloth, flour, sugar, seeds, coffee and other supplies in return for smoked meat, homemade clothing, sheep and cattle, corn and other types of farm produce, and, of course, all the beaver pelts they could get their hands on. Everyone usually went home happy, their bellies full, their wagons and canoes stocked with necessary supplies for another long winter ahead.

She closed her eyes and breathed deeply, knowing she shouldn't dawdle but, as ever, unable to control her daydreaming. She thought how strangely different the Indians were, frightening to look at sometimes, in spite of the fact that most of them got along well with the settlers. Most of those who came to the trade event were Susquehannock, but a few were Mohawk, Oneida and Onondaga. Sometimes even some Shawnee came, from the west and south. She couldn't always tell the difference, but her father could; and so could the long hunters who also came to trade.

They, too, were a strange breed, dressed in buckskin clothing and beaver hats, their long rifles always at their sides. A long hunter was a brooding sort of man, quiet, keeping to himself. He spent months at a time hunting for the trading companies. He seldom married, except perhaps Indian women, whose families looked after them when their men were away. Most white women couldn't put up with that kind of life. They needed men who would settle in one place and stay home to provide for them and protect them. That was the kind of man she wanted for herself someday.

Maybe this year her father would let her dance with some young man at the gathering. Her mother was always telling her how pretty she was, but she didn't see it herself. She still did not have the full breasts of a woman; her lips were too thin; she still had freckles; and, as far as she was concerned, her hair was much too straight and thin. Every time she tried to pin it up, it fell back down. Maybe no young man would even be interested in her.

Sleet suddenly filled the wind, stinging her face and reminding her to get busy and finish gathering the kindling. Her father would be angry if she took too long. He might double her chores for tomorrow if he had to come out here looking for her. She removed her gloves, holding them in her teeth while she tied her hood closer around her ears. She could hardly wait to get back to the cabin and drink the hot buttermilk she knew her mother would have waiting for her there.

She pulled her rabbit-skin gloves back over her hands and trudged through wet undergrowth that was fast turning to slush. She much preferred the drier snow that fell in midwinter. Today's temperatures created a dampness that seemed to make its way right through a person's clothing and down to the bone.

She picked up more dead sticks, then found a whole branch that was just old and slender enough for her to break it into pieces over her knee. She finished stacking the kindling and turned to go back to the cabin, then hesitated at the sound of breaking sticks to her right. A prickly sensation moved down her back. She closed her eyes momentarily and prayed it wasn't a mother bear with cubs.

The wind picked up again as she glanced to her right, sure she saw something move when the branches of a thick pine swayed in the wind. She debated a moment. Would it be best to stand still, or to run? It was hard to say where wild animals were involved. Still, when she'd seen the movement, she was sure she'd also seen a bright color.

She decided to proceed slowly, but again she sensed movement and could not resist whirling around to look toward her right. To her amazement, five painted and fur-clad Indians made their presence known, emerging from the pines like ghosts.

Mohawk? Susquehannock? Oneida? She couldn't be sure. Fear and apprehension engulfed her in a hot wave that made her feel light-headed. She was aware other settlers had experienced Indian trouble lately, but nothing really drastic. It all had something to do with the French wanting some of this land and using the Indians to help them get it.

One of the painted and tattooed warriors motioned

for her to come closer. She'd never known the Indians in these parts to be anything but friendly. Sometimes one or two would show up at her family's cabin, bringing fresh game, for which her mother would trade bread or cloth, sometimes sugar. Still, she was alone out here, and there was something very different about these men, the way they were painted, the distinctly unfriendly look in their dark eyes.

Suddenly, the one who'd beckoned her let out a chilling cry that made her nearly faint. All five of them bounded toward her then, their leader raising a tomahawk, his dark eyes gleaming with a hunger to kill!

Why wouldn't her feet move?

3

Terror filled Jess's veins with ice, rendering her motionless. It was not until the lead warrior nearly reached her that she found her senses and ran. The warrior's hatchet sliced downward so closely that she heard its whirring sound. Her chest ached with horror, so sure she was that at any moment the weapon would rip into her spine.

She ran through wet leaves, leaped over fallen logs. Behind her she heard two gunshots, then a chilling scream, not so much like a war cry, but more like someone horribly wounded. She was too terrified for it to make sense, or to stop to see what had caused the scream. She jumped a narrow stream, still feeling the ugly chill crawling down her back at the thought of the hideous hatchet slicing her in two. Shouts and cries continued behind her, the sounds fading as she kept running.

Soon! Soon she would reach the cabin, where her father and brother could close the wooden shutters and get out their long guns and finish off any Indians who might be following. She screamed for them as loudly as she could, then caught her foot on a branch buried under wet leaves. She went sprawling face first, sliding on her hands and jaw through black mud.

Now she was more certain than ever that she would die at any moment. She waited for a body to land on her, for the hatchet to come down, perhaps chopping off her head. Quickly, she rolled onto her back, thinking to fight as best she could. Only then did she realize no one had followed her!

Stunned, she managed to get to her feet, paying no attention to the fact that her face, hands and the whole front of her fur coat were covered with mud and leaves. She could still hear shouting in the distance. Part of her warned that she should keep running; but now she was curious. Why hadn't she been followed? The attacking Indians had most certainly been intent on killing or capturing her. What about the gunshots she'd heard? Had her brother or father been nearby? Were they in trouble?

Flicking off some of the mud, she cautiously snuck back toward where she'd left her sled full of wood.

She hid in the protection of fat pines whose lower branches grew close to the ground, then ducked behind large tree trunks, bending down to crawl in areas where her head might be seen. She thought she could hear men fighting, and her heart pounded with wonder and fear. She made her way close enough to see three Indians sprawled on the ground, one with his throat slit open, another with massive bleeding in his chest. The third man lay with a large hole in his face.

Two more warriors circled a man wearing buckskins. They were bent over and sneering, hatchets ready. The man in buckskins had long, dark hair, much like an Indian's, and he wore knee-high moccasins. Blood ran profusely from his right thigh, but the wound did not seem to affect his fighting skills. The fringes of his jacket and leggings danced wildly as he darted at the two warriors, swinging his own bloody hatchet. The Indian men jumped back, then one of them lunged, jabbing at the white man with a large, ugly knife. The man sucked in his belly as he withdrew, barely avoiding a slash to his middle.

The circling continued, the white man losing so much blood that Jess could not imagine how he could go on much longer. Suddenly, he flung his hatchet, landing it into the chest of one warrior. Jess winced and curled her lips at the thud of the weapon splitting bone. The white man swiftly pulled a knife and charged into the second Indian. They tumbled to the ground, rolling in the cold mud. Both men grunted and growled, their hair now tangled and muddy.

Jess had never seen such vicious fighting, and she marveled at the prowess of the white man, who apparently had taken on all five warriors, already killing four of them. When she opened her eyes again the last Indian was plunging his knife into the man's left shoulder. Before he could yank it out, the white man rammed his own blade into the Indian's side.

Jess's stomach turned at the warrior's grunt. Blood began spilling from his mouth onto the white man's face. The man managed to push the Indian's body off him, and Jess grimaced, squeezing her eyes shut again and swallowing back vomit. She'd heard tales of Indian fighting, but she'd never actually witnessed anything like this. This was nothing like the games men played at the trading event.

She remained squatting behind thick underbrush, feeling almost breathless. Tears began to sting her eyes as she realized that the man in buckskins had risked his life to save her. Maybe if she hadn't dawdled, none of this would have happened. But then, where had the white man come from? By his dress and looks, she surmised he was a long hunter, one of those wild men of the woods who did nothing but trap and hunt for a living. Had he, too, been hiding, watching her? Maybe he'd been enjoying his own fantasies of capturing her and dragging her off. How did she know he was any better than the savages who'd tried to kill her?

She opened her eyes again to see the hunter crawling away from the last Indian, his breathing labored. Now, in addition to his leg, blood oozed from his shoulder wound. He glanced around, as though sensing her presence. Jess remained hidden, not sure if she should show herself. Still, the man had saved her life.

He put his head down a moment, breathing heavily. Jess noticed one Indian move. It was the last one the white man had fought. Jess was amazed he was able to get to his knees and reach for a tomahawk that lay nearby.

"No!" Jess murmured. She darted out from behind the pine tree, frantically searching for a weapon. The first thing she saw was a fist-size rock. Not knowing what else to do, she picked it up and flung it at the Indian's head. Her movement had drawn his attention, and he was facing her just as the rock hit him, directly in the forehead. He simply stared at her a moment, looking shocked, then dropped the hatchet and fell face forward.

Jess stood in wide-eyed disbelief. Had she killed him? Most likely he was already dying as he'd made a last effort to kill the white man who'd stabbed him. Her gaze darted to the wounded white man, surely, she surmised, close to death. He lay on his side looking back at her. He actually managed a hint of a smile in spite of his condition, then nodded as though to approve of what she'd just done. Jess walked closer, and the man rolled onto his back. He watched her with dark eyes as she approached.

Blood ran down his left arm from his shoulder

wound, and he looked ready to pass out.

"I . . . my folks don't live far," Jess told him. "You're bad wounded, mister. If you follow me to our cabin, my folks can help you."

He put a bloody finger to his lips and seemed to struggle to hold his breath for a moment, listening intently. "There aren't any others out there," he finally said, his breathing labored again. "If there were, I'd hear . . . or smell them."

He reminded Jess of a wildcat, an animal that sensed danger without seeing it. "Who are they? We've always been friendly with the Indians around here."

"Ottawa," he answered weakly. "From Detroit. Don't belong in these parts." He closed his eyes. "Must be some of those . . . helping the French . . . take over this area."

"Take it over?"

He grimaced. "Can't talk more right now. Got to get . . . to your cabin."

He spoke haltingly, and his dark skin was becoming paler. She stepped even closer as he turned and got to his hands and knees. Jess looked around. "You got a horse somewhere?"

He raised up, still on his knees. "Left two horses farther back—my riding horse and a packhorse." He nodded toward the north. "That way—downwind of the Ottawa. I've been tracking them on foot for a ways to see where they were headed. When I saw them . . . watching you . . . I knew what they were thinking." He looked her over strangely, and Jess felt oddly embarrassed. He managed then to get to his feet. "I have . . . some supplies with my horses . . . traded some furs for them back at Logstown."

"Do you want me to find them for you?" Jess turned to go.

"No." He began to sway. "Your folks . . . can look for them," he explained. "These Indians . . . have to be buried quick . . . in case others come after them. If they find them dead . . . they might turn on the closest place for revenge. That would be your family's cabin."

Jess nodded. "I'll tell my pa. I'll try to help you to our cabin."

Still panting, he reached out. Jess held out her hands and stiffened to support him as he grasped hold and managed to stay on his feet. He leaned on her then, and she wondered how she could possibly help him all the way back to the cabin. He was a big man, tall and well built, too heavy for her to do him much good. His arm slid off her shoulder then, and he fell back to the ground.

Jess knelt closer. "Mister?"

"Get . . . help," he said weakly. He began to shiver.

Feeling obligated, Jess removed her raccoon coat and laid it over him. "I'll run as fast as I can!" She hesitated. "What's your name, mister? I mean . . . what if you die? We need a name for your marker."

He studied her with glazed eyes, this time actually smiling fully. Jess realized then what a terrible thing she'd just said. "I'm sorry—"

"Noah," he answered with a grunt. "Noah Wilde."

Jess heard shouting then, recognizing her father and her brother's voices. Gabe barked, and in moments the hound came bounding through the brush, loping up to her with tail wagging.

Jess stood up and shouted, "Over here! Hurry, Pa! A man's bad hurt!" She ran forward and in seconds her father was grasping her close.

"Thank God, child! We heard gunshots and shouts! What's happened?"

"Come with me!" Jess led them back to where the long hunter lay, now looking still and near death. "He saved my life, Pa! He fought all those Indians to keep them from taking me. I never saw anything like it. We've got to help him!"

"Lord have mercy!" Jonathan said softly. "Let's get him to the house, Sonny."

"I can take him, Pa." A tall and strong young man, Jess's brother bent down and pulled the long hunter to a sitting position, then put a shoulder to him and raised him up, staggering slightly under the hunter's weight as he managed to keep his balance. He started walking with the wounded man slung over his shoulder.

Jess followed with her father, who'd picked up the stranger's musket. "He said his name is Noah Wilde," she told her father. She looked back then, realizing Noah's tomahawk and knife were still embedded in the bodies of the last two Indians he'd killed. Her sled full of kindling sat in the midst of the slaughter, but she was not about to go back and walk in all that blood to get it.

She shivered, carrying her muddy and now blood-stained fur coat over her arm rather than putting it back on. She couldn't wait to reach the safety of the cabin, and she thought how much more ready she was now for that warm buttermilk.

4

This could be just the beginning." Jonathan Matthews pulled at his graying beard. He paced in front of the massive stone fireplace at one end of the family's log cabin and faced his eldest son.

"I don't like any of this," Sonny answered his father.

Jess knew better than to ask what was going on. Her father would just say it wasn't a woman's business. She hated it when she was left out of important matters. If her father thought her old enough to marry, then she was old enough to know about things like this, especially since it was she who almost lost her life. She'd said nothing about throwing the rock at the last Indian, not even sure herself yet of how she felt about that. The entire event had left her shaken and bewildered.

"Mr. Wilde can probably tell us what we need to know," Jonathan mused, "if he lives. I suspect he wasn't out there in the woods just looking for game.

He knows something about why those Indians were there. Jess says he told her they were Ottawa, from clear up by Detroit."

Now her father spoke as though she were not even in the room. Jess pressed her lips together in irritation. Her father sighed and sat down at the table, glancing toward the small, curtained-off room where Sonny usually slept.

Noah Wilde was in there, her mother still tending his wounds. Jess's father and brother had gone back and shoveled fast and hard to bury the dead Indians. Tomorrow they would go looking for the hunter's horses.

Jess felt like crying. She'd wanted to help the man who'd saved her, but her mother would have none of it. *You'd be seein' things you ought not to see,* she'd said. Instead, Jess was ordered to watch after Billy, who now lay with his head on her shoulder. She'd rocked her little brother to sleep, and he was beginning to feel very heavy.

"Rumor is the French are moving farther this way in more numbers than ever," Jonathan continued, running a callused hand through his hair and grumbling, "Your ma needs to give me another haircut."

"Makes no difference to me that they're setting up more forts and trading posts," Sonny told him. "But at the last gathering, folks were talking about regular settlers also coming this way. They think France is bringing over their poor and their prisoners to try to populate more of Canada and down into Detroit and those areas, sending over Catholic priests to reform the Indians and win them over."

Jonathan nodded. "That's the dangerous part. We saw that today." He shook his head. "The English, and us, we figure this territory to be ours. And the fact remains the English hold no love for the French, anyway. What I'm worried about is all that hatred will be fed to us colonists and we'll get caught up in a war started by two kings; a war we don't belong in. Long as we can stay here and farm and trade our goods for a fair price, whether it's with the English or the French, I don't much care about getting mixed up in any war."

They all glanced at the small bedroom when they heard a groan. Sonny scraped his chair on the plank floor as he shifted nervously. "Maybe we should kick out both the French *and* the English and run our *own* country. All the English want over here is free access to our lumber and farm goods, and the ability to expand their empire."

Jonathan shot him a look of stern warning. "Be careful, son. That's traitorous talk. Don't let anybody with a red coat hear you."

Sonny frowned. "I don't much care right now. This is *our* land, not France's *or* England's."

Jonathan held up his hand and scowled, nodding toward the bedroom again. "Right now we don't know where that man's loyalties lie! And the fact remains we are *colonists*. That won't change any time in the near future, if ever. We might as well learn to live under the king."

Sonny rose, taking his wolf-skin coat from a hook on the wall and pulling it on. "Maybe for now, but a lot of men my age aren't so sure we have to put up with red-coat rule forever." He picked up his long gun, and Gabe jumped up from where he'd been lying in front of the fire, wagging his tail as he trotted over to his master. "Ready for a walk, boy?" Sonny teased the dog. "Let's go!"

"You be careful out there, Sonny," Jonathan warned. "There just might be more of those Ottawa around. Stay close. You never know but that some of them might pay us a visit."

"Sure, Pa."

"You sure you covered that hole we dug for the Indians real good?"

"Plenty good. Only thing that could sniff them out would be Gabe, and the Indians don't use dogs for hunting."

"Don't underestimate their own abilities to sniff things out. You ask that hunter in there, he'll tell you. Fact is, *he* could probably sniff them out himself. Let's just hope it's a while before any others come around, and that we get a good, hard rain to wash away all the tracks and the smell of blood."

Sonny nodded. "It's getting close to dark. Figured I'd go look around a little more, see if I can find that man's horses and gear."

Jess felt a cold draft when her brother opened the door to go out. Gabe darted ahead of him, always ready for a good run. Sonny closed the door, and Jess and her father heard yet another groan from Sonny's room.

"Everything all right in there, Marlene?" Jonathan asked.

"I'm doing fine," Jess's mother answered. "Just keep that kettle of water hot over the fire."

"I already refilled it, Ma," Jess answered. "It's plenty hot."

Jonathan glanced at her. "How are *you* doin', child? That must have been pretty scary for you. You've said hardly a word since we brought back the hunter."

"I'm okay, Pa." She wanted to tell him how much she hated being called "child."

"You'd best put Billy down on me and your ma's bed and see to supper. You ought to be ready in case that man in there comes around and wants some hot broth or somethin', and I'm pretty hungry myself. It's been a hard day."

"Yes, sir." Jess carried Billy over to the small room where her parents slept and put him down, covering him. She noticed the little scar on his left hand from when he'd once tried to touch the flames in the fireplace. That one experiment had taught him a good lesson. Her mother swore that was the best way to teach a child what to stay away from. She didn't believe in spankings and yelling.

Her father, though, had a different mind-set. That was yet another lesson Jess and her brothers had learned early in life. She stirred the hot coals in the hearth and added two more pieces of wood, then used the iron poke to swing out the arm of the chimney crane, which held a black iron pot full of a mixture of chicken, potatoes and carrots. She donned her apron, using the end of it to lift the lid from the pot of simmering stew, kept warm since last night's supper. Food was never to be wasted. Once a big pot of anything was cooked, it was eaten at every meal until it was gone.

She slid the pot hook along the arm of the crane to keep the pot from hanging over the hottest part of the fire, so it wouldn't cook too hard. There was just about enough left for one more meal.

"You want me to make some dumplings, Pa? There's three big bowls of dough rising in the side oven. Ma made it early this morning, before any of us even left the house. I could use strips of it in the stew, kind of freshen it up with something extra. The dough needs kneading, anyway."

"That would be mighty nice."

Jess took out one bowl of puffy bread dough and set it on the table. She took a tin of flour from her mother's pantry and dipped her fist into it, then punched the center of the ball of dough and began kneading it.

"It won't take long for dumplings to cook," she told her father. She looked up when her mother finally came out of the room where the hunter lay. Jess hoped he would recover. "I'm making dumplings, Ma."

"That's a fine idea." Marlene turned to her husband. "While Jess is doing that, pour me some hot water into a clean wash bowl, please. Then mix a little cold water from the drinking bucket into it so I can wash my hands."

The woman's hands showed bloodstains, as did her apron. Jess could see she was worn out. Her mother's eyelids were puffy, and strands of her graying hair had come undone from the neat bun she'd fashioned at the back of her neck that morning.

Jess greatly admired her mother, a gentle woman who seemed too refined for living in the backwoods. She often talked nostalgically about Albany, the settlement she'd left to come here with Jonathan twelve years ago. Marlene's parents had both died since coming to New York from England, and Jess's father wanted to go someplace where he could find cheap land and build his own farm. Jess was only four then and barely remembered life in Albany, or what it was like to have neighbors. She knew her mother missed that life terribly; but she loved her husband, and a woman's place was with her man, wherever that might lead her.

Jess wished she was as pretty as her mother must have been when she was young. Her father often told her she looked like her mother, but no one could convince Jess that her mother hadn't been much prettier at her age. Now Marlene often lamented her dry, calloused hands and the wrinkles in her face. She often "escaped" to Albany when she told stories to Jess about life there, and Jess loved picturing it.

"How is he?" Jonathan asked.

"Fair," Marlene answered as she tried to retuck some of the falling strands of hair at her neck. "He's a big man—appears to be strong. He'll recover, I'm sure."

Jess continued kneading the dough, never interfering in a conversation between her mother and father.

"Considering how he handled those Ottawa, I don't doubt his strength," Jonathan answered.

Marlene walked closer to Jess. "He managed to ask if you were okay." She looked at her daughter lovingly, and Jess noticed an unexpected twinkle in the woman's soft brown eyes. Did it have something to do with Noah Wilde asking about her?

"He asked about *me?*"

Marlene nodded, and Jonathan rose to get a bucket of cold water from a corner of the room as though unconcerned with their conversation. Marlene glanced at him before looking lovingly at Jess again. "I thanked him for what he did for you." She kissed Jess's cheek. "I'm glad you're all right, Jess. Mr. Wilde told me you just might have saved his life in return."

Jess shrugged. "I just threw a rock at a man Mr. Wilde had already stabbed near to death. He looked like he was thinking to go after Mr. Wilde with a tomahawk, so I threw the rock at him and hit him in the forehead. He was about to die, anyway."

Marlene squeezed her hands. "Still, it was a brave thing to do." She walked over to where Jonathan prepared the bowl of water for her. Jess noticed the way her mother had of straightening herself even when weary, making herself seem taller than her five-foot-three-inch frame would allow.

While her mother washed, Jess glanced toward the curtained-off room where Noah lay resting. Why did the thought of him dying cause a stab of pain in her heart? She didn't even know the man!

She returned to kneading and pounding the ball of dough with more force than necessary, the strangeness of the day making her both anxious and excited. She wasn't sure what to think of any of it, or of her father's talk of war.

5

Jess forced down the wooden plunger of the butter churn, feeling the cream ooze through the holes. Already she could tell the butter was "coming," as her mother called it, meaning that soon she should add cold water to wash the butter and help it harden. Then she would add salt to bring out the flavor. She could already taste its fresh yellow goodness on a slice of warm bread.

After making dumplings for supper, she'd stayed up half the night kneading what was left of the bread dough. She'd been unable to sleep for thinking about the horrible, bloody fight of yesterday morning, and the man who lay in pain after saving her life. The least she could do was have fresh bread for him once he was able to sit up and eat. She'd already divided the dough into pans for one last rise and would soon bake the loaves in the stone oven built into the side of the fireplace. Maybe the smell of baking bread would inspire Noah Wilde to eat, since up to now he'd refused the broth her mother tried to feed him.

"Who's out there?"

Jess hesitated at the words, spoken in a deep voice from her brother's room, where the injured Noah lay. She turned, pushing a stringy piece of hair behind her ear and smoothing her apron. Her mother was outside hoeing her garden in preparation for a new planting of potatoes and vegetables. Billy was with her, playing in the dirt. Contrary to yesterday, the weather had warmed overnight, and they all had risen to a surprisingly pleasant morning, with no traces of the previous day's wet snow on the ground. Her mother blamed Pennsylvania's unpredictable weather in these parts on the wind and cloud movements getting caught between the Great Lakes to the west and the Allegheny mountains to the east.

With Sonny out hunting and her father tending to his chores, Jess was the only one in the house. Apparently, the hunter who called himself Noah needed something. She supposed she should go get her mother, but, she reasoned, the woman was busy and probably dirty from hoeing. In spite of being ordered yesterday to stay out of the room where their patient lay, Jess's curiosity was much too strong to deny. Being alone in the house when the poor man needed something seemed a good enough excuse to help him.

She swallowed nervously and walked to the doorway, pulling aside the blanket that served as a privacy curtain. She peered inside, noticing that Noah's muscled arms and shoulders were bare above where the blankets were tucked under his arms. An ugly, dark red gash on his left shoulder made her feel a little sick. It was stitched with sewing thread and tied off like the seam of a quilt. "Sir?" she spoke up. "Is there something you need?"

He turned to look at her, grimacing as though just that one movement of his head was painful. His long hair was spread out on the pillow, and Jess realized her mother must have managed to brush the dried mud from it and freshen his feather pillow. It seemed Marlene was efficient at everything she did, from cleaning to doctoring. Jess hoped to do as well as a grown woman.

Noah smiled weakly. "What I need is not something that's fit for you . . . to help me with," he told her. He looked her over with his deep brown eyes. "Where's your pa?"

Jess felt hot blood rising to her face. The poor man probably had to pee! She felt like a bumbling idiot. "He's outside taking care of chores." She pulled back, letting the curtain close so he couldn't see her. "My brother, Sonny, he's out hunting, and Ma is tending to her garden. Sonny said he'd for sure find your horses and supplies for you today."

"Good. I'm grateful to all of you." There came a pause before he spoke again. "Come on back in here."

Jess took a deep breath and moved just inside the doorway. Noah looked her over in a way that made her self-conscious. "Your ma said your name is Jessica."

"Yes, sir. Jessica Anne. Most just call me Jess."

He rubbed at his eyes with his right hand. "I seem to remember . . . you saving my life."

Jess felt a rush of flustered embarrassment. "Me?" She smiled nervously. "Heck, I didn't do anything much. I mean, I was flat-out scared. All I could think of was to throw that rock, but anybody could tell that Indian was already dying from your knife."

Noah looked up at the ceiling. "Well, he just might have had enough life left in him to finish mine." He turned to her again. "You're a brave young lady."

Brave young lady? The words made Jess's heart beat a little faster; to have a wild, experienced man like Noah Wilde call her brave . . . let alone a young lady. She would have thought he'd use the words "little girl." She stepped a little closer, secretly fascinated by his powerful-looking physique.

"That's something, you calling me brave," she said. "Lord knows you're just about the bravest man I ever knew, and a heck of a fighter. I'm the one who owes you my life. I can never thank you enough for what you did, and I'm awful sorry you're so bad hurt."

He closed his eyes and sighed. "Well, your ma is one heck of a doctor. I expect I'll survive."

Jess shrugged. "Out here a body has to learn their own doctoring, that's sure."

Noah lay quietly a moment. "How old are you, Jess?" he asked.

"Sixteen. How old are you?"

He managed another grin in spite of his pain. "Twenty-nine," he told her, facing her again.

Their gazes held for a moment, and Jess felt suddenly and surprisingly comfortable in his presence, as though he were not at all a stranger. "How did you happen to be right there when those Indians came yesterday?"

Noah shifted slightly, groaning with pain before answering. "Mostly coincidence. I was headed for Virginia. I saw those Ottawa and . . . followed them to see what they were up to. Then I spotted you. I could see . . . what they were planning, and I just . . . couldn't let it happen."

Jess felt an unfamiliar flutter in her chest. "You're a very honorable man, Mr. Wilde. I'll be eternally grateful."

He grinned. "Honorable sounds better than crazy. Most would consider me that for charging into five Ottawa warriors."

They smiled at each other and Jess found herself wondering if she had flour in her hair and on her face. She self-consciously pushed her hair behind her ears. "I prefer to think of it as honorable," she told him. "You're too humble, Mr. Wilde."

He looked her over in a way that made her feel more grownup. "Call me Noah."

Jess swallowed. "I really shouldn't be in here. My ma told me to stay out."

"She did, did she?"

Jess nodded and turned toward the door. "I'm making fresh bread and fresh-churned butter," she said, glad to think of something to change the subject. She looked back at him. "I hope you'll eat today."

"I'll try." He winced as he forced himself to sit up slightly, revealing more of his bare chest. Jess again looked away. "I have to finish churning the butter." She started out.

"Jess." He spoke her name as though he'd always known her.

"Yes?"

"I'm glad I happened along when I did yesterday."

Jess could feel her heartbeat in her ears. She couldn't help glancing back once more, meeting his dark gaze. "I've never seen a man fight like you did yesterday. You were like a wild bear. How'd you learn to fight like that?"

The look in his eyes turned to a surprising sadness, as though a sudden sorrow swept over him. He closed his eyes again. "When you live like I do, you learn the way of the Indian. You live and fight any way you have to."

Jess wondered if he had Indian blood, but she feared that was too personal a question to ask. She'd leave that to her father. "I'll get my pa for you." She left the room and walked to the door, going outside and calling for her father. When she saw Jonathan stop nailing a loose board on the horse shed and head for the house, she went back inside and put two loaves of bread in the side oven. She found herself hoping the bread would turn out just right, not yet sure just why she suddenly hoped to impress Mr. Noah Wilde with her baking.

She closed the oven door and whispered a quick prayer that Noah's pain and suffering would quickly end.

6

Have you heard about a place called Pickawillany?" Noah asked the question cautiously, eyeing the Matthews family members as he spoke. He sat with them around a rough-hewn wooden table. Marlene Matthews set the table with boiled potatoes, boiled venison, fresh bread and butter. Although still miserable after three days in bed, Noah was determined to get up and move around. Returning to Virginia as soon as possible was vital, and before doing that he wanted to talk about Pickawillany, not sure what Jonathan would think of his acting as a spy for the English . . . and the fact that he'd been at Pickawillany on the side of the French. He knew the whole family was curious about him; and he figured they deserved to know the truth, especially since he'd secretly taken a special interest in Jess.

"Heard about that place last fall at the trade gathering on the Monongahela," Jonathan answered him. "Word gets around in the backwoods surprisingly fast. Terrible slaughter of English traders, they say."

"A couple of them escaped to tell about it," Sonny added. "By now pretty much the whole eastern half of the country knows about Pickawillany, and they're mighty angry. They say the culprits were Detroit Miami and Ottawa, led by a chief called Pontiac, I think. Some Huron might have even been in on it."

Noah leaned back, remaining quiet as the others ate. Finally, he took a deep breath and spoke up again. "There were no Huron there," he told them. "Huron and Ottawa don't get along. Pontiac led the attack with his Ottawa Indians and the French-sympathizing Miami. Naturally, the whole thing was planned by the French."

The memory of the hideous acts of Charles Langlade and Chief Pontiac was still vivid. Worse was the memory of Johnny's awful death. The young man's last look of horror still haunted Noah. "I was there," he added. "I can tell you anything you want to know about it."

He expected the shock he saw on their faces, and was especially interested in Jess's reaction. She just stared in wide-eyed surprise.

"You one of those who escaped?" Jonathan asked.

"You know that wild Chief Pontiac?" Sonny asked before Noah could even answer the first question. A mixture of wonder and distrust flared in his eyes.

49

Noah poked at a piece of venison as he answered. "No man who lives the way I do can help but know a good many of the Iroquois, Miami, Ottawa, Huron, Mohawk, Susquehannock. I've dealt with all of them, mostly before they started taking sides between the French and the English," he answered Sonny.

Jonathan eyed him closely. "And whose side are *you* on? Is Wilde French or English? I've not heard the name before, and you haven't answered *my* question."

"I'm English," Noah replied. "And if you saw what the French and Ottawa did to my wife eight years ago at Albany, you'd know I could never befriend the French or any Indians who pledge themselves to them." He glanced at Jess again, and he saw something more now, pity, he supposed.

"What happened?" she asked.

Would the pain ever go away? "Let's just say she's dead." They all stopped eating momentarily.

"We're sorry about your wife," Marlene spoke up softly. "And you must understand, Noah, knowing you were at Pickawillany—"

"I understand," Noah told her. "I don't blame any of you for wondering about me."

There came an awkward moment of silence before Jonathan spoke up again. "So, how was it you were there, and how did you manage to escape?"

Now came the hard part. Noah held Jonathan's gaze boldly. "Sir, I am a spy for the English. I was with Pontiac and the French forces at Pickawillany."

"Oh, my goodness!" Marlene put a hand to her

breast, and Jess's mouth dropped open. Sonny and Jonathan both stiffened. Little Billy sat in a wooden high chair poking at his potatoes with his fingers, totally oblivious to the serious conversation taking place.

"A *spy?*" Sonny finally blurted out.

Noah looked straight at him. "I've been acting as a spy ever since my wife was killed at Albany. And the reason I was where I was three days ago is because I was heading for Virginia, to report to Governor Dinwiddie there. The French have big plans to invade and fortress the entire western frontier so that the English won't be able to push any farther west. I've got to get to Dinwiddie and reinforce what he's probably already being told—that we've got to strengthen the colonist militia and bring over more soldiers from England. Dinwiddie is the only English leader on this soil who takes the French threat seriously." He turned to Jonathan. "And I might add, sir, that you should take your family north to Fort Oswego, maybe even all the way to Albany, for the sake of safety. Your wife told me you both hail from there, as do I. My parents live there. My father might be French, but he's lived among the English for years and refuses to be involved in the actions of New France."

Jonathan frowned, plunging a fork into some potatoes. "Things can't be that bad yet. Besides, I can't leave this place. It's taken me twelve years to clear enough of the woods around here to farm." He held a forkful of potatoes over his plate as he finished.

"Things are going quite well for us. If I leave it all, someone will come in and benefit from all my hard work, take over my home and lands. I can't afford to risk that happening. Sonny and I are perfectly capable of standing on our own here." He shoveled the potatoes into his mouth.

Noah fought an urge to scold the man for his ignorance. "You saw what happened the other day," he reminded Jess's father. "If I hadn't been there, your daughter would be missing now, and probably wishing she were dead. I'm sure you've heard of some of the horrible events at Pickawillany. I've seen a lot of death and blood in my time, but the things that went on at Pickawillany stunned even me. The Iroquois, whether it's those who side with the French or with the English, take pride in their ability to bring exquisite pain to the enemy, in making them suffer. They often take heads and dismember the rest of the body. Women and children are murdered right alongside the men, or taken prisoner, which can sometimes be worse."

"Mr. Wilde!" Marlene exclaimed, putting a hand to her mouth. "We are at the table!"

Noah sighed, running a hand over his forehead. "I'm sorry, ma'am. I just hate the thought of families like you suffering at the hands of the Iroquois." He turned his gaze back to Jonathan. "Things are getting rough. The French are in the process of building forts all along Lake Erie and farther south. They are working hard at winning most Iroquois tribes to their side, bent on stopping any further migration west by the English, and determined none will ever move into the northern regions or northwest into Michigan. I think they are even thinking of moving into areas like this and pushing the English back east, discouraging most of the Iroquois from trading with the English companies. They want to lay claim to all of the interior and everything north and south of the western end of Lake Erie. It's very dangerous for single families to be living so far apart, so isolated from help. What could happen to your wife and daughter and your baby son isn't worth all the land in America. I know. It happened to my own wife."

Jonathan frowned. "The French would never come this far east."

"The Ottawa and Miami *would* come this far. You already know that."

Jonathan shook his head. "Maybe we can at least get in one last crop this year—trade that and the livestock at the gathering, or at Logstown, before leaving."

Noah saw the pain in the man's eyes.

"It's awful hard leaving all this after twelve years of such hard work," Jonathan said.

"I know that, sir," Noah answered. "I left a lot behind myself eight years ago, but for worse reasons. I no longer had a wife to share it with."

Jonathan pushed his plate away and excused himself from the table. "I'm going outside to smoke my pipe and think awhile," he told his wife. He turned, and taking his deerskin coat from a hook on a wall, he pulled it on and walked outside.

Noah glanced at Marlene. "I'm sorry, ma'am. It's just that if you'd seen what I've seen, and with that attack the other day, it just isn't safe to be here now. Things are only going to get worse."

Marlene nodded. "I understand." She looked at her son. "Sonny does, too, but we've worked so hard here." She looked back at Noah. "I'll talk to him. Surely we're safe for one more summer. Maybe then we can go back, and maybe just for a while. We have to hope all of this will be over soon and we can go back to our peaceful life here."

"I'm afraid it might not be any time soon, ma'am, but you can always hope for that." He looked around the table. "I'm sorry if I spoiled supper."

Sonny shrugged. "Pa always leaves when he gets something heavy on his mind," he told Noah. "I agree with you. We probably should leave, at least by the end of summer. That would still give us a good month or more before bad weather sets in."

Noah glanced at Jess, who simply sat staring at him, looking rather bewildered. The pretty young woman was his main concern. For the first time in years he was thinking seriously about a woman again. This one had heart, a strong character, and she was a damn good cook. Watching her family brought back memories of how he'd once lived before Mary's cruel death. For the first time since then he'd been having thoughts of maybe being able to live that way again. Before he left this place, he intended to see if Miss Jess

Matthews would mind if he came back to see her after speaking with the governor in Virginia. He could get back before the end of summer. He could even accompany Jess's family back to Albany, help protect them along the way—and get to know Jess better while he was at it.

"I would definitely leave before winter," he told Sonny. "And I'm glad you see the necessity. I just hope you can convince your father to go."

Sonny shook his head. "That won't be easy."

7

Jess carried a pail of milk up the three steps to the cabin porch, where Noah sat in her mother's rocker. His hair was tied behind his neck, and he wore a blue shirt that could be laced at the throat with rawhide cord. He'd left it open, revealing a few dark hairs that mingled with an interesting necklace. It looked like bear claws tied to beaded rawhide.

The man's physique and the open shirt reminded Jess of the day she'd seen him lying in bed, how lean and muscled his bare shoulders and arms were. The sudden memory made her feel ashamed, and she looked away when she walked past him.

"'Morning, Mr. Wilde."

"It's Noah, remember?"

Jess hesitated, secretly longing for an excuse to talk

to the man. "It just seems too familiar, I guess."

She carried the milk inside and set it on the table, wondering if Noah noticed how she'd pulled her hair up from the sides and held it there with combs. Sonny had told her once she looked pretty when she wore it that way, and that it made her look older.

She glanced at the door, left open for fresh air. It was a sunny, pleasant day, and her father and Sonny were out plowing up ground to plant potatoes. Her mother worked behind the horse shed plucking feathers from two fresh-killed chickens. Proper and ladylike as Marlene was, the woman had still learned how to correctly wring a chicken's neck to kill it quickly. She could laugh about it now, often commenting how she'd never done such a thing back in Albany. They would have a good supper tonight, fried chicken and all the trimmings.

Billy played in front of the house chasing the live, clucking chickens, and Jess realized this was her first chance to talk alone with Noah since he was feeling better. He'd practically invited a conversation, and she was curious about his life, especially after last night's conversation about Pickawillany. Secretly, she was almighty attracted to the man, for more reasons than his adventures. No one could deny he was brave and skilled, and handsome to boot. More than once she'd caught him looking at her in a way that made her feel all tingly inside.

It seemed strange to realize that she hated the thought of Noah leaving. He'd mentioned again this morning at breakfast that it was important for him to get to Alexandria, Virginia, as soon as possible, but Marlene insisted he wait at least several more days. He was still far too weak, and was not yet free of the danger of dreaded infection.

Jess quietly walked back to the door. "Noah?"

He glanced toward the door, the pipe he'd been quietly smoking still clamped between his teeth. "Yes, ma'am?"

She opened the door and stepped onto the porch, wondering at the fluttering feeling the man gave her. "Is it really true, that my pa should leave this place and go back east?"

The gentle, teasing look in his eyes turned to concern. "It's true."

"That would be real hard for him to do."

"I know that."

Jess shivered. "The things you told us—about the Iroquois and what they can do, what happened at Pickawillany—it scares me."

He took the pipe from his mouth and sighed. "It should. And after practically dying to keep you safe, I'd hate to have something happen to you after all, once I leave here."

Jess frowned, moving over to sit down on the top step. She leaned against a porch post and looked up at him. "Why? I mean, you never even knew me before that day those Indians came."

He studied her for a long, quiet moment. "Well, it's obvious you're a very nice young lady, from a good,

Christian family. Your mother is a fine lady, your father and brother good people. I'd just hate to see anything happen to any of you."

Jess looked down and toyed with a button on her skirt. "What will you do after you report in Virginia?"

He didn't answer right away. Finally, she looked at him again, to see him looking her over and grinning. What a handsome grin he had, straight, white teeth, a twinkle in his eyes. "You want the truth?"

She knitted her eyebrows in curiosity. "'Course I do."

"Well . . ." He rubbed his chin thoughtfully. "Fact is, I'd like to come back here and get to know you better, if your parents don't mind . . . and if *you* don't mind."

Jess's cheeks suddenly felt hot. She shrugged, pretending not to care either way. "I guess I wouldn't mind, if you've a mind to do that." Why did it thrill her to know he wanted to come back? She reminded herself that he was a long hunter, as well as an English spy, certainly not the kind to settle for long. And he was a lot older than she.

"Jessica."

He spoke the name softly. She met his gaze, suddenly wishing she wore a prettier dress, but a girl couldn't dress up when there were daily chores to do. "Yes?"

"You're full of questions, and I won't be around much longer. Go ahead and ask."

She thought a moment, then slowly stood up, walking to one end of the porch, wishing she knew more about men. "Well then, I guess I'm wondering what you did back in Albany before your wife . . ." Already she'd blundered, bringing up his dead wife! She looked at him with apology in her eyes.

"Before my wife was killed?"

"I'm sorry. I didn't mean—"

"It's all right." He put the pipe back between his lips and puffed on it for a moment. Jess could see the distant pain in his eyes. "I farmed," he finally answered. He puffed the pipe once more, then set it aside on the porch railing. "My father still farms there. It was a family thing, and we did pretty well. The farm is mine any time I want to go back and take it over."

Jess began to feel a little more comfortable. She stepped closer, clinging to a porch post. "What are your parents like?"

Noah looked out at Billy, who still dashed about the yard trying to catch a chicken, screaming and laughing every time one got away. "My mother is a very gracious Englishwoman. My father carries not just French but also Indian blood. His French father married a Mohawk woman."

"Then you *do* have Indian blood!" she blurted out. "I *knew* it!"

He studied her a moment, grinning. "You did, did you? Does that bother you?"

"No! But, if your father is French, how can you hate them like you do?"

Noah leaned back in the rocker. "I'm only one quarter French, and one-quarter Indian. The rest of me is English; but that's not the reason. After what the French did to my wife, it became easy to hate them. My father is as angry about things the French have done in the name of trading rights as I am. His own parents worked for a wealthy Englishman in Albany, who willed them a good piece of land that my father ultimately inherited. He became moderately wealthy and married my mother, who was from a good family, not wealthy, but highly respected. Her father was a teacher. She was well educated, and she in turn made sure I received a good deal of book learning."

"My mother has taught me, too. I can read and write," Jess told him proudly.

Noah nodded. "Good."

Their gazes held, and Jess felt suddenly more woman than girl. "So, you feel more English than French?"

"I do, although I speak French fluently. An Englishman was responsible for my folks owning land and doing well, and I grew up among the English. The fact that I speak French makes it easier for me to work as a spy."

"Was your wife English?"

He nodded. "She was. Actually, you remind me of her a little. She was small like you, had hair a lot like yours. And she was pretty—like you."

Jess smiled nervously. "Thank you." She glanced down. "Did you . . . have children?"

There came another long silence. Had she overstepped her bounds? "No," he finally answered.

"Mary was carrying when she was murdered. The baby died with her."

Jess felt a stab at her heart. "I'm so sorry! I never should have asked!" Again she cast him a look of deep apology.

"It's a natural question. Don't feel bad about it."

Jess folded her arms in front of her. "If you farmed, how did you get like you are now? I mean, a long hunter, a spy, able to fight Indians like you were one yourself?"

Noah shifted in the rocker, grimacing with pain when he did so. "Well, if a man is determined enough, he learns what he has to learn. I was determined to find a way to get back at the French, and the best way to do that was to hunt for game and furs, become a French trapper and trader. I knew that would help me be able to infiltrate French forts and trading posts. I already knew a bit about Indian ways because of my Mohawk relatives. I went to live with them awhile, made it a point to learn everything I could."

Jess sighed with wonder at the complicated nature of the man. "Do your mother and father know what you're doing?"

"They know. That's what makes the spying so hard. I have to be careful. It would be easy for people to claim my father is pro-French and accuse him of some kind of treachery. Since no one else in Albany knows I'm a spy, they might think because I'm gone for so long at a time that I'm up to something, that my father is involved in it, too. That's why I have to get back to Virginia and report, keep things on the up-and-up."

He reached for the pipe and pulled on it for a moment to keep the embers lit, then kept it in his hand as he continued.

"These are bad times, Jessica. No one trusts anyone. A man with a strong French accent like my father can wake up to find himself being dragged off to a hanging. I don't want to do anything to endanger him." He looked out at Billy again as he finished. "That's why I need to get to Governor Dinwiddie in Virginia and explain my presence at Pickawillany and why I couldn't do anything to help those people. It's a long story, but if I had warned them, some very fine people would have suffered, people who once helped save my life through a healing, just like your mother did."

Jess frowned, again moving to sit down on the top step. "It's all so confusing. I mean, we're all colonists, but the French and the English and the Indians are all mixed together so much so that a person hardly knows who to call friend and who to call enemy."

"That's right." Noah sighed deeply. "After what happened to my wife, our home burned, crops destroyed, I couldn't help deciding the French were the enemy. One thing I've learned, though, is that once you start that cycle of hatred, it just goes on and on. I saw that at Pickawillany, and being forced to pose as an ally of the French forced me to do things entirely against my convictions. It turned me into a person just as bad as those I spied against." He stared at his pipe, looking grim. "The experience told me I have to get out of this mess, quit doing what I'm doing and get on with life." He looked at her sadly. "Something just . . . I don't know . . . something changed. It's time to go home, I guess. I've had my fill of revenge. I want some peace. I want to settle again."

Jess felt her heart go out to him. She imagined what it might be like to make a home for a man like Noah Wilde, then looked away, fearing he might be able to read her thoughts. "The Bible says that hatred and revenge don't do a man much good," she told him. "The job of vengeance belongs to God alone, not man." She raised her gaze to see him studying her, as though trying to read her mind.

"Sometimes it's hard for man to accept that," he answered. "Maybe if I stay away from what I've been doing the last few years, I'll be able to put the past behind me and settle again."

Jess nodded. "I hope you can. I'm sure my folks would really appreciate you coming back here to help us move back east." *And so would I,* she wanted to add.

"If I can convince them to go."

Jess thought how she'd gladly go to Albany with the man, even if her parents decided to stay. She wanted to see Albany. More than that, she wanted to be with Noah Wilde. Realizing what a foolish thought that was, she forced herself to think of something else. "What's your necklace made of, Noah?"

He looked down, then put his hand to the necklace. "Bear claws. Miami Indians made it for me from the claws of a bear I'd killed."

"I've never seen anything like it."

Noah smiled with a hint of exasperation. "I hate to admit it, but the bear nearly killed me. Before he went down from my musket ball, he knocked me off a cliff and I broke a couple of ribs and was knocked unconscious. The weather was turning very cold. I might have lain there and frozen to death if a few Miami hadn't come along and found me. They took me to their village and nursed me back, skinned and gutted the bear and made this necklace for me as a sign of honor for managing to kill the thing. He was the biggest bear I've ever seen. Same for them."

"The necklace must be special to you."

"It is. I like to think it brings me good luck." He winked. "I was wearing it the first time I saw you."

Jess smiled and looked down again, not sure how to take his compliments.

Noah stood up then, wincing with pain. "I guess I'll be leaving out in a couple of days."

"Ma says you're not ready!" Jess rose and faced him, thinking how small she felt next to him. "Please wait a few more days."

He rubbed at the back of his neck. "I'll see. I'm worried about my father, though." He started to say something more, then stiffened. "Go grab Billy and get inside!" he told her quietly, watching something in the distance.

"What?"

"Iroquois are coming. Try not to show any alarm. Just do as I say." He moved to the steps and leaned against a support post. "They look like Susquehannock. Probably no real threat, but we'd better be careful." He looked back at her. "Hurry up!"

Swallowing back an alarm she'd never experienced before her attack four days earlier, Jess ran off the porch and grabbed Billy. She clung to the surprised boy as she ran back up the steps, glancing at Noah before hustling her little brother inside the cabin and closing the door.

8

Jess moved to a front window, her heart pounding. What if these Indians had come to kill and destroy? Until the vicious fighting she'd seen between Noah and the Ottawa, she'd never given much thought to the dangers the Indians presented. She had thought of them only as a curiosity. Her father and Sonny always treated them fairly but with caution, never with any real fear.

Now she knew fear, not just for her family, but for Noah Wilde. He was, after all, in no shape to fight anyone, if it came to that. He faced the Indians squarely and nodded to them, then said something in their own tongue. Jess's mother approached from the left, and Billy tugged at Jess to be allowed to go back outside.

"I wanna be with Mommy," he complained.

"Hush!" Jess ordered. "You stay still and be quiet or I'll take a switch to you, Billy Matthews!"

The boy stuck out his lower lip and sat down on the floor to pout. Jess watched her father and brother approach from the right, both men looking stiff and wary. They stopped several feet from the Indians, and Gabe sat obediently beside Sonny, growling low in his throat. Jess could see her brother commanding the well-trained hound to stay put and be quiet, just by a wave of his hand.

Noah continued conversing with the brightly dressed natives. Susquehannock, he'd told her. Jess knew now that any native could be pro-French or friend to the English. She had no doubt Noah was trying to determine just where these Indians' sympathies lay. Even from here she could see the worry in her mother's eyes, and Sonny and her father stood looking ready to pounce if and when necessary. Jess knew that if a fight broke out, Gabe would lunge into action, sinking his teeth into the enemy's flesh in defense of his master.

There were six of them, all men. Jess worried there could be more, for such men could melt into the surrounding woods like leaves and shadows. They seemed to be demanding something, but Noah shook his head, then called out to Jess's mother, "Do you have bread to spare?"

Marlene stepped cautiously closer. "Of course, if that's all they want."

"They've come a long way and are on their way to visit relatives. The last few days they've had trouble finding game, and the wild berries aren't ripe yet. They are wondering if you have any food to spare."

"You sure that's all they want?" Jonathan spoke up, stepping closer himself.

Noah hesitated, glancing back at the closed cabin door. "That's all," he answered, looking back at Jonathan. He turned to Marlene again. "Go on inside and rustle up what you can. They'll be grateful, and no Iroquois is going to turn on someone who is generous to them. These are Susquehannock. They're neutral in their dealings with the French and the English. These particular men are on a peaceful visiting trip."

Marlene hurried past the natives and onto the cabin porch, then rushed inside. "Help me gather some food," she told Jess. "And grab that light blanket off your bed, quickly. After what happened the other day I want to feed these natives and see them on their way. After that I would be pleased never to see another Indian the rest of the summer."

Jess obeyed, hurrying up the ladder to the loft and yanking a thin blanket from her bed. She climbed back down, and Marlene told her to spread the blanket over the table. Billy tried to hang on her skirt, but the woman shooed him away.

"Mommy will lie down with you when you nap in a little while," she reassured her son. "Right now I have something important to do. Be a good boy now and go sit down."

She laid two loaves of bread in the center of the blanket, telling Jess to grab a few potatoes. They both then added carrots, a few boiled eggs that had been cooked that same morning, and some jerked meat. Marlene gathered up the edges of the blanket and twisted them together, then carried the bundle of food to the door.

"Stay inside," she told Jess. She glanced at Billy. "You stay here with your sister and mind her," she ordered. She walked out. Jess hurried back to the window to watch, resenting the intrusion for the simple fact that the Susquehannock had broken up her conversation with Noah. She'd enjoyed the private minutes with him, enjoyed talking with him and the way it made her feel more like a woman than a young girl. For some reason she felt very womanly and special when he looked at her, and she found herself hoping she would get another chance to speak alone with him.

She watched through the window again as her mother handed out the bundle of food to Noah. "Take it to them yourself," he told her. "Getting it from the woman of the household will earn you great respect and assure no harm will come to your family."

Jess could feel her mother's uneasiness. "All right." Marlene walked out to the natives and handed out the food. They actually appeared to be grateful, looking inside the bundle and smiling and nodding. One of them removed the colorful blanket wrapped around his shoulders and handed it to Marlene, who accepted it graciously, then walked back to the porch, giving Noah a look of relief.

One of the older natives then shouted something to Noah, pointing toward the cabin. Noah shook his head and answered in their tongue. Whatever they were discussing, the older Indian seemed a little irate and argued with Noah for several minutes. Noah continued to protest and made a motion with his arm as though to wave them off. Finally, the older one seemed to calm down. He turned and barked something to the others, and all the natives left together.

Marlene turned and came inside, rolling her eyes at Jess. "Thank God they're gone," she told her. "I never used to worry when natives showed up, but ever since those Indians tried to make off with you . . . ." She walked up and gave Jess a quick hug, and Billy grabbed his mother's skirt and tugged. Marlene turned and picked the boy up, giving him a hug also.

"I feel the same way," Jess told her mother. "I was never scared of them before. I'm glad Noah was here. I wonder what they were arguing about."

Noah and the men came inside then, Jonathan grumbling that he had enough to worry about with spring planting without having to wonder when natives would show up making demands. "Never used to be a problem," he complained.

"What was that old man arguing about?" Sonny asked Noah.

Noah glanced at Jess, then turned to Sonny. "Well, the Iroquois have a custom of sharing their young women with honored visitors. He thought your daughter should be offered to him for the night, as a gesture of trust and friendship."

Marlene gasped, and Jess's eyes widened at the horrible thought. Anger filled Jonathan's and Sonny's eyes. "I'd kill every one of them first!" Sonny declared.

Noah set his pipe on the table. "Don't get too upset. To them it's not an insult but rather an honor. The young woman is supposed to be more than happy to fulfill her welcoming duties, you might say. It's custom. That's why I had to argue with the old man. He felt insulted that I refused to send Jess out to him." He grimaced and rubbed his left arm. "I made him understand that's just not our way. You can go on with whatever all of you were doing. I'm afraid I need to lie back down for a while."

Jonathan sighed and ran a hand through his hair. "Well, I'm glad you were here to set things straight with them," he told Noah. "We're obliged for everything you've done to help out."

Noah faced him with a warning look. "Do you see now why you have to consider leaving here?"

Jonathan scowled and turned toward the door. "I'll think about it. You'll have my answer when you come back from Virginia. I appreciate your offer to accompany us back to New York. I'm just not real sure yet what I'll do." He walked out.

Sonny nodded to Noah. "Thanks, Noah." He turned to Jess. "You stick close to the cabin." He hoisted his long gun and left to finish his chores, grumbling about Indians on his way out.

Noah glanced at Jess again. "Sonny's advice is true. Stay close and be aware." He turned to Marlene. "I'm aching everywhere. I guess you're right about waiting a few more days before I leave."

"You'd better go ahead and lie down," Marlene told him. "Those wounds are still very tender." She sighed and turned to Jess as Noah limped back into Sonny's room. "There is plenty to do in here—more bread to knead, and perhaps you could bake a berry pie for supper. There are still some dried blueberries in the storage shelter."

"Yes, ma'am."

Marlene ordered Billy to stay inside with his sister for a while. The boy pouted but obeyed, and after her mother left Jess walked to the table to check on three bowls of rising bread dough. She shivered at the thought of being handed over to the natives as a welcome gift, then glanced at the curtained doorway to Sonny's room. She couldn't help wondering if and how often Noah Wilde had been offered young Indian maidens as welcome gifts. Had he accepted? The thought made her heart rush with painful jealousy and anger.

9

"He likes you."

Jess turned at the sound of Noah's voice. She felt a pleasant excitement at his presence in the stock shed, where she curried one of his horses, a buckskin gelding. Its mane and tail and all four legs were black.

"He's a pretty horse," she answered, running a hand over the animal's shoulder. "Tallest horse I've ever seen. We don't see many horses around here. Most folks just own oxen, like Pa. They're better suited for plowing and such." She came around to the right side of the horse, closer to where Noah stood just outside the stall. "What's his name?" she asked, again brushing the horse vigorously.

"Just Buck. Seemed fitting enough. The gray one over there, that's Slowpoke. I call him that because I use him for a packhorse and I'm constantly jerking at him to keep up."

Jess smiled. "I had a black horse once, but she wasn't well formed like this one. She died last year. I miss her. She was real gentle." She stopped working and looked at Noah. "Pa doesn't believe in having such things just for pets. He says if an animal can't serve some purpose on a farm, it doesn't belong there. Blackie got sick so he shot her." She sighed. "I cried for three days." She began brushing Buck more gently, feeling Noah's eyes on her. After a moment of quiet he offered solace.

"Sometimes men just have a different way of looking at things," he told her. "When your primary purpose is survival, there's no room for sentiment."

Jess frowned, facing him again. "Like when you had to help the French at Pickawillany?"

A terrible sadness showed in his eyes, and Jess felt sorry for the question.

"Something like that," he finally answered. He looked her over in that way he had of stirring pleasant, womanly feelings in Jess. He'd been with her family for eight days now, but they had not been alone since four days ago when she talked with him on the porch. Still, as he visited with her family at meals and became more relaxed and friendly with them, Jess was beginning to feel close to the man. Several times she'd caught Noah watching her as though he wanted to tell her something, often in ways that showed great admiration, even desire. Had she simply imagined it? She hoped not.

"I don't much understand how men think," she told him with a nervous smile. "My pa can be mean as a bear, and then he'll turn around and apologize or be real nice to my ma. I've heard him cuss and I've seen him cry. He didn't know I saw him. It was after Ma lost a baby. That was before Billy was born. I think he was more upset that my ma almost died than he was about the baby."

"I can understand that."

Jess set the brush aside and turned, facing Noah. "I guess you could." She studied his dark eyes, thinking how strange it would be to see a big, wild man like Noah Wilde cry. Surely he'd cried when his wife was murdered. Maybe he'd let his anger and revenge take the place of crying. Her mother told her once that sometimes men were like that—took out their feelings in other ways. Jess, on the other hand, had trouble hiding her own feelings, like those she was beginning to experience whenever Noah Wilde was near. "Have you given more thought to quitting what you're doing and going home to settle again?" she asked.

He limped around the end of the stall to come inside and face her. "I have." He reached out and petted Buck's rump with his left hand, wincing when he did so. "It's what I want to do, but it depends on a lot of things."

"What things?" Jess asked, surprised at her own forthrightness.

Noah shrugged. "Oh, I don't know . . . what I'm told when I get to Virginia; how my parents are doing; how serious things are getting between the French and the English. I have no doubt they are *very* serious by now, after Pickawillany."

He leaned his right shoulder against the wall, studying her so fondly that Jess felt a rush of desire that embarrassed her. She stepped back slightly.

"It also depends on your pa, and you," he told her.

"Me?"

He smiled, a teasing look in his eyes. "Well, like I

told you the other day, if I can talk your pa into leaving here, I'd like to return and help get you back to Albany. At the same time, I'll be thinking even more seriously about staying once I get there. And if a man is going to settle, he ought to have a woman at his side. I was hoping maybe you'd give that some thought."

"Me? You hardly know me!"

He kept smiling as he shook his head. "I know you well enough to know you can cook and you work hard. I know you're pretty and that you have a soft heart. And I know you're a scrapper. You didn't run away when that Indian rose up to try to finish me off. You landed that rock right square in his forehead."

Jess didn't mind the compliments, but they surprised her, considering the man seemed to be saying she had all the qualities that made a good wife. *What about love?* she wanted to ask, but was too bashful. A man and woman ought to be in love to marry. She'd learned enough about Noah Wilde to know she could love him easy enough; but right now he confused her, the way he beat around the bush about what exactly he wanted of her.

She looked down at the straw-covered floor. "I guess we won't know much else until you come back and we travel back to New York," she told him. "I mean, we've got to know each other pretty good these last many days, just by all the talking and such." She looked up to meet his gaze again. "I guess we know each other good enough to give consideration to . . . to what you're thinking. If you decided . . . I mean, if things worked out like you think, you'd have to talk to my pa and all that. And on the way to New York, we'd have that much more time to talk and find out even more about each other." She turned away. "This is all kind of strange and surprising. In a lot of ways you're still almost a stranger, Noah. I'm . . . I appreciate your compliments, and you're a right handsome man and all; but you have some things to settle in your mind . . . and with those others waiting for you in Virginia. I expect there are a lot of things you won't know your-self until you go there."

"I expect so." She felt him move closer, felt a big hand on her shoulder. "All I know is that I believe in fate. And fate brought me to those woods last week just in time. To me that's a sign that you have some importance in my life. I almost died keeping those Indians from getting hold of you, and I don't even know why I did it. I guess for one flash of a moment I saw Mary standing there, Indians ready to attack her."

Jess swallowed, finding the courage to turn and look up at him. So close! He stood so close! "I'm not Mary. That's one thing you'd have to deal with."

He smiled again. Were those tears she detected in his eyes?

"No, you definitely are not Mary. I don't mean to be comparing. I'm just explaining why I reacted like I did in that moment. And I wanted you to understand why I feel you're important to me, in spite of the short time I've known you."

Jess felt her heart race. "I guess I feel the same way. I've never before met a man who believed in fate. I believe the same thing. You sure are different from other men. Pa would say it was silly to believe in such things."

He touched her face so gently that Jess could hardly believe this was the same man who'd slaughtered five Iroquois with the fierceness of a wild grizzly. He could break her in half, have his way with her any time he wanted, but she felt no fear. She almost felt as though she'd always known him. He brushed a few strands of hair behind her ear.

"I'm not your pa. But I'm also not so different from most men. I'm just lonely, and searching for some peace."

He leaned closer, and Jess stood rigid as he lightly kissed her forehead. He moved away from her then, turning to leave. "Give it all some thought, Jess. I'll be leaving in two more days."

"You're not well enough!" she blurted out, screaming on the inside that she never wanted him to leave.

He glanced back at her. "I'm well enough." He looked her over again. "Well enough to know it's time for me to leave before I change my mind. I have responsibilities to tend to, Jess, and my father to think about. If I don't show up, people might make trouble for him. I just want you to think about what I've told you."

Jess nodded. "I will, Noah." She watched in wonder as he limped away. Nothing felt real at the moment. Not many days ago she'd been wondering about dancing with some young man at the next gathering. Now here had come a full-grown, experienced man whose courage and skill no one could doubt; an educated man who owned a farm in Albany; a handsome man who'd been leading a life of violence and revenge for many years and who now was ready to give it all up—for her! Did she dare allow herself to fall in love with him? Would he leave here and never come back? Did he feel any love for her, or did he just think he *might* be able to love her someday?

She put a hand to where he'd kissed her, feeling on fire. Already she knew there was no argument in her own heart about "allowing" herself to love Noah Wilde. Senseless as it seemed, she knew it had already happened. She loved the man with every fiber of her being.

10

Jess awoke to a gentle pressure on her shoulder. "Jess." She recognized her mother's voice and turned to see the woman crouched beside the wooden and rope-spring bed she shared with her little brother.

"What is it, Mama?" She sat up and rubbed at her eyes, not sure what time it was. A slice of moonlight filtered through the tiny window of the loft, enough to see her mother's face relatively well once her eyes adjusted.

"Your father is sleeping, so I thought I'd take the opportunity to talk to you," Marlene answered quietly. "Billy is sleeping, too."

Jess swung her legs over the edge of the bed. "Talk about what?"

Marlene sighed, moving to sit down in a wooden chair near the bed. "About Noah Wilde."

Jess felt a rush of excitement at the very mention of Noah's name. She frowned, not sure what to expect. "Noah? Why?"

"I think you know why, darling. You're in love with him, aren't you?"

"In love?" At first Jess felt defensive. Did her mother think there was something wrong with that? "I . . . I'm not sure. Why do you think that?"

Marlene smiled. "Because I was your age once. And I know exactly how men like Noah Wilde appear to girls who have not experienced much of life beyond their own family and home. I don't doubt that his last name is quite descriptive of the man himself."

Wild? "I realize he's led a life of roaming and fighting and spying for years, but he's ready to give all that up now," Jess told her mother. "That's why he told Pa that he wants to come back here and help us get back to Albany. He intends to go there himself and settle again."

Marlene nodded. "I'm sure he's thinking that way,

darling. And I'm sure he's sincere; but it isn't always easy for a man to settle again after living such a life. He's still restless and angry and grieving."

"I could change all of that. I know he's thinking of settling with me as his wife once we all get to Albany. I can tell by the way he talks. He hasn't said he loves me, Mama, but I know he's thinking it. After losing his wife and baby—"

Marlene put a hand to her mouth in surprise. "Baby?"

Jess felt like crying at the thought of it. "He told me earlier today that his wife was carrying when she was murdered."

"Oh, my!" Marlene shook her head. "He's surely a torn man." She leaned back in the chair and closed her eyes for a moment. "I saw him go into the horse shed today when you were out there currying the horses. What else happened in there, Jess?"

"What else? Nothing! We just talked. He seemed to need to talk, so I listened."

"Nothing else?"

Jess felt embarrassed. "Well . . . before he left he . . . he kissed me on the forehead. That's all."

Marlene sighed again. "I'm not against the man, Jess. He seems honest, and Lord knows we owe him for nearly dying to keep you safe. I just want to warn you that he would be a lot of man for any woman to take on, let alone a sixteen-year-old woman-child who's never been courted, not even by a man closer to her own age who is as inexperienced as she is."

Jess shrugged. "Pa keeps saying I'm old enough to be thinking about marriage."

"Yes, you are; but I'm sure he was thinking of one of the younger men who come to the gathering."

Jess thought about such young men in comparison with Noah. "No young man has ever grabbed my heart and made it sing like Noah Wilde has. I know he's older and experienced in things I don't know anything about, but when I'm with him I feel so safe, Mama, like nothing in this world can harm me as long as Noah is at my side. I know with all my being that he would be a loyal, caring, protective husband. It's *because* of all his knowledge and experienced ways that he'd make a good husband. It would be to my benefit to marry a man like that, a man who's already been married, who owns property, who knows all the right people. Don't you think that would be better than marrying a young man who doesn't know what he's about? Who doesn't know what he really wants?"

Marlene reached out and grasped Jess's hands. "You have a point. It's just that a man like that can be quite a handful. I see more troubles coming over this French and Indian problem, and Noah is right in the middle of it all. I fear it won't be as easy for him to get out of his situation as he thinks it will be. He's very valuable to the English because he knows the ways of both the French and the Indians. He even speaks their languages. They just might keep after him to continue helping them, and he might feel bound to do just that. Where would that leave you? You'd be home worrying constantly over whether or not he'll ever come back, or be killed or tortured or imprisoned. I see hard years ahead, Jess."

Jess pulled off her nightcap. "If that's true, then it will be hard for all of us, Mama. It's already hard for you and Pa, having to consider giving up everything you've worked for over the last twelve years. And if war is to come, wouldn't I be safer being with Noah?"

Marlene smiled sadly. "You'd be safe in body, but your heart could be shattered by something terrible happening to Noah."

"Yes, ma'am. That's a risk we all take, don't we? Pa could have died that year Sonny's gun went off and hit him in the side. Those Indians could have attacked and killed Sonny and Pa if they'd come upon them first. Nobody knows where life will lead them. You've told me that many times."

Marlene squeezed her hands. "So I have."

Jess thought about Noah, who now slept in a storage shed, feeling he was putting the family out by sleeping in the house. "Have you talked to Pa about any of this?" she asked. "He likes Noah, doesn't he?"

"Oh, yes, very much. But he worries, too, considering the very things we've just talked about. Of course, Noah hasn't really voiced his intentions over you or what he wants once he returns to Albany; but your father and I both see it in his eyes—and in yours."

"You do?"

"You don't hide it very well, Jess."

Jess swallowed, wondering if Noah saw it, too. Surely he did, and that made her feel humiliated. "Oh, no," she said softly.

Marlene laughed softly. "There is nothing wrong with wearing your heart on your sleeve, Jess. A young girl's passion is difficult to hide. I felt the same passion for your father. That's probably hard for you to imagine, us being the age we are now."

"No, it isn't. Anybody can see how much you love Pa. And you're so pretty, Mama, and refined. It still shows, even though you've lived away from the city for so long. I know in my heart it took a lot for you to leave there and come out here to the wilderness. You had to love Pa a lot to do that."

Marlene touched her cheek. "Well, thank you for the compliment. And, yes, I did—and still do love your father very much." She rose. "I just want you to know you can talk to me, Jess, about anything. And I have a feeling your father will be talking with Noah about a few things, man to man, I guess you'd say. I think he wants to get an idea of Noah's intentions. It will help your father decide if we should leave here when Noah returns."

"He won't embarrass me, will he? I mean, I don't want Noah to know how I feel. Maybe he's already guessed, but I don't want anybody to tell him flat out. He might not have any of the feelings I think he has. Maybe it's just my imagination."

"Well, intuition tells me it's not your imagination at all. I just think Noah is wrestling over a lot of things on the inside, wondering if he should impose his wild and restless life on someone so young and innocent. It's just possible he'll make no decisions until he reports in Virginia and finds out what's going on there. I'm sure he's experiencing torn loyalties right now, arguing both sides, which is probably why he's said nothing truly serious to you about feelings he might have. He's wise enough to weigh all the facts."

Marlene leaned forward and kissed Jess's cheek. "Get back to sleep. I just felt I had to discuss this with you a little." She squeezed Jess's hands again and descended the loft ladder.

Jess sighed and lay back down, not bothering to put her nightcap back on. Her mother's words weighed heavily on her heart. She was relieved to realize her mother and father suspected her feelings and were trying to be understanding, but she also worried about some of her mother's comments about Noah. Would he go to Virginia and discover something there that would keep him from returning, something that would make him decide he should not impose on her life?

How could he have come to mean so much to her so soon? She could hardly bear the thought of him going away forever. She would want to die if he didn't come back.

11

Jess slowly turned to the sweet tune Sonny played on his fiddle. She felt beautiful tonight because of the way Noah looked at her now as they danced together. His warm hand grasped hers gently, his other hand was at her waist, and his very touch made her heart beat faster.

Billy danced around them, giggling and holding his favorite blanket. There was little room in the cabin for dancing, but Marlene and Jonathan had decided Noah's last night here should be special. Jess had helped her mother cook a grand meal of roasted pork, along with sweet potatoes taken from the dugout beneath the cabin, where vegetables were kept through the winter. Jess made fresh biscuits, and the butter she'd churned a few days earlier made them even more delicious. Things could not be more wonderful—except for the fact that Noah was leaving in the morning.

How she hated the thought of him going away! He'd been here only ten days, but those days had become so memorable. In those ten days she'd fallen in love. The feeling was as natural and real as if she'd known him for months. They were meant to be together. She felt no doubts. Noah was ready to love again. He'd not actually told her he loved her, but that look in his eyes

. . . it was so happy. She felt proud that dancing with her made him feel that way. She thought, if she were his wife, how safe she would always feel with him. She already knew that each day he was away would seem like the longest day she'd ever lived through. She wanted to cry at the thought of watching him leave.

Marlene hummed along with Sonny's playing. In spite of his sore leg and shoulder, Noah managed to finish the dance. How handsome he looked tonight, his dark hair tied at the side of his neck and hanging over one shoulder. His white shirt was gathered at the neck, where it met a stiff collar that buttoned at his throat. The dropped shoulders of the shirt met gathered, cuffed, three-quarter-length sleeves. Jess had no doubt it was probably the dressiest shirt he'd packed—and he'd worn it just for her. Otherwise he wore deerskin leggings and moccasins, having nothing else dressy with him. The man was a grand mixture of educated gentleman and wild frontiersman. Jess was sure he could handle himself in both worlds.

Tonight Jess wore a green linen dress her mother had made her for a dance at the gathering last fall. She'd danced only with her father and Sonny, not even caring much whether young men there might have an eye for her. She'd felt no attraction to any of them. Noah was the first man who'd stirred these wonderful feelings in her. She was glad for the dress, which her mother often said made her eyes look even greener and prettier.

She wore a white, ruffled pinafore over the dress, and her mother had pulled her hair up and pinned it in big curls, a style that made her look older. Her mother had even allowed Jess to wear a little color on her cheeks, knowing she wanted to look her best tonight.

Sonny began playing faster, until the pace became too much for Noah's leg. He laughed as he limped to a chair. Jess sat down in a rocker near him while her mother sliced into a fresh-baked berry pie and insisted Noah have a piece. Noah ate the pie and drank coffee with Jonathan and Sonny, then the three men smoked and talked for a good hour.

Jess thought how this was one of the happiest times she could remember. She wanted it to last forever, but her joy was dimmed by worry over the more immediate future. Noah had again urged Jonathan to prepare to leave, but Jonathan insisted on one more growing season first. He'd asked Noah to return and help with the harvest in the fall. Then he could help herd all the livestock and crops to the trading post in Logstown, where Jonathan wanted to sell all he could; he would need money when he returned to Albany. He'd told Noah that Sonny would build an extra wagon for hauling the furniture and dishes and whatever things Marlene had accumulated in their twelve years here, things that meant a lot to her.

"Leaving here will be the hardest thing we've ever done," Jonathan now said sadly. He sat gazing at the fireplace as he spoke. Marlene sat near Jess on the other side of the room, with Billy on her lap, and Jess could tell the woman was practically ready to cry. In spite of longing to go home to Albany all these years, Jess knew her mother would find it very difficult to leave here now. This had become home, and when a person put so much time and hard work into something, it hurt to leave, especially knowing others might come along and burn down whatever was left behind.

"The lives of your family are more important," Noah reminded Jess's father.

"I know, I know." The man leaned forward, resting his elbows on his knees. He sighed deeply, and Jess felt her heart wrench, realizing how sad her father was. "How long do you think this mess will go on?"

Noah rubbed his sore leg. "I wish I knew, Jonathan." He puffed on his pipe for a moment. "The main problem is that both the French and the English have the Iroquois involved. The longer this goes on, the more divided the Iroquois will become, so we'll be mixed up in their own war against each other over hard feelings for taking sides. That kind of war worries me the most. Settlers will be caught in the middle. Once the Iroquois are angered and go on the warpath . . ." He hesitated before continuing. "I can't begin to explain their brutality, especially not in front of women. Right now probably the only Iroquois the English can call friend are the Mohawks—maybe the Oneida and some of the Susquehannocks. Pretty much all of the Ottawa, the Huron, Senecas, Onondagas, Delawares, Shawnee—they're all pro-French. I'm afraid it's going to take years for things to settle, and before that ever happens, I see all-out war ahead."

Noah glanced at Jess, and her heart warmed at the concern in his eyes. He looked back at Jonathan. "I'm wondering if I might have a word alone with your daughter before I leave in the morning. I'll be gone by sunrise. I have everything packed." He looked over at Marlene. "Thank you, ma'am, for the bread and potatoes you've given me to take along."

"It's the least we can do," Marlene answered. She managed a smile. "You go ahead out on the porch with Jess and speak with her alone if you wish."

"Thank you." Noah set his pipe aside and rose, limping to the door. Jess's heart pounded harder when he opened it and motioned for her to join him outside. She glanced at her mother, who smiled her approval, then rose and walked out with Noah, her mind racing with the possibilities of why he wanted to see her alone.

12

Noah grasped Jess's arm and pulled her aside, away from the front window. "I need to talk to you alone once more, Jess." He leaned close. Something in his masculine presence made Jess feel as though she were on fire.

"What is it, Noah?"

His reply was to meet her mouth with his own,

parting her lips in a deep, sweet, warm kiss. Pleased and surprised, Jess felt she would melt into him. No man had ever kissed her like this. She'd known only fatherly or brotherly kisses on the cheek, and little Billy's sloppy, innocent baby kisses.

Unable to control her joy and passion, Jess threw her arms around Noah's neck. He reacted by lifting her right off her feet as the kiss lingered, and Jess decided this was the best first kiss a woman could ask for. Noah finally left her mouth for just a moment, trailing his lips over her cheek to her neck as he crushed her close. When he met her lips again, Jess offered her mouth willingly, returning the kiss with open lips, tasting his sweet mouth, feeling a wild, wonderful awakening deep inside she'd never known. She felt wicked and wanton and all woman, and she knew she wanted to be this man's wife. She wasn't one bit afraid of what that meant. She could think of nothing more wonderful than mating with Noah Wilde and letting him awaken the woman inside aching to be released. She was confident he would be gentle and loving. She was never more sure in her life of what she wanted, and that was to belong to Noah, in mind, in spirit, in body. He left her lips again, kissing her eyes, her forehead, her hair.

"Don't go, Noah, please, don't go!" she whispered. "I love you. I'll be afraid without you."

He held her close, his stronger right arm around her waist while gripping the back of her neck with his left hand. "I have no choice," he answered softly.

Again he kissed her eyes. "I'll be back in plenty of time to take care of you. When I come back, I want you to be my wife. Tell me you'll marry me, Jess. I love you."

He'd finally said it. He loved her! Jess wanted to shout and sing. "You know I'll marry you," she answered. Their lips met again, and Jess whimpered when he ran his left hand down her shoulder and over her right breast, gently squeezing, sending flames through her blood. Was it terribly brazen of her to allow him to touch her that way? Why couldn't she bring herself to protest? He squeezed harder, his kiss deepening as he groaned from his own desire.

So, this was love. This was what it was like to want a man so badly that you would follow him to the ends of the earth to be with him. Now she knew why her mother had left everything that mattered to her to come out here with her father.

Noah moved both arms around her then, holding her close, clinging to her almost desperately. "I'll come back as soon as I can," he told her. "I'll probably be gone before you even get up in the morning, Jess."

"But I'll never sleep, anyway," she answered. "Let me come out to the shed and sit with you until you leave."

"No!" He kissed her hair. "The way I'm feeling right now, something could happen we would both regret." He sighed. "If anything happens and I don't make it back—"

"Don't say that!" Jess leaned back and studied his

dark eyes in the brightly moonlit night. "Nothing will happen!"

"If it did, I'd never forgive myself for stealing what doesn't rightly belong to me yet. And if something should go wrong, Jess, I'll write you. In the meantime, you watch yourself, and you make sure your father heads east by fall if I'm not back yet."

"Please don't talk that way! You'll be back. How long will it take you to do what you have to do?"

"No more than a month."

"That sounds like forever!"

"It does to me, too. I'm sorry, Jess, but I have to do this. I'm obligated. I'll think about you every minute I'm gone."

"You know I'll be doing the same. I love you, Noah Wilde. I never thought I'd fall in love so fast, but I have. You were right about us. There's a reason we met like we did, and this is it. We're supposed to be together."

He pulled her close again and kissed her once more, a long, passionate kiss of promise. He held her a moment longer before pulling away and placing his hands on either side of her face. "I'm glad I came along when I did, Jess, glad I met you and your family. This is the happiest I've felt in eight years." He kissed her hair, then stepped back. "You'd best go inside. If we stay out here too long it won't look good."

"I don't want to stop touching you."

"And I sure as hell don't want to stop touching you, but we've got to get this done with, Jess. I owe it to my father to go back first and report."

Jess could not stop her tears. "Tell me once more. Tell me you love me and you'll be back."

He brushed at her tears with the back of his hand. "I love you. Nothing can keep me from coming back for you, Jess Matthews." He took her hand and raised it to his lips, kissing her palm, then squeezed her hand and turned away, walking off the porch.

Jess watched him in the moonlight until he disappeared into the shed, where his horses were already packed and waiting for the trip to Virginia. She wanted to run to him, beg him not to go, throw herself at him like a wanton woman.

She stood there a little longer, wiping her eyes and tucking her hair into its pins, fighting her desire. She grasped a porch post, and looked up at the stars and a full moon. "Please, God, take care of him. Make sure he comes back," she whispered. She could not stop more tears, and her head began to ache, as did her heart and her insides, which longed to physically be one with him.

Finally, she breathed deeply for self-control and reluctantly turned to go inside. She again smoothed back the sides of her hair, which during their passionate kisses had tumbled from the pins. She wiped at her cheeks once more, sure all the color must be gone from them now, then went through the door, saying nothing to her parents but "Good night."

She climbed the wooden ladder to the loft, where Billy had already been put to bed. She slowly undressed, wondering what it would be like to lie next to Noah in the night, letting him make love to her. She pulled on her nightgown, then unpinned her hair and shook it loose. She tied on her nightcap and lay down on the feather bed next to Billy.

She could not stop more tears then, nor the deep longing to have Noah Wilde lying beside her. Her weary tears finally led to an exhausted sleep, the sleep she didn't think she'd be able to find. When she awoke, she was surprised to realize the sun was already up. She could hear her mother moving around downstairs.

Noah! Quickly, she sat up and pulled on her robe, wrapping it closely around herself. She threw off her nightcap and hurriedly climbed down the ladder, then headed for the door.

"Jess!" her mother called to her.

Jess stopped and turned.

"He's already gone, darling."

Jess felt as though someone had run a sword through her heart. Still barefoot, she turned and hurried outside to the end of the porch, from where she could see the shed. The door stood open, and from the way the rising sun caused a shaft of light to fall inside the door, she could see Noah's horses were gone.

It all seemed so unreal. For a brief moment she wondered if any of the events of the past ten days had really taken place; but then she touched her lips and remembered Noah Wilde's kisses. Yes, everything had been real . . . too real . . . too wonderful.

She ran to the shed, hoping to at least catch a scent of him. She pushed back the shed door and felt a keen emptiness. Her heart rushed when she noticed Noah's bear-claw necklace hanging over the stall. She rushed to pick it up. A lump rose in her throat as she fingered the necklace, then kissed it. He'd told her it was special to him, that he felt it protected him and brought good luck. He'd left it for her, surely as a symbol of his love.

13

"Sit down, Noah." Governor Dinwiddie spoke the command with unusual curtness. Noah sat down gingerly in a velvet chair, more sore than he'd expected he'd be after ten days of constant riding. "I'm tired and haven't even had a chance to turn down my bed at the boardinghouse," he told the governor with irritation. "I didn't think when I sent that messenger that I'd have to come here so quickly. I didn't even think you'd be here this late in the day."

"You well know how anxious I would be to see you. I didn't want to wait until tomorrow, Noah."

"Why did I have to leave my musket and pistol with those militiamen outside?" Noah asked, upset at being treated like the enemy when he'd arrived at the governor's home. He faced the governor's desk and watched impatiently as Dinwiddie patted his powdered wig and waved him off.

"I don't like guns and such. You know that, Noah. I despise violence." Dinwiddie straightened the wide cuffs of his purple ottoman outer coat, then sat down in an oak and leather chair behind a large, polished desk. The man then fidgeted with a ruffled tie that decorated the throat of his white satin vest. Noah thought he seemed unusually nervous.

"Well, sir, if you detest violence so much that you can't even look at a long gun or a pistol, it's a good thing you've stayed away from the frontier regions. I assure you, violence is a way of life there, usually with knives and tomahawks. I have very sore and ugly scars on my left shoulder and right thigh to prove it."

Dinwiddie sighed and walked around to the front of his desk, again making Noah wonder at his restlessness. Noah noticed that the large tongue of the man's black shoes sported silver buckles, a status symbol among the wealthy. Dinwiddie leaned forward and eyed Noah with a scolding air.

"Tell me, Noah, the injuries you mentioned, did you get them at Pickawillany? If so, whom were you fighting, the English . . . or the French?"

Noah became alert, wary of the man's strangely threatening attitude. "Neither," he said flatly. "I got them fighting Ottawa Indians in Pennsylvania, where they did *not* belong, I might add. That's what I'm here to report. Things are much worse out there than you know."

Dinwiddie, a middle-aged man of average looks,

studied him intently. "Are they, now? And I suppose you have an explanation as to why you have arrived here nearly a year after the awful massacre of English traders at Pickawillany?"

Why did the man keep referring to Pickawillany? Noah turned slightly in his chair so he could stretch his long legs out in front of him without bumping Dinwiddie's legs. "Governor, I was at Pickawillany with the French, per your orders, I might remind you. They had sent other scouts ahead. I was trying to keep their confidence. There was no way I could have warned the people there of what was coming. I had to pretend to be with the French in every respect. Besides being led by the very vicious Ottawa Chief Pontiac, that attack was also led by Charles Langlade, a half-breed whose sole purpose at Pickawillany was to kill Miami Chief Unemakemi, against whom he carried a vicious hatred. Do you want to know how Unemakemi died?"

Dinwiddie sniffed. "You are a very able man, Noah. Surely you could have—"

"Langlade pressed his knees on the chief's shattered arms to hold him down while he sliced open the chief's chest and reached inside to rip out the man's heart, holding it out while the blood vessels were still attached and Unemakemi was still alive, staring at his own heart! Langlade sliced through the blood vessels to sever the heart from them, then took a bite out of it while it was still throbbing." He noticed Dinwiddie pale. The man drew in his breath and stood up, walking to a window.

"I don't need such details, Noah."

"I think you do! Some of the prisoners that were taken also had their hearts cut out and eaten. I don't think you have any idea of the brutality of the Iroquois, Governor. They can be your best friends or your worst enemies, depending on how fairly they are treated. Right now the French treat them a hundred times better than the English, and if we don't do something about it, every Iroquois tribe between here and Illinois Territory will side with the French. Colonists will die like Chief Unemakemi died. As far as Pickawillany, I can hold my own against five, maybe six Indians at once. I've done it. But I was there with several hundred Indians and French soldiers. There was nothing I could do."

Dinwiddie scowled. "For God's sake, Noah, Johnny Peidt was there! He—"

"I know he was there!" Noah interrupted. "I saw him die, and there was nothing I could do! It haunts me day and night, but that's the cost of spying, Governor."

Dinwiddie paced, fists clenched. "This is a damn mess!"

"Don't go judging what happened out there if you haven't been in the same situation yourself, Governor. I did what I was *ordered* to do. You should be aware that the French are sending out troops in full force to build forts all along the western border and even into areas that belong to English settlers. Their plan is to stop all future westward movement by the English, and to use the Iroquois to help them do it. That means more disasters like Pickawillany!"

Dinwiddie stopped pacing and stood at a window, toying with his ruffled cravat. "None of that explains why you didn't come back here right away."

Noah frowned with disgust, wondering how any man who lived in civilized parts could ever understand what was truly happening along the frontier. "I can't be two men at once. I was with the French. They asked me to scout for them as they returned to Montreal. After what they witnessed, I don't think they were terribly trusting of Langlade. And by then I had gained their full confidence. I was only obeying your orders by staying with them to continue to learn what I could. I went to Montreal, which took several weeks. I decided to stay on there and see what I could learn over the winter. Then I headed back south with the excuse that spring was coming and I wanted to hunt for furs to sell to French traders. I had no such intentions, but it was the only logical excuse for leaving. I was lucky even to get permission to go. I was on my way through Pennsylvania when I came across a young lady about to be attacked and stolen away by Detroit Ottawa. It happened near the junction of the Allegheny and Monongahela rivers."

"*Detroit* Ottawa?" Dinwiddie clasped his hands behind his back and turned. "That's not good."

"Of course it isn't." Noah felt frustrated and angry at the fact that it had taken Dinwiddie all this time to truly see the dangerous trend taking place. "They were snooping around for a reason, probably sent south by Pontiac himself. If we aren't careful, the French will push their way past outlying English settlements and keep going till they have us pushed all the way to the coast."

"Never!" Dinwiddie sighed. "What happened with the attack on the girl? I take it that's how you were wounded."

"It is. I managed to kill the whole lot of them, but I almost lost my own life." Noah thought about Jess. She was all he *could* think about. God, how he missed her! "The young lady's family helped me. I came straight here as soon as I was well enough. You should know that the French are sending troops and supplies south to reinforce their establishments at Fort Presque Isle and Fort Le Boeuf, with plans to take over Venango and head farther south along the Allegheny, maybe even establish a fort at its junction with the Monongahela."

Dinwiddie pursed his lips in thought as he moved back around his desk, his head bowed. His face reddened as he stood silent, his white wig making his skin appear even redder. "We will stop that movement!" he declared. He faced Noah then. "By God, we will *stop* it! We will build forts of our own and make more of an effort to win the help of the Iroquois."

Noah straightened in his chair. "That won't be easy. Most of the Iroquois favor the French, and they don't like splitting loyalties, with the possibility of fighting each other. The Mohawks are your best bet, but even so, they are pretty adamant about not getting involved."

"I know that only too well. Governors Clinton of New York and Governor Hamilton of Pennsylvania and I all met with Mohawks and Oneidas. One old Oneida man, called Sconondoa, gave a long speech about how the Iroquois need to stick together against all white men, French and English. We will have to promise them the world on a platter to get them to help us."

Noah leaned forward. "Whatever you decide, I won't be able to help you, Governor." He stood, towering over Dinwiddie, who looked up at him with a frown.

"What do you mean?"

"I mean I'm quitting. What happened at Pickawillany was the final blow, being with the French and unable to help those poor victims. I've had my revenge for what happened to Mary. I want to settle again, get on with my life. I want children, and I want to farm again, maybe settle outside of Albany near my parents."

Dinwiddie put up his hand as though to tell him to be still. "You can't do that."

"What?" Noah felt his anger rising.

Dinwiddie walked to the door of his study and opened it, speaking to someone in the great room. "Send them in." He turned back to Noah, clearing his throat and looking fearfully nervous. "Noah, I believe you know how much I value the friendship of Judge Fairfax."

Before Noah could even reply, several militiamen burst into the room, holding muskets aimed at him. Confused, Noah stiffened, his hands moving into fists.

"Please don't, Noah," Dinwiddie told him. "This is hard enough for me. I don't want to have to report to your father that you've been killed. I like the man, but what has to be done, has to be done."

"What is going on here!" Noah raged, backing away. Some of the militiamen moved behind him.

"Noah, if you try to fight, they'll shoot you!" Dinwiddie warned. "This isn't a bunch of Indians armed only with knives and tomahawks. These are Virginia militia, and they will do as I order and shoot you if you dare try to fight or get away."

Noah eyed each man, and he knew damn well they would obey the governor's orders to shoot. So, this was why he'd been ordered to turn over his weapons! He had no recourse for the moment but to obey Dinwiddie. "What the hell is this?" he seethed, glaring at Dinwiddie.

Dinwiddie scratched at his chin, obviously confident now that he was backed by armed men. "Noah, in spite of my appreciation for your help in the past, I am afraid I have to have you imprisoned for a few months."

"What!"

Dinwiddie backed away as Noah stepped closer.

One of the militiamen waved his musket at Noah. "Step back, Mr. Wilde!"

Noah shot the man a look that made him swallow, then turned his gaze back to Dinwiddie. "Explain yourself!"

Dinwiddie cleared his throat and toyed with his ruffled tie again. "Hear me out, Noah. The Honorable Mr. Fairfax is enraged over the death of Johnny Peidt, and over the general slaughter of the English traders at Pickawillany. He has become even more enraged that it took you this long to get back here to explain."

"I told you why I couldn't return right away."

"That won't matter to Fairfax, although I promise to explain your plight to the man. For now I have to have you arrested, Noah. Fairfax blames you directly for not warning the citizens of Pickawillany of the coming of the French and Ottawa. In his eyes you failed in your mission. If you had not returned when you did, he was ready to have your father arrested as a conspirator. The man is French but living among the English. You know his precarious position."

"He's married to an Englishwoman! You know that."

"That doesn't matter to Fairfax. Besides . . ." Dinwiddie looked down. "Your mother is dead, Noah."

Noah felt stunned. His lovely mother—dead! A stabbing grief engulfed him. He should have been with her and his father. "How?" he asked.

"A fever, probably consumption, I'm told. I'm sorry to have to tell you this way, under these circumstances. Still, with your mother gone, your father is more vulnerable now to rumors about the French, especially after Pickawillany. People are angry, and becoming more restless and distrustful. Someone has to pay in some way. That someone, I'm afraid, is you. The best I can do for you is make your plea to Fairfax and urge him to allow you to prove your loyalty in some way."

"I *have* proven my loyalty, many times over! I could have been killed at Pickawillany as easily as anyone else; and if I'd been discovered as a spy, the French would have had me hanged or imprisoned, probably tortured first! And this is the thanks I get?"

Dinwiddie again put up his hand in a patronizing wave. "Now, now, Noah, relax. I'll have you out in no time at all."

"I made a promise to someone!" Noah steamed. "I have to return to Pennsylvania as soon as possible. You make sure I'm able to do that!"

Dinwiddie nodded. "All right, I'll see to it. I'm sorry for this, Noah, but it's actually for your own good, and your father's."

"No, it isn't," Noah answered, his jaw flexing in anger. "It's for *your* own good! You're doing this to lick the shoes of Judge Fairfax and win his favor!"

Dinwiddie pressed his lips tightly, a rush of sudden anger flashing in his blue eyes. He glared at Noah momentarily, then turned away. "Take him away," he said calmly.

Two of the volunteers jabbed muskets into Noah's

back, while the rest continued to surround him, obviously wary of Noah's size and skill. Noah looked back at Dinwiddie. "You bastard!" he seethed. He walked out with the soldiers, worried not for himself, but for Jess. Dinwiddie had better keep his word about getting him out of this soon.

14

Late September 1753

Jess laid her handmade shirts on the wagon gate. Two men quickly walked over to look at them, one of them accompanied by a woman Jess supposed was his wife. She felt sorry for her because of her husband's short temper and impatience. He kept telling her to hurry and make up her mind, scowling, even grabbing her arm roughly once. Jess thought how Noah would never treat her that way . . . if she ever saw him again.

Where was he? She refused to believe he'd lied about coming back, as Sonny had suggested. Her father grumbled that he didn't know *what* to believe, but her mother was sure Noah had every intention of returning.

No matter what she did, all summer and autumn, whether it was planting potatoes and vegetables, weeding them, digging and picking them, sorting and loading them, making the shirts, helping with all the chores, feeding the chickens and collecting their eggs, stacking wood, helping with laundry, eating, sleeping, watching Billy—it didn't matter: every minute of every day and night was spent thinking about Noah.

Was he hurt? Dead? No, not Noah! She felt his presence, day and night. She knew it sounded silly to others when she told them so, but she just knew he was alive . . . somewhere. Something had kept him from coming back, something he couldn't help. Before he left he'd even mentioned the possibility: *If something happens . . .*

She took money from the ornery settler for two shirts. He grasped his wife's arm and yanked her away, grumbling that she could have made the shirts herself. The woman silently followed, and Jess couldn't help wondering how she was treated by her mean husband when out of the public eye.

A second man eyeing the shirts was obviously a long hunter, but he was slovenly and smelly, not clean and handsome like Noah. The man fingered through the shirts, and Jess noticed how soiled were his buckskins. She wondered if he would bother cleaning up before putting on the shirt she'd put so much work into.

A few more men looked the shirts over, and she bargained with them while her father and brother unloaded more potatoes and corn at the trading post, where other settlers and a few apparently friendly Indians wandered around doing their own trading.

Logstown was as civilized a place as could be found

in western Pennsylvania, but according to Jess's mother, it couldn't hold a candle to Albany, where there were hundreds, maybe even over a thousand more people, more than one street to the town, churches and preachers, even schools. She tried to imagine what that would be like, and how happy she'd be there with Noah and his parents, a full woman, Mrs. Noah Wilde. She liked the sound of it; but as each day passed with no sign of Noah, she wondered more and more if the day would ever come that her dreams would become real.

There had been no gathering this season at the confluence of the Monongahela and Allegheny. Settlers were too wary of the Indians that usually gathered there, afraid now that they could not be trusted as in the past. Jess's father was forced to come to Logstown to sell his produce and livestock. Jess worried he would change his mind about leaving. In spite of the troubles developing with the French and the Indians, many men here voiced their determination to stick it out and stay put. They were too proud to "run," had worked too hard to build what they had. They enjoyed a freedom here they would never know back east, and they intended to keep things the way they were.

Jess's father seemed to be reconsidering his decision. If only Noah would return, Jess was sure he could talk her father into sticking with his decision. She hoped that even if Noah didn't return, if they went to Albany, she could find his parents and learn what had happened to him. If he came here and found them gone, he would know where they were. He would still be able to find her.

"Sir?" She spoke to the long hunter who lingered, still picking through the shirts. His hands and finger-nails were dirty, and he needed a shave. He was the last sort of man she would normally speak to, but she would do anything to find out about Noah.

The man glanced at her with pale blue eyes that looked puffy. She guessed by the smell of his breath that the puffy eyes were from too much whiskey. "Yes, ma'am?" he answered.

"I . . . I don't mean to seem forward," she told him, "but I am just wondering if you know a man by the name of Noah Wilde. He's a long hunter, like you. He's originally from Albany."

The man squinted his eyes as though in thought. "Don't believe I've ever met him." He grinned, showing brown teeth. "He a relative, or somebody you're sweet on?"

"I . . . he's just a friend of the family. We haven't seen him for months, and we're worried about him."

The man shrugged. "He's probably holed up with some squaw someplace."

He winked at her, and Jess wanted to hit him, knowing he was deliberately trying to upset her. "Is that the way men like you live, in sin and drunken-ness?" she sneered.

The man laughed. "That's the kind of life *all* men would like to live." He laughed again. "Honey, when you live in the wilds, you live like the Indians. And now especially, a man has to stay friendly with them, figurin' you can't be too sure which ones will offer a squaw, and which ones might just decide to cut your heart out instead. Maybe *that's* what's happened to your Noah Wilde. Maybe some dog is lickin' his lips from—"

"Stop it!" Jess interrupted, wanting to cry. "Do you want a shirt or not? If not, please go away!"

The man chuckled again. "Sorry, little lady." He picked out a blue wool shirt. "I'll take this one. Did you make these yourself?"

"Yes." Jess struggled to keep her tears from showing.

"Well, you're a right good seamstress, I'll say that." He slipped a gold coin into the palm of her hand and winked at her, leaning close so that she frowned from the smell of his breath. "If I come across your Noah Wilde, I'll be sure to tell him you were askin' about him," he told her. "What's your name?"

Jess slipped the coin into the pocket of her checkered pinafore. "Never mind," she answered. She began straightening the three shirts that were left, and the man walked away, chuckling.

A lump rose in Jess's throat, and tears blurred her vision. "Noah!" she whispered. Had he thought twice about his promises? Maybe he'd decided he'd acted foolishly and didn't love her for the right reasons. Maybe he wasn't dead or hurt at all. It was the not knowing that drove her crazy. She had not even seen a letter or a messenger with an explanation. With hints of war, the troubles with the Iroquois, any number of things could have happened, especially with Noah being a spy.

"Jess!"

Jess turned to greet her mother, who untied her bonnet and removed it to fan herself as she walked across the street. It was an unusually hot day for September. "Your father sold most of the cattle and all the produce," the woman told her, looking relieved. "We made good money this time, and he's decided for certain to go home to Albany."

Jess felt the first happiness she'd known in months. "He did?" She embraced her mother. "I'm glad. Maybe there I can at least find Noah's parents. Maybe Noah will even still get here before we finish packing!"

Marlene tied her hat around her neck, but did not put it back on. "Jess," she said with grave concern. "Maybe it's time you stopped thinking so much about Noah."

Jess wished she could get rid of the constant tight pain in her chest. "But you said yourself—"

"I know what I said, darling." Marlene grasped Jess's hands. "Jess, things are very unpredictable right now. The fact remains you don't know what has happened to Noah. If God means for him to return, he will. Believe me, I understand how you feel, and it breaks my heart to see you hurting. But you have to face the fact that something may have happened to Noah, that he could even be dead."

"No! I don't believe it."

"He seemed to be a man of his word, Jess. And I have a feeling he's the kind of man who wouldn't let anything *but* death stop him. I know the reality of that is hard to accept, but I think it's time to begin letting go. We'll go to Albany, and until we get there I want you to begin preparing yourself for the possibility of never seeing Noah Wilde again. If his parents are there, maybe then you can learn the truth. I'm just afraid of what that truth is."

Tears slipped out of Jess's eyes, and she quickly wiped them away. "He's alive. I know it. I *will* see him again. I know it in my heart."

Marlene closed her eyes and sighed. "I hope you're right. I pray about it every day, Jess. That's all you can do, too. Right now let's think about your father. This is the hardest decision he's ever made, harder than coming out here in the first place. He'll need us, Jess. For the time being we have to talk this up to him, tell him what a wise decision he's made on behalf of the family and that we're all happy about it."

Jess swallowed back more tears. "I'll help, Mama."

Marlene kissed her cheek and left, and Jess watched her go, again hoping she would grow to have her mother's wisdom and strength. Two more men approached then, and Jess sold the rest of her shirts. She looked across the street, where her mother had gone to greet Jonathan as he came out of the trading post. They briefly embraced, and Jess knew then what a traumatic decision this was for both of them. Her father never usually showed any kind of affection to her mother in public. To do so only meant he was hurting deeply.

15

Early October 1753

"Mon fils!" Jacques Wilde greeted his son with open arms.

Noah embraced the man, glad to finally see with his own eyes that Jacques was well and safe. *"Père! Comment ça va?"*

"That is not the question, my son. It is *you* for whom I am concerned! How could Dinwiddie do this to you? And how are they treating you?"

"As you can see, not very well," Noah answered. He glanced at the New York militiaman who guarded the eight-by-ten-foot solid log and windowless room where he'd been kept since being marched here to Fort William Henry in New York five months ago. The guard scowled at both Noah and his father before closing the thick, solid door to the dark, damp room. The only light then was a small shaft that came through a twelve-inch-square barred window in the door.

Noah, long accustomed to the near darkness, led his father to a wooden bench, where they sat down. "This is the only piece of furniture in here," Noah explained. "I sleep on the dirt floor and have a lidded pot for . . ." He stood up again and paced. "Damn them all! After all I've done for them, this is what I get! I hardly know where my loyalties lie anymore, Father."

"Oh, my son, my son! This is my fault. It is because I am French that they are doing this! I should be the one in here."

"That's ridiculous. This isn't your fault. This is simply because of William Fairfax, and the fact that I was at Pickawillany when Johnny Peidt was murdered." Noah walked back to his father and sat down, putting an arm around his shoulders. "I'm glad to see you, to know you're all right. I'm so sorry about Mother. I should have been with the both of you."

"You could not help it. You did not know." Jacques sighed. "I would have come all the way to Virginia to see you and speak with Dinwiddie before he even sent you up here," the man fumed, raising a fist, "if not for also being ill. There was a lot of sickness in Albany. Then later I was told I would not be allowed to visit with you, something about delivering messages from the French. I was furious! I have been pleading almost daily with Governor Clinton to let me see you since you were brought up here to New York. Finally, he spoke with William Fairfax, who said I could come. That Clinton, and Dinwiddie, too, they will not pee without Fairfax's approval!"

Noah hugged the man's shoulders. "I've thought of ways to escape, but I was afraid you'd suffer for it.

Besides that, Dinwiddie promised I'd be out of here quickly. I thought he'd keep his promise, but obviously he does not intend to. Here it is October, and not a word from him! Did Clinton give any hint of letting me out of here?"

Jacques shook his head. "It is not fair what they have done. You have devoted many years to spying for the English. And after losing your own wife to a terrible death at the hands of the French, how could they think you would have betrayed them in any way?"

"They don't. This is nothing more than blaming the handiest person they could find for Pickawillany. Dinwiddie and the bunch of them are embarrassed over it, after being so confident the French were not a threat. This helps them save face."

"But Dinwiddie and Clinton—all of them—they know you so well! It's because of them that you were with the French at Pickawillany in the first place!" Jacques wiped his eyes and nose as he spoke.

"All the more reason to punish me," Noah answered. "It makes Dinwiddie look better in Fairfax's eyes. I think he's just biding his time now, until Fairfax calms down. Then Dinwiddie will find a way to show I'm making amends for whatever it is I supposedly did wrong. I'm not concerned for myself. It's Jess I'm worried about. I can't even write her. They'll carry letters to you for me, but they won't take one all the way to the wilds of Pennsylvania, especially since what happened at Pickawillany."

"I am glad you could at least write me, son. When

you told me about the lovely young woman Jessica, my heart ached for you. I am glad you have found someone to fill your life again, sorry you cannot go to her."

Noah rested his elbows on his knees and hung his head. Jess! What must she be thinking by now? He could imagine the terrible disappointment she must be feeling. Was she safe? Had her father kept his promise to move the family to Albany?

"I feel so torn in loyalties now, Father," Noah explained.

This time Jacques put an arm around his son's shoulders. "I understand, Noah. I am a Frenchman among the English. People I used to call friend now turn away when they see me. Things have been very bad since Pickawillany. What happened there was in the newspapers for weeks. Your mother and I worried so about you, wondering if you, too, were there, what might have happened to you. She died not knowing."

Noah groaned with grief, his hands balling into fists as he rose and paced again. "I'm so sorry about that."

"She is with you now in spirit, Noah. She knows and understands, I am sure. She will watch over you."

Noah faced his father, then knelt in front of him. "I don't know what to do anymore, Father. I have responsibilities to you, to Jess; I have my vow to help the English, my promise to Mary that I would avenge her death. By now Jess probably thinks I've deserted her, that I never meant any of the promises I made her." He bent over and pounded a fist on the dirt floor.

"Damn! I've got to get out of here! I've got to at least get a message to her."

Jacques thought a moment. "Son, I could go and try to find this young woman you love. I could take your letter to her myself."

Noah raised up and shook his head. "I can't let you do that."

"It is the least I can do. Your beautiful mother is buried at the farm, and I have not the heart to stay there alone any longer."

"No!" Noah insisted, facing Jacques. "I won't hear of you going out there! It's much too dangerous now." He pressed both hands against a wall and hung his head in thought. "I could easily escape this place, but that wouldn't solve anything. They would only find a way to punish you for it, use you to get me back here. I'd probably be shot, either during the escape or once they found a way to make me come back, and that wouldn't do Jess any good."

He sighed, sitting down next to Jacques again. "I appreciate your offer to take a letter, but Jess's family lives deep in western Pennsylvania, on the other side of the Alleghenies. It would be a terrible trip for you. Besides that, it's just possible they are already heading east. The plan was to come back to Albany as soon as harvest was over, if not sooner. The best thing you can do is stay at the farm. If they make it, you should be there to greet them and explain what has happened. You can let them live at the farm for the time being." He put a hand on his father's arm. "They're good people. Mr. Matthews and his son can help you with the farm, and Mrs. Matthews is a wonderful woman and a damn good cook. So is Jess. I think their presence would help bring happiness back to the farm, Father." He closed his eyes. "We just have to pray they come here and that they make it safely."

Jacques put a hand over Noah's. "You must keep the faith, son. The Sacred Mother will take care of this young woman you love. I, too, tried to find someone to take a letter to this young woman you love, but I could not find one volunteer. And so we have to let God watch out for her and bring her to you. Surely you are meant to be together."

Noah again felt the sharp pain in his heart that plagued him constantly. He could see Jess so clearly, smell her hair, remember the taste of her mouth, the feel of her firm breast. "Try once more to talk to Clinton and Fairfax, Father. Maybe you can go to Virginia now that you're well and talk to Dinwiddie. Something has to be done. I have to get out of here. Tell Dinwiddie I'll go on one last mission for him, if that's what it takes. I told him I was quitting. Tell him if there is anything I can do, anything to help, anything to get me out of here . . . ."

"I will tell him, son. In the meantime you must pray and have courage. This young woman, I am sure she still loves you and believes in you. She, too, will not give up. She will wait for you."

Noah walked to the door to peer through the small window, breathing deeply of the fresh air from out-

117

side. "I'm going crazy in here. If I don't get out soon I *will* do the wrong thing and try to escape. You're the only reason I hold back, as well as knowing I'd never be able to come back to Albany and settle there with Jess." He turned to face his father. "Right now it would be easy for me to kill Dinwiddie with my bare hands!"

Jacques rose and walked over to speak softly to him. "Be careful who might hear you, son. These are dangerous times." He led Noah away from the door. "It is only a rumor now, and because of all this trouble with the French, the colonists do not think there is much merit to it; but I have heard there are some young people who speak of the day when this country will belong just to the colonists, without English rule."

Noah frowned. "An overthrow of the king?"

Jacques shrugged. "Something like that. It sounds like foolish talk for now, but the way you have been treated is just one example of why some are thinking the English have no business enforcing their laws on us. We are far from England, and when people risk their lives for something as the colonists have done to settle this land, they begin to think it should belong to them, that they should run it themselves."

Noah grinned and nodded. "I totally agree. Do you think that will ever happen?"

"Who knows? For now we have the French to worry about. That sounds strange, coming from a Frenchman, but it is true just the same." Jacques grasped Noah's arms. "Let's get through this crisis first, Noah. You can only take one thing at a time. You cannot fight both the English and the French, let alone the Iroquois. For now you must fight for *yourself* and for the woman you love, wherever that leads you."

Noah nodded. "Right now Jess is the only thing that really matters to me, besides you."

Jacques smiled sadly. "I am glad that finally, after all these years, you have found another woman to love. My son's heart sings again."

Noah turned away, again going to the door window. "Not at the moment, Father. Not until I'm with Jess again."

16

Mid-October 1853

Jess felt her life changing before her eyes. It all started the day the Indians had attacked her, and Noah stopped them. Nothing had been the same since then. Noah Wilde's kiss had changed her from an innocent young girl only daydreaming about a beau, to a woman dreaming about lying with a grown man and letting him capture her innocence. Now she helped pack the wagon that would take her and her family away from the only home she could remember. She would go to a real town, meet new people, maybe find Noah.

The cabin was nearly empty, the stock pens also empty. She had rounded up the chickens into wooden pens her father hung on the sides of the wagon. The chickens and Gabe were the only animals going with them, other than the oxen that would pull the wagon.

Her mother had cried off and on for the last two days, taking down curtains, packing china she'd brought all the way from Albany. Now it would be carried back again. Next spring the fields would lie empty. All the months of cutting trees and hitching oxen to the stumps to pull them out, the hard, hard work of getting the land ready to cultivate—all that would not matter now. Within days weeds would start growing, and new young trees would sprout by next spring.

"We can probably never come back," her father had said sadly last night, tears in his eyes. "By the time we would be able to do so, we would have to start all over clearing the land, and I would be too old by then."

Jess now fought tears herself as she set a small bushel of potatoes in the wagon, part of the food they would take with them. She felt sorry for her father, and angry at the French for starting this. The threat of war was changing her whole life, and destroying her father's happiness. She'd mentioned that when they reached Albany they could probably stay with Noah's parents at least for a while, or with some other family; but Jonathan Matthews was a proud man.

"We'll not be putting others out," he'd told her.

"We'll find our own place as soon as we can."

The trouble was, according to him, things were more expensive in Albany, and all the land was already taken. Jonathan fretted that they would not enjoy the freedom there they'd enjoyed here, and he would probably never again own so much land that was all his own. He would probably end up working for someone else, as would Sonny; and he worried he would never be able to properly support her mother. It just wouldn't be the same. The only one who would never know the difference would be little Billy, who ran around playing now while they packed.

Noah. Where was Noah? This would all be easier if he were around. The trip back would be wonderful and exciting. She helped pack with a heavy heart. None of this was like she thought it would be, and her father's unhappiness weighed on her.

"Someone's coming," Sonny announced.

Noah? Jess walked to the front of the wagon, where Sonny had been hitching the oxen that would pull it. She shaded her eyes at the sight of someone approaching, leading one horse packed with supplies. It was not Noah. It was a woman. Jess's parents came out of the house to wait, and as the woman came closer, Jess could see it was the same woman she'd met at Logstown, the one with the rude husband. She was deeply disappointed that it was not Noah; but that disappointment turned to pity when the woman reached them. Her face was swollen and purple. She blinked back tears as she approached Marlene.

"I remembered hearin' you talk back in Logstown about goin' east," the woman told Jess's mother. She had difficulty speaking because of her swollen lips and, Jess guessed, a sore jaw. "My name is Harriet Phillips. I'm wonderin' if I might travel with you."

Marlene looked at her husband, then back to Mrs. Phillips. "That's up to my husband, Mrs. Phillips." She reached out and touched the woman's arm. "What on earth has happened to you? Is there anything I can do to help?"

The woman looked down. "No," she said quietly. "My husband . . . got a little drunk."

"Dear God," Marlene muttered.

Tears ran down Mrs. Phillips's cheeks as she raised her head to look at Jonathan. "I finally . . . I had to hit him, don't you see? I had to defend myself."

"Of course you did," Jonathan told her.

She shook her head. "I hit him with a poker stick." She looked down again. "I killed him. I didn't mean to. It just happened." She sniffed and dabbed gently at her swollen nose with a handkerchief. "Now I have to get away from here. I don't want other folks to know, and I've got no children. I can't stay in this place alone and survive. And I'm scared of Indians."

She met Marlene's gaze again. "It all happened four days ago. We live south of here, not far from Logstown. I quick packed up, and I followed the trail this way, hopin' I'd find your place. I been scared to death the whole way, bein' in the woods alone, what with all that we hear about the Indians."

She fixed her gaze on Jonathan again. "I just thought you should know the truth. You might not want me along after all."

Jess was astonished. She could not imagine a man beating his wife. Her father had never been anything but good and gentle to her mother. It seemed that with the Indian attack and now this, she was just becoming awakened to a whole different side of life, aware of the violent side of man.

"What happened is your affair," Jonathan told her. "You're welcome to come along with us."

Mrs. Phillips looked up at him. "I thank you. I brung my own food. I'll keep to myself and won't be no trouble."

"You don't have to do that, Mrs. Phillips. My daughter and I will enjoy the company." Marlene put an arm around the woman. "Why don't you come sit down on the porch while we finish packing? You must be so very tired, let alone the fact that you're obviously injured. We'll he staying one more night before we leave out early in the morning. That will give you time to rest before we—"

"Indians!" Sonny shouted, running to grab his musket from the wagon.

Jess whirled to see at least twenty nearly naked warriors running from the woods behind the wagon. Shrieks and war cries could be heard from behind the cabin, and she turned to see perhaps ten more warriors coming at them from the other direction. She ran to grab Billy, but a warrior reached the boy first. He snatched Billy up and ran off with the screaming child.

"No!" Jess screamed. She started to run after him, then felt a blow to her head that momentarily stunned her. She reeled forward but was caught when someone wrapped a strong arm under her chin and dragged her backward. From then on all Jess could do was watch . . . watch . . . This time there was no Noah Wilde to help her, or the rest of her family.

17

The arm around Jess's neck gripped her like a vise, and with his other hand her abductor held a large knife against her mouth, just under her nose. She dared not move. Never had she known such terror, nor such horror. The very air came alive with war cries, mixed with the desperate screams of her own parents, and Mrs. Phillips.

Sonny already lay dying from an arrow in his chest. A warrior covered with tattoos chopped off his head while he was still alive, and Jess felt numb of all physical and emotional feelings. It was the only way to bear what she was witnessing. Her father fought briefly, swinging his long gun at warriors who came at him in a cruel teasing. He'd got off one shot, killing one warrior, and that was all he'd had time for. Now they dodged and darted at him with knife and tomahawk, cutting, slicing, bludgeoning, until finally Jonathan crumbled to the ground, where the attackers continued hacking away until the man was in pieces.

Jess's mother was dragged into the house along with Mrs. Phillips. Minutes later the abductors came outside, and Jess saw smoke coming from the doorway and one window. She heard her mother's screams, and she knew that she and Mrs. Phillips must be tied inside, destined to be burned alive.

Mama, Jess agonized to herself. How could this be? How could any man behave this way? Why were they doing this to people who'd never brought harm to them? More black smoke billowed from the cabin, the precious little place Jess had called home all her life. Flames began to show themselves at the windows, and as the fire began consuming more of the cabin, the screams inside grew to unbearable horror. Jess groaned with indescribable agony. She felt faint, waiting for whatever hideous pain these painted warriors intended for her.

The cabin was soon engulfed in flames, while the warriors outside grouped together to overturn the wagon she and her family had just finished packing. They spilled out its contents, while three of them killed the oxen by planting hatchets in their brains.

The animals crumbled to the ground, and the chicken cages broke open. Chickens squawked and scattered, feathers flying. A few of them were caught and killed by chopping off their heads, and those who killed them held them up by the feet, screaming wildly as blood dripped from the open necks.

Others began sorting through whatever valuables they could find, among them a couple of Jess's mother's dresses, probably for some Indian woman to wear. They took some of Jonathan's tools, part of the food, Marlene's hand mirror and comb, some blankets, one quilt made by Jess's grandmother that had been brought here twelve years ago by Marlene. Jess could hardly stand the thought of these natives using it. They grabbed her father's hand pistol and a few pots and pans, loading everything onto a couple of packhorses they had brought with them.

Jess waited for her own horrible death, praying it would happen quickly. The screams of the women inside the cabin had long ceased, and the roof had caved in.

The native who'd held Jess throughout the ordeal suddenly let go of her and took the knife away from her face. He grasped her arm, and she turned to look at him, surprised at how young he was, as young or younger than Sonny. Half his face was painted black, and his head was mostly shaved except for a narrow roach down the middle that led to longer hair at the back, into which feathers were tied. The shaved part of his head was also painted black. From his pierced nose hung a rawhide loop with a blue stone that came to the center of his lips. Strangely, Jess felt nothing, not even fear. She simply waited for whatever was to come, facing her abductor squarely. She suspected he wanted to hear her scream, wanted to see terror in her eyes. She would not oblige him.

Mama! No. She would not, could not think about what she'd just witnessed. It was impossible to comprehend. Instead, a strong instinct for survival emboldened her. Her abductor looked her over, felt her hair, while most of the others gathered around him, shrieking and celebrating, some of them even laughing as they held up some of the bounty they'd gathered from the wagon. Jess refused to look at her mother's dress.

No! Don't think about it! Don't look at the quilt or the mirror. Don't cry! Be brave! Hold back the vomit that wants to spew from your mouth! Noah would tell her to have courage, be strong.

Noah! Why had she thought of him in this dire moment? He should have been here, yet she was glad he was not. Against all of this, even Noah would not have survived, not even with the protection of the bear-claw necklace, which now was lost somewhere amid the ruined wagon supplies. Since she had not been killed, Jess gradually began to realize that she'd been saved to keep as a slave. She did not fear rape, since she'd heard Noah explain once that young Iroquois warriors never raped. Only French soldiers did that. The warriors only killed, or took captives, sometimes to raise as their own. She could only hope in that small good fortune, and pray that Billy would end up in the same camp. Billy was out there somewhere. He, too, had surely been taken captive and not killed. A remnant of the love shared by Marlene and

Jonathan Matthews remained.

Whatever her own fate might be, Jess vowed then and there, as she faced her captor, that she would do whatever was necessary to stay alive and be strong for her little brother—and until Noah could find them. Surely he would try once he came back and saw what had happened here.

Her abductor pulled her over to where the oxen lay dead. Jess only glanced at them, feeling sorry for the poor faithful animals. The young Indian then cut off some of the rawhide straps that made up part of the hitch gear and used one strap to tie Jess's wrists together in front of her. He tied another strap around her neck, then kept hold of the other end as he jerked her along, leading her off into the woods.

18

Third Week of October 1753

Noah wanted nothing more than to kick his horse into a gallop and ride away from the militiamen who accompanied him back to Alexandria. He could hardly stand wondering what might have happened to Jess by now, but he told himself to be patient. He was at least free for the moment, and if he wanted to stay that way, he had to at least see what it was that had caused Governor Dinwiddie to finally send for him.

He hoped his father would be all right alone at the empty farmhouse. Jacques had stayed an extra day at Fort William Henry, intending to go to Dinwiddie himself and plead with him for Noah's freedom; but before the man could leave, Noah was informed that Dinwiddie was setting him free and that he was to report to him in Virginia. Noah insisted his father go home, where he'd be safe, promising to get news to him as soon as possible.

Governor Dinwiddie most likely had plans for Noah's services again; right now, Noah didn't much care what it was as long as he did not have to return to the dark, hellish cell he'd lived in for the past several months. The first part of this journey had been spent on a sailing vessel from New York to Virginia, and the fresh, cold air in Noah's face had felt wonderful. After disembarking, they had ridden inland to Alexandria and were now approaching the governor's home.

Jess! Soon he might be able to go to her. His belongings and horses had been returned to him, except for his weapons, which the militiamen told him would be held until after he spoke with Dinwiddie. He was "almost" free, depending on what it was Dinwiddie wanted.

He dismounted in front of the brick mansion and was followed up the walkway by the armed militiamen. Upon reaching the door he turned to face them. "Haven't you fellows figured out by now that you don't need to guard me like some kind of murderer? We've traveled together for almost two weeks and know one another pretty well."

"Got to follow orders, Noah," one called Ben answered. He gave Noah a slight wink. "That's the way it is."

Noah shook his head, thinking how well armed the colonists were now. He could not get his father's comment out of his mind—that some were thinking of running this country on their own, without the blessings of the king of England. Considering how nonchalantly the English were treating the French and Indian threat, they would likely be even more careless about considering their own colonists a threat. That could be of great benefit to the colonists if they ever decided to turn on the red coats.

As Jacques had reminded him, his only concern now was the French—and Jess. He used the large, brass door knocker to announce his presence, and a gentlemanly Negro man with gray hair opened the door, bowing slightly.

"I am here to see Governor Dinwiddie, at his request," Noah told him.

"Please come in, sir. I will announce you."

Noah waited impatiently, looking around the opulent entranceway and feeling irked at how well the governor had been living while he was kept in a dark, smelly hole of a cell since last May. Now most of the leaves were off the trees, and in the last two days the weather had turned to a bone-chilling cold that foretold of winter close at hand. He could see his breath today, and the deerskin jacket he'd worn over his white dress shirt suddenly was not warm enough. Besides that, he chided himself for wearing a dress shirt at all. Dinwiddie didn't deserve his taking any special pains about how he looked.

Dinwiddie himself greeted him, fancy cuffed coat, ruffled shirt, satin vest and all; and he was actually grinning and putting out his hand as he approached. "Noah! I see you survived just fine! I'm happy to be able to set you free!"

Noah could think of other things he would prefer to do to the man than shake hands with him, but he reached out anyway, making sure to squeeze the man's hand just hard enough to remind him of his very unhappy situation. He gave no indication of being grateful for his sudden "freedom."

"Governor," he answered without a smile. "Perhaps you could call off your militia. It's damn unnecessary to have them watch me and you know it. And I'd like my weapons returned."

Dinwiddie chuckled. "Oh, no, not until I inform you of the conditions of your freedom, Noah. And I assure you, it's nothing that will be at all taxing for a man like you. Do this one thing for me, and everything will be settled between us." He motioned for Noah to follow him down a carpeted hallway to the same office where he'd informed Noah of his arrest.

Noah thought to himself how easy it would be now to kill the man with no weapons at all. One snap of the neck would do it. He followed Dinwiddie into the office and took a seat across from the desk. The governor opened a silver box and offered Noah a cigar. "I'm sure a good smoke would taste wonderful right now."

Noah just glared warily at the man. "No thanks. Get to the point, Governor. What do I have to do to earn my final freedom?"

Dinwiddie frowned. "Come now, Noah. They did feed you well, didn't they? I ordered them to do so, you know."

"I wrote and told you I needed to get out by August at the latest. It is now October."

The governor waved him off. "Two months. How much difference can that make? I received a letter from your father explaining why you needed to be released. I'm sure your little lady is fine, Noah. After all, we aren't at war yet, and what I want you to do will help assure that never happens. And believe me, I would have let you out sooner, but I had to wait for just the right opportunity to appease Lord Fairfax. That opportunity has come along, and I am quite excited about it. The best part is, this mission will take you directly to western Pennsylvania, exactly where you want to go! In fact, you will be leaving in two days, and I will be giving you money to stock whatever supplies you deem necessary."

Noah lost a little of his belligerence. "What's the sudden urgency?"

Dinwiddie sat down and leaned back in his leather chair, grinning quite smugly. "The urgency is due to orders from King George himself. I wrote him about the need to take some kind of action to protect our western frontier, just as you advised we should do. That is another reason I had to keep you at Fort William Henry for so long. I was waiting for the king's reply. He has given me permission to dispatch someone to French strongholds on the Allegheny, and in particular at Presque Isle and Venango, warning them that any further movements into English territory will possibly result in war between France and England. We are ready to defend our western territories to the fullest."

The governor leaned forward, resting his arms on his desk. "I've had a slight problem with the House of Burgesses—a little misunderstanding over spending the necessary money to beef up our troops—but I'm sure it can be settled. Besides, I have the king's permission, and that is all I need. The men in the House still do not fully realize the threat we are facing from the French, but I do, Noah. I believe your warnings, and I intend to act on them."

Noah studied him intently, hardly able to believe he was really going to be able to go to Pennsylvania. "Surely you don't expect me to be the one to carry your threatening message," he told the governor. "I'm supposed to be of French persuasion, remember? I could run into Frenchmen who know me and think I'm one of them. Such a message would seem a little strange, coming from me."

Dinwiddie chuckled. "Of course I don't expect you to actually carry the message; but I convinced Fairfax to let you act as a guide for the person who *will* take the message, a young man of only twenty who has shown remarkable abilities in soldiering and loyalty to the king. He is the half brother of Lawrence Washington, who was a dear friend of Fairfax but died not long ago. Fairfax would like to give this young man a chance for a star military career, so I have given him the rank of major and have made him adjutant of Virginia's Southern Military District, at a salary of one hundred pounds per year, I might add. His name is George Washington, and I see a great career ahead for him."

Noah could hardly believe his ears. "Twenty? Has he ever been out in the wilds of the Appalachians?"

"Oh, I know that sounds young, and I doubt he has been anyplace like that, but he is sturdy and loyal and eager. And he is very intelligent. He is right now stocking his supplies. You will be his guide, but always remember that Major Washington is in charge. He will choose more men along the way, probably at Will's Creek, where he will stock up on even more supplies at the Ohio Company storehouse. All his decisions regarding additional men are his to make. Your only job is to guide and protect him until such time as he reaches the confluence of the Monongahela and Allegheny, and perhaps on to Logstown. I have told him that if he feels he has enough men and the proper interpreters by then, you will be allowed to go your own way. Fairfax does not know that. Young Washington understands your plight, and I hope you have understood mine. I did what I had to do, Noah, and now I have found an excuse to get you out of imprisonment and help you get back to Pennsylvania without raising eyebrows. Fairfax knows the skilled man that you are and is confident you will protect young Washington to the best of your abilities. He has told me that with this last mission, you will be forgiven for Pickawillany."

"There is nothing to forgive," Noah growled.

Dinwiddie leaned back again, resting his hands on his belly. "I pulled strings for this one, Noah. I hope there are no hard feelings. I truly do regret having had to arrest you."

Noah couldn't decide whether he wanted to thank the man or hit him. It all depended on what he found in Pennsylvania. "I suppose I should thank you, Governor, but considering where I've been the last five months, that's a little hard to do."

"I don't blame you, Noah. I'm doing this partly for your father, you know. His petitions to me were quite touching. And I can fully understand your urgent desire to get back to Pennsylvania; but I am sure the little farm girl you are so struck with is just fine. Things really are not all that bad yet."

Noah stood up. "I'll find that out when I get there. For your sake, I hope you're right."

Dinwiddie sobered. "Noah! Is that a threat?"

"Yes, sir, it is. Jess Matthews is the first woman I've cared about since Mary was killed."

The governor grinned. "Noah, I do believe you

worry a little too much. As I said, I trust your warning that England must act forcefully against the French, but there is no real danger yet to the outlying settlers."

Noah could see that in spite of his decision to send a warning to the French outposts, Dinwiddie and probably most others still did not grasp the full measure of the danger involved. "You're forgetting this isn't just a threat from the French. They have a good three-quarters of the Iroquois Nation behind them. Fighting the French is one thing. Fighting the Iroquois is quite another."

Dinwiddie rose. "Well, you certainly should know. Perhaps this trip back out there will prove you wrong, or right. That's part of the reason for the mission. When Major Washington reports back to me, we will then decide what further measures should be taken. We may even begin building forts along the western frontier, army posts, something much more formidable than the few trading posts and settlements we have there now. As long as I have the king's permission, we can do whatever needs doing." He walked around his desk and put out his hand again. "Good luck, Noah, and do forgive me."

Noah shook the man's hand grudgingly. "Forgiveness is out of the question," he answered. "Just tell me when I go to meet George Washington."

Looking slightly miffed, Dinwiddie turned away. "I've reserved a room for you at the Peachtree Hotel. Washington will come there in the morning and speak with you before you leave. He'd like to hear your opinions on the situation on the frontier. He has letters with him that he will deliver to the French, warning them to leave the area and pose no more threats to English settlers, or suffer the consequences."

Noah thought how foolish it was just to send letters. A large troop of militia and red coats—a true show of force—would serve the purpose much better. Instead, they were "threatening" the French with a few letters and a twenty-year-old major who'd never trekked the western frontier. Young George Washington was in for a surprise, especially leaving for the wilds this time of year. God only knew how much colder it might get.

19

Mid-November 1753

Jess shivered into her grandmother's quilt, grateful that the warriors who'd brought her on this forced march had allowed her to warm herself with something familiar. From what she had been able to determine by the sun, the few times it had peeked through the almost constantly gray sky, she had been herded north, half dragged most of the way by the leather leash around her neck.

For the first many days, perhaps two weeks, she guessed, her neck had been horribly painful and bled. Now, when she ran her fingers between the noose and her skin, she could feel scabbing. She wondered if she might be permanently scarred. One thing was certain, her emotions and memories would be scarred forever. She guessed it had been at least a month since the horrible slaughter of her family. In all that time she had not been able to cry. She'd forced herself to feel no emotion at all, except that of determined survival. God only knew what had happened to Billy, or what would eventually happen to her.

Her fate couldn't be any worse than what she'd endured so far. The warriors had led her on a constant, daily journey. The first many days her legs and feet ached so that she longed for death. She couldn't help but marvel at the stamina and animal-like instincts of the Iroquois. How they could possibly know where they were going amazed her. They knew the woods like the panther or the deer.

Noah, she groaned inwardly. He knew this land as well as any Iroquois. If he was alive, he would try to find her. Had he discovered the old homestead yet—seen the carnage left there? He no doubt was an excellent tracker; but after a month of travel, and with a weather change that brought almost constant cold rain and sometimes new snow, the tracks of her abductors and their scent would have vanished by now.

She could not allow hopelessness. Somehow . . . somehow she would be saved from this hell. She had to cling to that belief, or just lie down and die. And there was Billy to think about. Poor little Billy. She might see him again, be able to hold and comfort him.

Thank God he'd been whisked away before witnessing the awful death of his mother and father and his big brother—and poor, faithful Gabe.

She sat in a cave now with her abductors, while outside a cold rain mixed with snow pummeled the leaf- and needle-covered ground and the bare trees. The weather could not be more bleak, nor could the outlook for her own future. About the only thing she had to be grateful for besides her grandmother's quilt was the fact that these natives had not abused her in any way, other than the horrible noose around her neck. They never bothered her when she had to stop to relieve herself, and they made sure she had water to drink.

She'd hardly eaten, since most of the time the still- painted warriors tried to feed her raw meat, which they ate with considerable enthusiasm. She finally forced herself to eat just to stay alive and to have the energy to keep up with these creatures of the forest. In spite of their seemingly bloodthirsty, cruel ways, they now seemed rather ordinary. They talked, actually joked, with each other, laughing and sharing their food. They bathed in streams, no matter how cold it was, and many of them could be considered handsome. But always there was that wild look in their dark eyes, the look of an animal, a look that said they almost detested her, probably just because she was white and her family had settled in land they considered their own.

And why shouldn't they? They were here first, and

when she saw how they behaved in the forest, it struck her that this truly was Indian country. These natives fit the forest like the fox or the squirrel or the bear. It was as though they were a part of it, like the trees and grass.

Why had her father wanted to come here? Look what it had led to. What was it about man that made him always want to explore new places, conquer new lands? That's what all this was about, wasn't it? The French wanted this land. The English wanted this land. The Iroquois seemed to think it belonged solely to them, and she was beginning to understand they were more a part of it than any white man of any nationality.

She could not imagine why she was having such thoughts, considering what these creatures had done to her family. Maybe she was simply going crazy. She certainly had every reason to. There was not a bone or muscle in her body that did not scream to rest and be left alone. Her stomach often cramped from lack of proper food. She could not even imagine how she must look. She wore the same dress in which she'd been captured, and it was now in shreds. Her leather boots were so worn that the sole of one of them had come loose and constantly flapped, often causing her to trip. Her stockings were wet and her feet freezing. Her hair by now had to be a stringy, dirty mess, and she felt sick from the cold.

She watched the others eat and talk. There were nine of them, all young. The warrior who had first abducted her at knifepoint left them after finishing raw rabbit meat, coming over to where Jess sat and holding out a rabbit leg. His hands were bloody from ripping the leg from the rabbit's body; but repulsed as Jess was by the sight, she took the leg from him, realizing this was the only nourishment she would get for perhaps another day. She would die without it.

She held the young man's eyes boldly as she bit into the raw meat, suspecting the only reason she still lived was because her abductor respected her bravery, and the fact that she had not cried and complained. She chewed and swallowed, surprised that such food no longer made her want to vomit.

As she chewed on the rabbit meat, she stiffened warily when the warrior removed her worn, leather shoes. She deliberately showed no reaction when he reached up under her dress and pulled down her knee-high stockings, thinking how it didn't matter any more what he might do. Then, to her pleasant amazement, the warrior replaced her shoes and stockings with a pair of winter moccasins that came up to her knees. They were a little big, but incredibly and deliciously warm on her sore, freezing feet. Amazingly, she saw a hint of feeling in the young man's eyes. He'd actually done something to help her! She finished the rabbit leg and threw down the bone, wiping blood from her mouth.

She was not going to die some horrible death. She could tell from the simple fact that her abductor seemed to care that she was fed and warm. She did not even cringe when he took out the same big knife he'd held under her nose during her attack. He moved it toward her face. She sat very still while, to her astonishment and great relief, he used the knife to cut the leather noose from her neck.

He nodded to her and actually smiled a little, then left her, going to the supply bag he carried over his shoulder when traveling and taking out a beaded pouch. He brought the pouch over to where she sat, opening it and dipping his fingers into it. He began smearing something greasy and smelly over the sores on her neck. Whatever he used, it was soothing. When he finished, he nodded again, as though to reassure her she'd be all right.

One of the others said something to him then, and the young warrior frowned, turning and answering rather angrily. Jess guessed the other warrior had made fun of him trying to help her. He turned back to Jess and took hold of her hands, rubbing the rest of the greasy balm onto her dried skin. He wiped the rest of it into her hair, and when she thought about it, she realized the greasy ointment would actually help keep water from reaching her scalp, a kind of protection in inclement weather.

Was he being kind or just cruelly clever? Jess reasoned that probably the only reason he was helping her at all was so that she would be in decent shape when he got her wherever he was taking her, in case he wanted to sell her to someone. Surely it was not out of the kindness of his heart. Men who committed the

kind of atrocious, vicious cruelty her family had suffered could not possibly have hearts. She supposed the
young man figured he'd taken her far enough away
from home that she would no longer try to run away.
She would be completely lost, and he knew it. She had
no choice now but to stay with him and the others,
until they reached whatever destination lay ahead.

She took the back of her hand and rubbed it against
her dry, chapped lips, ignoring the smell of the ointment. A person did what was necessary to survive out
here, and survive she would, for Billy, in memory of
her beloved family . . . and for Noah.

20

Late-November 1753

Noah could not remember a worse autumn. Storm
after storm hampered their travel, but George Washington stood up to the elements better than Noah
thought he might. The young man seemed determined
to accomplish his mission come hell or high water;
and it seemed they would face worse than that.

For the moment they were holed up at Will's Creek,
having taken the Nemacolin Trail in order to stock up
on even more supplies. They were camped outside the
storehouse, their tents weighed down from the drizzle
of rain, snow and ice outside. The wind was picking

up, and Noah smelled an all-out blizzard coming. He grumbled inwardly at how the weather was slowing them down. If he were alone, he would keep right on going and not make so many stops. Time was of the essence in reaching Jess, but he would keep his promise to Dinwiddie to accompany Major Washington at least that far. It was his only assurance of complete freedom from then on.

Everyone was bundled into winter garb, and Noah was glad for his own fur moccasins and his wolf-skin coat. Washington, the servants he'd brought with him, and some of the militia with their small party all wore wool, which Noah considered much too heavy, especially when it was wet. Too much exposure caused wool to become heavy and smelly, but rain and snow could not penetrate the wolf's fur Noah wore. Washington especially insisted on dressing as a proper representative of the English government, but Noah figured common sense was better than worrying about impressing others.

In spite of the fact that George Washington was obviously a pet of William Fairfax, and had brought along personal servants, Noah could not help liking him. He wasn't even sure why, except that in spite of the young man's apparently high-class upbringing— he had even brought along his own fencing instructor—George Washington seemed a hale and hardy fellow, game for adventure and bent on proving himself worthy of the responsibilities given him. He was not arrogant, and he listened well, respecting

Noah's knowledge of the wilderness. Young George in return did a good job of commanding the small group of men and winning their respect.

Noah looked up from where he sat on a crate inside one of the larger tents as Washington ducked inside, followed by a buckskin-clad man wearing a beaver hat and carrying a musket. The man nodded to Noah, and Noah returned the gesture.

"Mr. Wilde, this is Christopher Gist," Washington told Noah. "I've hired him to continue guiding me once we reach the confluence of the Monongahela and Allegheny. I have also hired a trader named William Davison. He apparently understands most of the various Iroquois tongues. I know that you do, too, but I also know you will likely leave us once we reach Logstown or its vicinity."

Noah nodded. "I'm glad you understand, Major."

The young man grinned as he, too, sat down on a crate. Gist removed his beaver hat and sat on a log. He adjusted the deerskin coat he wore, the hair side turned inward.

"Goddamn cold," Gist muttered, chewing on an unlit cigar. "Instinct tells me we'll have weather like this the whole way."

"I figure the same," Noah told the man.

"I've hired four other men," Washington told Noah. "More numbers won't hurt if we run into Indian trouble."

Noah nodded. "Smart thinking."

Washington rubbed his hands together. "I do wish

you could stay with us, Mr. Wilde. You speak French, you know the Indian dialects, and I don't doubt you're a good man to have around in case of trouble."

One of the young major's servants brought in three tin cups filled with hot coffee, handing one to Noah one to George Washington and the third to Gist. Noah nodded his thanks, wrapping his cold hands around the cup. "Thanks for the vote of confidence," he told Washington. "If I find out the family I'm concerned about has left their farm as I warned them to do, I'll stay on with you, as long as I can send someone with a message to tell them where I am and what I'm doing. If they haven't left, or if I see there has been trouble, I'll have to leave your party from that point."

"I understand. Governor Dinwiddie filled me in. I hope you find everything in fine order."

Noah felt the tight squeeze in his chest again. "So do I. My biggest concern is a certain young lady I left behind almost seven months ago."

Washington grinned. "I understand that, too." He sighed, rubbing his eyes, then taking a drink of his coffee while Noah did the same.

"Just what do you really think you can accomplish on this trip, Major?" Noah asked.

Washington shrugged. "A solid threat, I suppose. I'll be delivering letters at various French posts that have encroached on English territory. The letters contain a strong warning that they had better pull back or expect a good deal of trouble from England. The king has given his permission to begin putting pressure on French influences here."

Noah thought a moment. Washington was traveling with only a few men, and some of them were not even part of the militia or the king's men. They were servants and interpreters. He really had nothing with him to back up voiced threats.

"I hate to tell you this, Major, but letters are not going to be of much use against the French," he told Washington, staring at his coffee as he spoke. "You will find out yourself what Dinwiddie and Clinton and Fairfax and all the others still don't realize. The French influence has spread far and wide, all through the Great Lakes, Detroit, all along the Monongahela and Allegheny and this side of Lake Erie and Lake Ontario. You already know what they did at Pickawillany, and they've moved in on the Ohio River area. Worse than any of that, they have most of the Iroquois Nation on their side. I'm afraid the English have done a poor job of staying friends with the Iroquois, and the French offer them better trading deals. The French have worked hard at showing the Iroquois that they are much better friends to them than the English."

He sipped more coffee before meeting Washington's gaze. "If all of this leads to war, which I am convinced it will, all the settlers west of the Susquehanna and Mohawk Rivers will be in dire danger. The Iroquois are not a foe to take lightly. They don't fight in the ways the white man is used to fighting, and they don't stop to feel sorry for anyone, woman, baby, horse, cow or otherwise. If you ever have to fight them, you had better make up your mind to fight dirty and to the death, because that's what they will do. Honor, gender, rank and status have nothing to do with who they fight and who they kill—or the way they kill. They'll cut out a man's heart, land a tomahawk in his skull, cut off his head and/or other body parts. It wouldn't matter if he was the king of England, and it won't matter if he wears a red coat or buckskins. They can be your best friend or your worst enemy, and England would be wise to keep them as friends."

"He's right there, Major," Christopher Gist offered. "And you'd be better off taking a lot more men on this mission, red-coated soldiers, in fact. I don't expect there will be trouble, but a few men and a couple of letters won't have much effect on the French at Fort Le Boeuf or at Venango. Most likely they will laugh at the letters once we leave. They might be courteous to your face, but don't doubt their determination to take over all the trade with the Indians and force England out of it, as well as force out all the settlers."

Washington sighed, swallowing. He smiled nervously at Noah. "Well then, the way things are going, you were right to tell your friends near Logstown to leave."

Noah drank the rest of his coffee. "I'm sure I was. The question is, did they take my advice?" He looked at Gist. "Have you heard of any trouble between

Indians and settlers up around Logstown?"

Gist shrugged. "I ain't been there since last summer. I know there was plenty talk of folks getting out, but a lot of them are just too stubborn. If anything has been happening, I haven't heard; but then this bad weather set in early. Perhaps because of that most of them have decided to stick it out one more winter rather than travel in this mess. I do know that last summer most of the settlers were determined to get in one more crop, and most didn't seem too concerned about leaving."

Noah set his cup aside. "That's what I'm worried about." He stood up, having to bend his head because he was too tall for the tent. "Excuse me, Major." He ducked outside, squinting at snow that blew into his face. He put the hood of his jacket over his head and walked over to check his horse and packhorse, cursing the weather that was slowing his progress. He could only pray that Jonathan Matthews was one of the few colonists in the Allegheny country who'd decided to leave.

21

Jess lost all track of time, her thoughts fuzzy and confused. She hardly cared if it was day or night; and the attack against her family seemed more like a horrible nightmare, buried deeper and deeper in the recesses of her mind and heart. She was beginning to feel like a forest animal finding ways to survive against enemy predators and the elements. Even her memory of Noah was fading, as she came to realize more and more just how alone she truly was. If she could hang on to her determination to live, if for nothing more than to defy her attackers, she believed she would somehow find a way back to the world she once knew. Someone would find the remains at her homestead and realize that she and Billy were not among them. People would start asking around, looking for them, wouldn't they?

Still, she knew she was being taken deeper into Indian country, where few whites dared to tread. Those who did were likely French, since they had kept heading north. Her only salvation for the moment was that her young captor continued to make sure she was kept warm. She'd been given a fur cape with a hood, which she guessed was made from beaver skins, and she still wore the winter moccasins he'd given her.

The weather had slowed the progress of the war party. Several times they had spent two or three days hovering in caves or makeshift tents. Through it all she'd suffered no harm. Her neck seemed to be healing, but without a mirror she had no idea if she'd been scarred. Her main physical problem was that she simply was not accustomed to such constant travel, surviving the elements without being in a warm cabin, drinking hot buttermilk and eating warm biscuits, tending a fire that warmed homemade soup and hot coffee . . .

No! She must not think of those things. It would be a long time, if ever, before she enjoyed them again, and she hardly cared if she did, since she could not share them with her family—or Noah.

Such distant memories. The person she was two months ago no longer existed. Perhaps before all of this was over, she wouldn't even know how to live like a normal human being. Maybe the people in her old world would no longer accept her in their lives. She remembered talk she'd heard once about a woman who'd been an Indian captive.

She'll never be the same, her mother had said.

Her husband doesn't want her back, she remembered Sonny saying. *He went back east—took their daughter with him and left his wife behind.*

How sad, Jess's mother had answered.

Yes, how sad. How could people not have sympathy for a woman who suffered what she was suffering now, the numbing fear, the gut-wrenching memories, the horror of not knowing what lay ahead, the agony of wondering if she would ever again see a white person. Maybe even Noah, if he would happen to ever find her, would no longer want her.

There was no sense in trying to escape. She was no longer bound to her captor by leather ties; she didn't need them now. After all, where would she go alone in the dead of winter? These men knew how to survive, and she would die without them. They all knew it. She could see it in the domineering look in her captor's eyes. He was confident, even arrogant about it. Sometimes she wanted to slap him, or spit in his face; but she needed him, and that irked her.

She trudged through deep snow, following her abductor's pathway until he and the others suddenly halted. They began whispering among themselves, and her captor suddenly walked back to her and clamped a strong hand over her mouth. He said something to her in his own tongue, his tone firm and threatening. She did not have to understand him to catch his meaning.

He wrapped his other arm around her middle as he dragged her forward, following the others as they crouched and proceeded quietly. Her abductor took his hand from her mouth, then took out his big knife and flashed it before her eyes, again threatening her. She looked past the knife, through a small break in the underbrush, and she caught a glimpse of what looked like a log fort.

It must be an English fort! A quick scan caused her to catch sight of something red along the fort's parapets. A red coat! An English soldier! She could cry out, scream! *Scream!* How easy it would be, but there was the glinting knife in front of her eyes. She could almost feel it slitting her throat, or sinking into her side. She wanted to live, to survive. An innate sense of pride told her she would rather go on suffering, proving to her abductor that just because she was a white captive she would not crumble and scream for help at the first sign of aid. She was not afraid.

She felt his tight grip at her ribs; she knew what he

would do if she called out, and she knew he thought she would try, anyway. Hard as it was to keep quiet, she did just that. She had to think of Billy. If somehow their paths should cross, she would have to be there for her little brother. Her mother would want that.

Her abductor forced her to crouch as they made their way through thick pines. She looked back to see the fort behind them, and she wondered if she'd just missed her last chance at saving herself from this whole new world of brutality and hardship.

22

Second Week of December 1753

"What a splendid place to build a fortress!" Major Washington shouted the words above a cold wind. He rode his horse to the edge of a point of land that jutted into the confluence of the Monongahela and Allegheny. Snow blew into his face, but he didn't even seem to notice it. "I can hardly believe the French have not already dug in here," he shouted to Noah, who sat his horse beside him.

"Or the English, for that matter," Noah shouted in reply. "I've always thought myself this would be a good place for at least a trading post." He pointed across the Monongahela. "Out there in the distance, that's the Ohio. From here you can see anyone coming

153

east on the Ohio, south down the Allegheny, or north along the Monongahela. From whatever direction the French might come, this would be a good place to stop them, Major."

Washington grinned. "It certainly would!" He turned to face Noah. "By God, I believe I will recommend to Governor Dinwiddie that we build a fort right here! In spite of the misery of this trip, I am already anxious to come back and help do just that."

"Good," Noah answered, nodding. "That means the settlers in this area would be a lot safer."

"Speaking of which, Mr. Wilde, as soon as we reach Logstown, you may leave our party to seek out the family about whom you've been so concerned. I hope you will be so kind as to stay with us the next day or so that it will take to get to the little settlement. According to you and Gist, there will probably be Indians there. I wish to make sure Mr. Gist is adept at speaking with them and interpreting for me before I let you go."

Close, so close! Finally Noah would have the chance to see Jess! "Yes, sir, I'll stay with you until then."

"From there we go on to Venango, then Fort Le Boeuf."

"You'll be deeper in French territory by then, Major. But you have Monsieur van Braam to interpret for you then. I don't really think there is any danger at this point from the French." Snow was beginning to stick to Washington's eyelashes. "You're not approaching them with a large contingent of soldiers. It's pretty obvious you're only on a mission of discovery. Still, as I said, the French you find aren't going to think much of a letter of warning. They'll brush it off as nothing. If you come back next year and start building a fort here, that will be something much different. I would be sure to bring enough men to defend yourselves against an attack."

Washington nodded. "You should know, Mr. Wilde. I will take your suggestions seriously." He looked back out over the wide river. "Do you have any idea who might be in charge at Venango?"

"Probably Captain Daniel Joncaire. He'll be obliging, probably try to impress you with wine and a fancy dinner, if my guess is right. But he won't want to take any responsibility answering your threatening letters. He'll be glad to know you're headed on north to Fort Le Boeuf. That way he can wash his hands of this and let the commander there handle it. That will probably be Captain Henri Marin. However, I can tell you he was very ill the last I saw him. He may have already been replaced."

"How about Indians? We haven't seen any yet."

"You will at Logstown, probably Senecas and Cayugas. If you're lucky, the Seneca chief Monakaduto will be there. He would rather see the English get a foothold there than the French. He might even agree to accompany you to Venango and Fort Le Boeuf. I think you should take this mission as a chance to win some of the Indians in this area to English favor. Treat Monakaduto and the other chiefs with respect, and they will do the same with you. The English call Monakaduto 'Half King,' because he favors giving his loyalty to the king of England."

Noah turned his horse and faced the major. "I have to tell you, sir, that whether you would have had allowed it or not, I would have to leave you at Logstown anyway. I can't risk going with you into French fortresses. I might be recognized. As far as they know, I'm a French sympathizer, a French trader and guide. I can't be seen riding with an English major on a mission to warn the French to get out of here, let alone the fact that if I'm recognized, it might mean trouble for you."

Washington's horse whinnied and shook snow from its mane. "I understand, Mr. Wilde. And contrary to your treatment by Governor Dinwiddie, I have to say I appreciate the fact that you have risked your life more than once to help us, and that you even took a chance leaving the young lady you care about just to go to Virginia to report. I'm sorry that got you into so much trouble. From what you've told me about Pickawillany, I can see why you were helpless to do anything about that." He grinned. "And I hope I never have to face the Iroquois in battle."

"Major, I hope you don't either." Noah urged his horse forward, riding up to Christopher Gist. "I'll be leaving once we reach Logstown," he told the scout. "You'll have to make sure the major and these other men treat Monakaduto properly. You know as well as

I do how precarious our relationships are with the Iroquois and other tribes."

Gist grinned wryly. "I sure do. This is a useless mission, far as I'm concerned. Might repair the relations between the English and the Indians, but it won't do a damn thing to deter the French. You believe that, too, don't you?"

Noah looked back at Washington, who had turned back again to scan the landscape. "I've explained that to the young major, but I'm not sure he truly realizes how futile his threatening letters will be." He looked back at Gist. "He's all excited about what a good site this will be to build a fort. He plans to come back here next year and do just that. What's your opinion of it?"

Gist chuckled. "My opinion is we are headed for war, Noah. That your opinion?"

Noah smiled but felt sad inside. "I'm sorry to say I agree, and it will be an ugly one if the Iroquois are involved. If I find the young lady I'm looking for after we reach Logstown, I intend to go settle with her someplace safe and let the French and the English and the Iroquois go at it, if that's what they're determined to do. I've had my fill of it over the last eight years, and I'm tired of trying to make men like Dinwiddie and Fairfax and others understand how serious all this is. I think Dinwiddie has a pretty good idea. He's the only one who's written the king about it and who's working to fortify the border areas. The problem is, it's too late, as far as I'm concerned. Things are going to get very ugly, and I don't want to stay around and watch it."

"Well, sir, I hope you don't have to. I hope you find your lady friend is just fine and you can head back east and rejoin your father and live happily ever after."

Noah laughed. "Well, now, that paints a pretty picture." He nodded to Gist and rode back to where he'd tied his packhorse. He hoped to hell Gist's wishes would come true. He'd find out soon enough.

23

Another vicious blizzard pummeled Noah as his horse struggled through deep snow along the narrow road leading east from Logstown. For some reason the west wind seemed to be picking up more moisture than usual this year as it moved across Lake Erie. When that wind butted up against the Appalachians, it swirled backward, dropping most of that moisture on western Pennsylvania.

He cursed the weather and cursed himself for not taking Washington's advice and staying on at Logstown; but he was too close now. He couldn't spend one more day waiting to see Jess, if she was still here. If not, he would breathe a great sigh of relief and head home. Maybe by now the whole family was with his father in Albany.

No one in Logstown had heard anything from any of

the settlers since the fall trading. Winter had set in early, and most folks hibernated in such weather, having already procured supplies they would need for the winter. He did at least learn from the owner of a trade-goods store who remembered the Matthews family that Jonathan had sold his cattle and pigs to another family in Logstown. He'd also traded a good deal of tools and implements, as well as his plow horses, to the trader for money rather than more supplies.

"Far as I can remember, he planned to pack up and leave for Albany," the trader told Noah.

That was good news; but with winter setting in so early, Noah wanted to make sure the family had actually left. If not, maybe there were things they needed by now. If they were gone, he'd follow the natural trail east and make sure they had not become stranded somewhere in the mountains.

His good thoughts soon vanished when, in a rush of wind that took a swirl from the east, he caught the scent of charred wood. He strained to see ahead, but was still too far away to catch a view of the family cabin. The smell was not that of fresh-burned wood, but rather that of something that had burned a long time ago, charred so badly that it still stank. To catch that kind of smell in such cold weather could only mean that whatever had burned was a large structure.

The cabin? Surely Jonathan hadn't burned down his own house. Could he have been that angry and disappointed at having to leave? He'd said something about

Indians maybe coming along and burning it, or some other settlers moving in and taking over. Maybe he'd burned it down himself so neither could happen. Noah didn't even want to consider the other possibilities.

Snow mixed with sleet slashed at his face as he forced his horse to keep going. He clung to the reins of his packhorse, having to jerk at them occasionally to urge the reluctant animal to keep up. Finally he came in sight of the homestead, and already he could see the stone chimney of the fireplace jutting into the air with nothing around it.

"My God," he muttered. There certainly would be no warm cabin to sleep in tonight. He could hardly believe Jonathan would really do this, and when he came closer he realized that indeed this was not the man's doing. Not only did the cabin lay in black ruins, but in front of it lay an overturned wagon, also burned.

Noah felt as though someone had slammed him in the chest with a tomahawk. He knew without looking any further that this was the work of Indians. "Jess!" he groaned. He dismounted, trudging through snow to reach the wagon, where he began a frantic search, praying he would find no bodies.

"Goddamn snow!" he growled, kicking and digging at the items in the wagon, finding a wet, frozen dress here; black, frozen potatoes there; a few tools; an open trunk that had obviously been looted.

He plowed through the snow toward the cabin, then tripped on something. He reached down and dug away at the snow to find a body, a large man wearing a checkered shirt. Sonny always wore checkered shirts. "No, God, no!"

Apparently, cold weather had set in early enough after Sonny's death that the body was still fairly well preserved, enough that Noah could see several stab wounds. An arrow was still stuck in his chest. Shoving away more snow revealed the horror that Sonny's head was missing. Oh yes, this was the work of Iroquois!

A strong wind blew at the snow, revealing a man's hand nearby. Noah knew it was surely Jonathan's. He wanted to weep for them both, but he could not stop for such things. He had to keep digging. He had to hope he wouldn't find Jess's body! And what about Billy? Poor little Billy. Frantically, he pushed the snow away from around Jonathan, grimacing when he realized the hand he'd seen had been severed from the body. As he uncovered the body he found only parts. The poor man had been chopped to pieces!

The lump in Noah's throat nearly choked him. He blinked back tears so he could see better as he rose and looked around. He noticed two bodies not far from Sonny's and Jonathan's. The wind had swept most of the front yard nearly bare except for where it had caught on the two men's bodies and swirled into a drift on the other side of them. Their shaved heads and painted faces showed them to be Indians, and their near-naked bodies were proof this massacre had taken place while the weather was still warm, probably October.

He turned his attention to the burned cabin. He'd known Indians to burn people alive. The last thing he wanted to do was walk into that rubble, for fear of what he might find there, but he had to know. He forced his feet to move, thinking how much he hated Dinwiddie at the moment. How he would love slowly killing the man right now! He hated himself, too. He never should have left. If not for his parents, and his own belief that he had to do his duty and report to Dinwiddie . . .

Nothing made sense anymore. He'd lost one woman he loved to this mess. Now perhaps his vow of revenge had cost him yet another. What the hell was he going to do with himself if Jess was dead? What was there left to live for? And where did his loyalties lie now? French or English, it didn't make much difference to him anymore. All that mattered was that Jess not be dead.

He noticed Gabe's body then, near where the steps to the house should have been. He didn't doubt Sonny's faithful dog had made a valiant effort to save his master, only to be met with a knife or a tomahawk. He sighed deeply before making his way carefully over what was left of the porch and through the snow-covered rubble of the cabin, kicking at boards.

A little voice told him he was unlikely to find Billy. Boys that age were usually stolen away to be raised by some Iroquois woman who'd lost a child to death, or who was barren. Sometimes children were taken for spite, in retaliation for losing a child to another tribe in battle. In this case, an Iroquois child could have been lost to a white man's disease; thus, a white child would have been stolen in revenge. In an all-out battle between tribes, children would usually be murdered right along with their mothers; but this was a single raid against a defenseless family. The warriors would look for bounty, not just stolen goods, but bounty in human form. He could only pray that was all that had happened to Billy. The child would at least be raised in love, then, and his little mind and heart learn to forget his real mother.

He tripped over charred wood, kicked it away, then nearly lost his breath when he saw a leather shoe. Dreading what might go with it, he gently kicked away the snow above it to see a blackened leg. "Please, God, don't do this to me," he muttered. Feeling sick at what he had to do, he knelt down and began brushing away more snow. The wind helped, blowing it away as he pushed and batted at it.

Gradually, his efforts revealed a blackened near-skeleton of a body, the face burned away, a little hair left on top of the head. From what he could tell, the hair was dark, not light like Jess's. Grimacing, he looked for the left hand, and on the black bone of her left ring finger was a gold wedding band, mostly melted and stuck to the flesh.

"Mrs. Matthews," he whispered. Such a good woman . . . such a terrible way to die! Tears stung his eyes. He wished there were a way to comfort her, hold her, apologize. Then, to his deepening horror, he noticed the remnants of another dress. Struggling against more weeping, he brushed yet more snow away, realizing then there were pieces of rawhide strips around the two bodies, and what looked like the remains of a chair between them. They'd apparently been tied to the chair and burned alive.

"Don't let it be her," he groaned. He'd found two men, Sonny and Jonathan. He'd found Marlene Matthews. If there was one woman's body left, whose else could it be but Jess's? Yet for some reason he felt in his heart she was alive somewhere. He should always trust his senses and suspicions, shouldn't he?

The blackened bones of this body revealed someone much taller than Jess, and what was left of her hair looked gray. *Gray!* Who could it possibly be? Frantically he beat more snow away, found the left hand. He actually grinned through his tears when he realized that it, too, bore a melted wedding band! Jess wouldn't have married after he left. Never! This was someone else. Maybe she'd been another captive the raiders had decided to get rid of in trade for Jess.

Jess was young. Jess was pretty, and strong. She'd make an excellent slave, but his good thoughts faded as he realized she would also make an excellent wife for some older warrior. She would bring a lot of useful items in trade. She might even be traded to some vile Frenchman who dealt in prostitution.

He rose, hardly aware now of the biting wind and blowing snow. Physically, he felt nothing. Emotionally, he felt everything. He wiped at his eyes, remembering what a loving, happy household this had been. He could almost see a fire in the fireplace, where a black pot still hung, perhaps their last meal before leaving for Albany. He turned to look out at the wagon, realizing he'd been so engrossed in finding human bodies that he hadn't even noticed the two stiff, dead bodies of the oxen.

They were all accounted for—Sonny, Jonathan, Gabe, Mrs. Matthews, and some poor woman who'd somehow ended up in the wrong place at the wrong time, or who perhaps had already been a captive. There was no telling now. He should bury what was left of the bodies, but with the snow so deep and the ground frozen, it would be next to impossible. Besides that, his time would be better spent at the moment in looking around as best he could to make sure there were no other bodies. If he was lucky, he would find nothing. And if he found nothing, he had to make up for valuable lost time by starting a search.

Where in God's name should he start? It was far too late to try to do any tracking; that was impossible now. He would have to follow his instincts. The first Indians who'd attacked this place had been Detroit Ottawa. Still, the dead bodies appeared to be Delaware. Either way, his Miami friends around Detroit just might know something. That was the only logical place to start. It was going to be god-awful traveling in this mean weather. He'd have to hope to God that neither he nor the horses froze to death in the effort.

He noticed another mound near the oxen. Rushing over, he saw it was another Indian. Jonathan and Sonny had apparently put up a valiant fight, even though they were most likely attacked by surprise. He walked back to kneel by their bodies and prayed for all the dead. Tears spilled down his cheeks as he threw back his head and prayed for Jess and Billy, that they were alive and had not suffered some horrible torture. He himself was now their only hope of being found, he was sure. And find them he would, or die trying!

24

Jess and her captors approached a fort, the Indians making no effort to hide themselves. Jess had no idea where they were or what fort this might be, but apparently whoever lived here was friendly with her abductors. That meant this was most likely a French post. Other Indians, including women and children, greeted them upon arrival.

In spite of the bright sunshine, the weather remained bitterly cold. Jess shivered as she rose and stepped out of the canoe. At first she was surrounded by several women, who all chattered at once, some touching her hair. One older lady spoke with Jess's abductor. He soon grabbed Jess's wrist and jerked her away. She thought at first he would take her into the fort, where maybe a Frenchman inside would have pity on her and help her. However, her abductor led her to one side of the fort and down a pathway worn into the snow that led into deeper woods beyond the fort.

They approached what looked to Jess like a house made of tree branches. It was extremely long, and smoke curled from the top of it in several places. She'd heard about Iroquois longhouses but had never seen one. She guessed this was such a structure. Upon entering through a door at one end that was sheltered with hides, she was amazed at how warm it was inside, as well as the size of the interior, much bigger than she'd imagined such a place would be.

Her abductor said something to a wrinkled old woman who'd spoken to him earlier, then left. The old woman shoved Jess, urging her to the left side of the longhouse. The two sides were separated by walls of tree trunks and branches, so that the structure seemed to be divided in half, with what looked like living quarters for several families running along each side.

Jess gladly sat down near a fire, as instructed by the old woman and a younger woman who joined her. It was obvious the younger one took orders from the older one. Was she perhaps a slave, stolen from another Iroquois tribe?

The old woman pointed a finger at Jess as though to warn her to stay put. It was an order she didn't mind obeying, since she was too tired to do anything else. She removed her cape and leaned forward to enjoy the warmth of the fire, but she didn't sit there long before she was ordered to stand up again.

The old woman barked something at the younger one, and both proceeded to rip off Jess's clothes. Jess screamed for them to stop, but her protests led only to being struck across the back with a slender branch by the old woman. She gasped at the quick pain, and after having seen what had happened to her family, she feared some kind of horrible beating or mutilation if she protested any further.

Jess wanted to die of embarrassment, but it was only then that she noticed other women in the warm structure wore only aprons, their breasts bare. Some nursed children. A few naked men sat around fires, as though it were nothing to be unclothed; to Jess's relief but also her wonder, the men paid no attention to her nakedness. The other occupants of the longhouse appeared to be families. Mothers cuddled their children tenderly, a sight that astounded Jess, considering the cruelty these people could show their enemies.

Left standing only in the winter moccasins her abductor had given her, Jess covered her breasts and waited as the older woman picked through several deerskin tunics. She chose one that had a cape attached to it that looked to Jess like otter fur. The woman handed it to Jess, who eagerly pulled the tunic over her head to cover her nakedness.

"White woman need be warm," the woman said. "No get sick."

She spoke English! Jess felt a thread of hope. This was the first person she'd come across who spoke her language. "Thank you," Jess told her.

"Sit!" the woman told her.

Jess obeyed, and the younger woman brought her a piece of meat that had been cooked over an open fire nearby. Jess looked up to see holes in the roof where smoke could escape. She gratefully took the meat, the first cooked meat she'd had since being abducted. She didn't much care what it was, as long as it was hot and not raw.

She nodded her thanks and gave the younger woman half a smile, hoping that by some miracle, as long as she had to live among these people, she could perhaps make friends with some of them. However, the woman gave Jess a look of disdain as she sat down near her, picking up what looked like a belt onto which she was sewing beads.

Jess turned to the older woman. "I . . . my name is Jess. What is yours?"

The woman simply sat staring at her and did not reply. "Can you tell me where I am?"

Frowning in a way that made her thousands of wrinkles look even worse, the old woman glanced at the younger one before replying. "La Présentation," she answered, in what sounded to Jess like a French accent. "I am called Mona."

It felt good to be able to communicate with someone in her own language, even the enemy. "French soldiers—are there some here?" she asked.

The old woman shrugged. "Not in cold time. Priest here. Father Piquet." She suddenly smiled. "We Christian!"

Jess brightened. "Christian!" She pointed to her chest. "I am Christian, too!"

The woman scowled at her again. "English Christian no good. Only French and Iroquois."

Jess wondered at the remark. Did this woman really even know what being Christian meant? She glanced at the younger woman, who had her eyes on her work and said nothing. Jess surmised she was not allowed to speak unless given permission. She took a last bite of the meat and set the bone aside, licking her fingers. A rather starved-looking black dog hurried over from another apartment within the dwelling and grabbed the bone.

Jess watched the dog run off, then turned again to Mona. "Can you tell me who the man is who brought me here? Is he going to leave me here? What will he do with me?"

The woman grinned slightly again. "My nephew. He is called Tonnerre. French name—means Thunder. You find him easy to see?"

"Easy to see?" Jess thought a moment. Did she mean easy to look at? No, not with that pierced nose and painted face; not when he could hold a knife under her nose and threaten to disfigure or kill her; not when he stood and watched his friends massacre her family. "Yes," she lied, not wanting to offend the woman. "Will we stay here?"

The old woman shook her head. "One night. You go far yet, to the north."

Jess's heart fell. This was the first place she'd

landed where there was at least a slim possibility she could get help. "Why? It's so cold. Why can't we stay here?"

"Tonnerre no live here." With a bony finger she pointed the way. "North. He live north. Take you there. Save you."

Jess frowned. "Save me?"

"For wife. Long time. Delaware men no marry for long time. Three, maybe four more seasons for Tonnerre."

Four years? Did that mean the young man would not try to force himself on her for that long? Maybe someone would find her by then. "What . . . what will I do while I wait?" she asked.

The old woman shrugged. "Be slave. Serve Tonnerre's grandfather, a Delaware chief. Help his wives."

From things she'd witnessed thus far, Jess dared not try to imagine what it would be like to be a slave to these people. And wife to Tonnerre? Never! She would find a way to kill herself first. Besides that, she wasn't sure what the custom was for a slave regarding what she'd heard about young maidens being offered to visitors. Would she be included in that strange form of hospitality?

Her mind raced with the possibilities of being spared by these people. Should she mention Noah's name? Maybe they knew him and considered him a friend. She was in French territory now. Surely she couldn't get Noah in trouble by mentioning his name. If these people knew Noah, telling them she was his woman might get her out of this mess—but they might wonder how that could be, since Noah was supposed to be French. If he did come looking for her, she didn't want to make things more difficult for him by saying something now that could get him in trouble later.

She would wait. Maybe things wouldn't be as bad as she thought when they reached their destination. If she could see that Tonnerre did not intend to wait three or four years to take her, then she would use Noah's name as a last effort to ward off his advances. For all she knew, it wouldn't make any difference to these people. Right now she had to pray Noah was alive and would look for her.

"You sleep now!" the old woman ordered. "Tonnerre say you rest. Go in morning."

Jess felt a heavy disappointment. Much as she ached to be home and wake up from this awful nightmare, she was grateful to at least be someplace where there were women and children, where it was warm, where the food was bearable. The thought of heading back out into the cold made her want to cry, but she still refused to allow that weakness to show.

In spite of the old woman's order, she ventured one more question. "Do you know . . . did anyone come here with a little white boy about two summers in age? Is there a little white boy here?"

Mona shook her head. "No white boy."

Billy . . . where was her little brother? "Is there any way I might be able to speak with a French soldier, or with Father Piquet?"

172

Mona again shook her head. "Soldiers, priest—they not have say in Delaware warrior ways. They afraid of Delaware. Special afraid of Tonnerre."

Delaware. So, at least she knew which tribe of Iroquois had abducted her. "But a priest . . . a Christian should care," she protested.

"Piquet our friend. He no help you. You are English! He teach us how English crucify Christ, who was Frenchman!"

"What!"

"It is true!" Mona told her, pointing a finger at her. "It is very bad what English did to Jesus Christ! Jesus' wife . . . she have Jesus' son. Son is king of France. English must suffer for what they do to king's father."

Jess could not believe her ears. A priest was teaching such lies to the Iroquois? "You *believe* that?"

The old woman suddenly turned angry. "Piquet no lie! *You* lie!"

"But what he told you . . . it isn't true!"

"You see? English lie to turn Delaware against their friends and brothers, the French." She stood up, walking over to pick up the switch she'd used earlier. "You sleep now, or Mona whip you!"

Savage disappointment swept through Jess. She couldn't even expect help from a priest! And for such a man to teach the Iroquois such lies about Jesus was incomprehensible. She lay down on a mat, choosing not to risk being stripped and beaten in front of others.

Flashes of how her parents and brother had died hit her when she closed her eyes, combined with feelings of incredible hopelessness; but she knew that if she broke down and cried, all the strength and determination would flow out of her with her tears. She would wait, wait and cry later—after she found Billy, or until she could cry in Noah Wilde's arms.

25

Early January 1754

Cold Foot welcomed Noah into his private wigwam. Noah breathed a sigh of relief at the warmth inside the old Indian's large and roomy hut. He'd left Buck and Slowpoke with a young Miami boy to tend, asking him to dig the ice out of their hooves and giving the boy two rabbit skins for his help.

Cold Foot directed Noah to sit down near the central fire, then offered him a tobacco-filled pipe he'd already lit.

"It is good to see you, my friend," the old Indian told Noah. "I offer you my pipe in honor of our long acquaintance."

"I'm happy to see you, too," Noah replied in the Indian's native tongue. He untied the wolf-skin coat he wore and pulled it off, then took the pipe. Cold Foot then ordered his wife to come and remove Noah's knee-high winter moccasins. She smiled at Noah as she knelt in front of him and Noah held out one foot. He took several short draws on the pipe as she removed one wet, snow-encrusted moccasin.

"Feels damn good to sit by a fire and smoke," Noah told Cold Foot. He held out his other foot, and Cold Foot's wife removed that moccasin also, then set both shoes near the fire to warm and dry them.

"I appreciate your hospitality," Noah continued. "I've been traveling for weeks, and this is the worst winter I can remember in a long time. I had to use snowshoes a good deal of the way. Even the horses had a hard time of it. I'm surprised they didn't die on me."

Cold Foot nodded. "Indeed, this has been a very bad winter. Tell me, what causes you to travel in such weather? How far have you come?"

"From far in the east, a place called Alexandria. I went first to Logstown in Pennsylvania, then came here."

Cold Foot frowned. "Why do you travel so far in this weather? This is a time for men to settle in their longhouses and wigwams and tell stories to the children."

Noah watched the flicker of the fire's flames, worried over how in God's name Jess could survive such a winter. Maybe she'd been left behind somewhere to freeze to death. He could hardly stand the thought of how she might have suffered, or that it was all because he'd left her.

"I would like nothing better, my friend, but a lot of things have happened since I left here nearly a year and a half ago for Pickawillany."

Cold Foot nodded, honor and respect showing in his dark eyes. "I asked you not to warn those people. From the stories I heard upon Pontiac's return, it was obvious you heeded my plea. For this I thank you, and will always carry great respect for you; but I feel great sorrow for the Miami people who died there."

Noah took a few more puffs on the pipe. "As do I. And in turn, I will always honor and respect you, Cold Foot, for never letting anyone know I was spying for the English."

Cold Foot smiled sadly. "It is too bad what all this trouble between the English and the French is costing us Iroquois, and even white men like you." He turned to his wife again, a sturdy woman whose wrinkled face, Noah thought, still reflected the beauty she must have possessed at a young age. "Bring our friend some of that good French wine," Cold Foot told her.

The woman walked over and took a bottle from near the outside wall of the round, grass hut, where the wine would stay cooler. The wigwam was built much the same way as a longhouse, but was much more private.

"It was bad at Pickawillany, was it not?" Cold Foot asked Noah.

Noah nodded, remembering that bloody day. "Very bad. Many lives were lost. It hurt my heart." He took a tin cup of wine from Cold Foot's wife and thanked her, then turned his attention back to Cold Foot.

"Charles Langlade cut out Unemakemi's heart while Unemakemi was still alive."

Cold Foot sighed, shaking his head. "The same thing could have happened to me if that man knew the truth." Tears showed in the old man's eyes. "You would have liked to warn those Miami."

Noah looked back at the fire. "It's done now," he said quietly. "I returned north and stayed the winter in Canada. My real troubles started last spring when I headed back south. I came through Pennsylvania, where I met an English family and became very close to their young daughter."

He decided not to mention the fight with the Ottawa who'd attacked Jess. He'd killed five Ottawa warriors, and he was back in Miami and Ottawa territory now. This was Pontiac's stomping grounds. If the blood-thirsty Ottawa leader had any idea it was Noah who'd killed the five warriors, he would never make it out of here alive.

"I had to get back to Virginia to report to those who'd sent me out here," he explained to Cold Foot. "When I got there I was imprisoned. They accused me of betraying the English by not warning those at Pick-awillany."

Cold Foot frowned. "I do not understand. There was nothing you could have done."

"I tried to explain that, but it didn't matter." He took a drink of the wine. "What does matter is that by the time I was released and could come back here to marry the young woman I cared about, I found her family's cabin burned, the farm destroyed. I found the bodies of her father and brother and her mother, as well as of one other woman. I don't think the other woman was the one I came back for. The skeleton of the second woman was someone taller than Jess, so I believe Jess was stolen away."

He looked pleadingly at Cold Foot. "The Indian bodies I found looked like Delaware. I couldn't be sure, and I couldn't believe the Delaware would raid that far south. I know they seldom come to this area, but I need to know if you are aware of any of the Indians in this region, Ottawa, Miami, Delaware or any other, who have been raiding down in the area of Fort Le Boeuf. Have you heard about any white prisoners being brought here? Any young women? Jess also had a little brother named Billy. Has anyone brought a little boy here, perhaps about two years old?"

Cold Foot thought a moment, then shook his head. "I have heard of no raiding to the south recently, except for Pickawillany. Nor do I know of any white prisoners. If I could help you, I would, my friend, but I cannot."

Noah drank more wine, wanting nothing more right now than to get drunk. Maybe it would help kill the pain in his heart. "This was the only place I could think of to come, Cold Foot. I don't know where else to go from here. Because of the snow it was impossible to track whoever did it. Their tracks had long been covered." He studied the old man intently. "Do you have any advice for me? Where should I go from here?"

The old man pursed his lips and stared at the fire, thinking for several minutes before answering. "I am not sure what to tell you. If the young woman and her little brother were spared, it was most likely to make a slave of the woman, and to have the boy adopted by an Iroquois woman. In either case, it would not be easy winning them back."

"I am well aware of that, my friend. I will do whatever it takes to get them back, even risk my life. I just want to know where I should go from here to keep looking."

Cold Foot shook his head. "Perhaps you should talk to Chief Pontiac, or to Charles Langlade. I am aware that Langlade is at Fort Detroit even now."

Noah had little desire to come into contact with either man, both of whom could be dangerous if crossed; and it did not take much to rile either of them. "I'm not sure I should talk to them," Noah answered. "The girl I'm looking for is English. They might wonder why I care."

Cold Foot nodded. "Perhaps you could tell him that you and some other French traders had been doing your own raiding in the area, to kick out the English. You could say that you came upon the cabin and saw what had happened, that you were surprised to see Indians had been there before you, and you wonder if Pontiac knows who has been raiding so far south."

Noah finished his wine and held out the cup, asking

Cold Foot's wife if he could have more. "I'll give you some red beads for another cup," he told her. The woman laughed lightly and refilled the cup.

"I have venison to cook. You would like some?" she asked.

"I'd be very grateful," Noah answered. He looked at Cold Foot. "Is an honorable Miami leader telling me to lie to Pontiac?" he asked, still grinning.

Cold Foot sighed. "I suppose I am. It is not our way to avoid the truth, but you are my friend, and I am sorry you have lost this young woman who means much to you. If lying is the only way to find out if they know something, then that is what you must do." He grinned himself then. "Besides, *you* would be the one who is lying. I only planted the idea. And I have long ago learned that it is easy for the white man to lie."

Noah chuckled. It felt good to find something to laugh about. "I suppose most Iroquois would see it that way. God knows enough promises have been broken." The words stabbed at his heart. He'd broken the one most important promise of all—the promise to come back for Jess by the end of last summer.

"Be careful, my friend," Cold Foot continued. "You walk a dangerous path. Everyone here in French Territory, especially in this area of Detroit and Fort Pontchartrain, thinks you are one of them. They might think you have come back to help them again."

Noah sipped more wine, well aware of the fix he could get himself into by being back here; but if he could still find Jess alive, it would be worth the risk.

"Once I leave here, I may never see you again, Cold Foot. But I will always remember you fondly."

Cold Foot smiled sadly. "As I will remember you, Noah Wilde. There is much ahead of us in this struggle, and none of it will be over soon, I fear. There are many more long, cold winters ahead, and I do not speak just of the weather."

Noah thought how he could bear just about anything that was to come, as long as he had Jess Matthews by his side. If he never found her, it mattered little to him what the future held. He would have failed her, just as he'd failed Mary by being gone when she was attacked. He'd lived with that memory for going on nine years now. If Jess met the same fate . . .

He held out the cup. "Fill it again," he told Cold Foot's wife.

26

Noah had never thought of Fort Detroit as being at all ominous. He'd walked in and out of the large, well-guarded post many times, never feeling threatened. He reminded himself he still needn't be. No one knew anything different about him. He was Noah Wilde, hunter, trapper, trader—and sometimes a man in the service of the French. He had to get out of here this time without having to commit himself to any more scouting, if possible.

Luckily, he'd learned that Governor Duquesne was not here. He was in Montreal. If anyone would be likely to try to corner him into more work for the French, it would be Duquesne. Trouble was, the one in charge for the moment was none other than Charles Langlade, or so one of the traders outside the fort had told him.

He'd ridden a well-worn path through the snow from Cold Foot's village to Fort Detroit, a trek of only about ten miles. Wigwams, longhouses and log houses surrounded the fort, some well-kept, others nothing more than tumbling shanties. The air smelled of wood smoke mixed with cooked meat. At times that smell was overcome by the smell of horse manure and wet dogs, which ran everywhere, barking and romping. Some snarled at each other over a discarded bone or old meat.

Indians moved about as easily as did the French soldiers and traders. Most were Ottawa, Pontiac's men, some were Miami. It was hard telling where Chief Pontiac might be, and Noah hoped that wherever that was, he'd stay put. Usually in the dead of such a hard winter, no Iroquois would venture out to raid. Those who'd attacked Jess's family would not have expected winter to set in so soon or so hard.

He was even more concerned about finding Jess now that he'd learned she was not in the area. He'd been so sure she'd be here, since this was one of the closest and largest Indian and French settlements far enough from English settlements to hide a white captive. Now he wasn't really sure where to continue the search. Jess could be anywhere from northern Michigan into Canada or south into Ohio, even clear down in Tennessee or in upper New York. The possibilities were endless.

He rode through the wide doors of the wooden stockade, nodding to a French soldier he recognized.

"Allo, Monsieur Wilde," the soldier spoke up.

"Allo, soldat. Où est Monsieur Langlade?"

The soldier nodded toward the officers' quarters. *"Monsieur Langlade est lieutenant de nos jours."*

Lieutenant! Charles Langlade was a lieutenant over French soldiers now? Noah shuddered to think of the man who'd ripped the heart out of Unemakemi being in charge of soldiers who might make war against English settlements. Langlade was as vicious or worse in war than most any Indian, including Pontiac, and that was saying a lot. The man literally thirsted for other people's blood. No man wanted to be on Langlade's hate list.

Still, other than Governor Marquis Duquesne, Charles Langlade was the one person most likely to know about any raiding that might be taking place. Dreading even having to see the French trader again, Noah rode over to the officers' quarters and dismounted, tying his lead horse and saying a quick prayer for the wisdom to speak without giving himself away. He had no doubt he could hold his own against Langlade, even though the man was just about the same size and vicious as a damned grizzly. Having to fight him was not so much his concern, if matters ever came to that. His concern was that the man was now an officer in the French army, which meant that anyone who harmed or killed him, especially when that person was a common trader, could most likely expect to be hung or shot for it. And that was only if the killer first survived whatever Langlade's Iroquois followers would do to him. Most likely, Chief Pontiac would get to him first, and Pontiac's methods of making a man suffer for his "crimes" were something Noah didn't even care to think about.

He walked onto the stoop outside and knocked on a thick, wooden door. A private opened it, asking his name and why he was there. Noah obliged the man, speaking in French, keeping in mind not to show any English traits. Langlade was clever, and suspicious of everyone, even under normal circumstances.

"Noah!" he heard Langlade exclaim from another room. "Send him in!" The words were spoken in French, and Noah felt at least slightly relieved to know Langlade seemed to be in a good mood. The private came out and motioned for Noah to enter. He promptly did so, finding Langlade standing behind an ornate desk. He wore a French lieutenant's uniform, but the coat hung open, revealing a chest covered with dark hair. Only Charles Langlade would so defile proper uniform code. The vision of the man literally covered in Unemakemi's blood, some of it even running down his chin, came roaring back to Noah's memory. He almost made a face at the thought of it.

"Mon ami," Noah replied. He put out his hand, making sure to speak only in French. "I see it's 'Lieutenant' now."

Langlade grinned proudly, and Noah thought how handsome the man would be, a fine mixture of French and Indian, a well-built man with a nice smile—if not for the blood that had dripped from those teeth, teeth that had bitten into a man's beating heart.

They shook hands, and Noah did not miss the warning squeeze from the lieutenant. He squeezed back, in the way men had of measuring one another's strength.

"Oui, my friend," Langlade told him. "After leading the Ottawa and the French soldiers at Pickawillany and bringing back English captives, Governor Duquesne made me a lieutenant! What do you think of that?" The man walked around behind his desk and opened a drawer.

"I think it was a very wise decision," Noah lied. "You're a born leader."

"Oui, mon ami, and I find I am enjoying it!" The man handed out a cigar. "Have a smoke with me, old friend," he told Noah. "I have not seen you since we returned from Pickawillany. Where have you been, Noah? I could use your services again. There is much to be done, much to be done!" He sat down and put his feet up on his desk, shouting then at the private outside the door to come in and light a stick from the heating stove to light their cigars.

"I spent the summer hunting," Noah answered. The

private lit his cigar, and Noah took several puffs, enjoying the flavor while Langlade's cigar was lit.

"Fine tobacco, eh?" Langlade asked. "When you are an officer, you enjoy only the best. You only need to impress Governor Duquesne." He chuckled and took several puffs on his own cigar, waving the private away. Noah could tell the young man was glad to leave. "Now, why did you not return here in the fall?" Langlade asked him.

Noah shrugged. "I decided to head west after leaving Canada. I went all the way to Fort St. Joseph, spent some time there with a very obliging Potawatomi squaw, did some hunting and trading. Then I headed back this way and decided to check out English movements and settlements this side of the Alleghenies. They're still pushing west, you know."

"Oh, I certainly do know that. I can tell you plans are in the making to put an end to that. Some of the Iroquois are already raiding to the south, and I can assure you that French soldiers are soon to follow."

Noah took great hope in the man's comment. He knew something! He smiled, reminding himself not to appear too eager. "I figured as much," he told Langlade. "At any rate, I went back into the Ohio Valley to do a little more hunting, then headed back to the English settlements. I have to admit I'd spotted a very young, very pretty English girl I'd intended to kidnap and take north with me."

Langlade frowned. "An English girl? You can have any young Iroquois woman you want—probably any young French girl, for that matter, you handsome bastard. Why did you set your eyes on an English girl?"

Noah kept up the sly smile. "Maybe because the English ones are forbidden, and she'd most likely fight me tooth and nail. Makes them that much more desirable."

Langlade finally smiled again. He nodded, clamping the cigar between his teeth. "Ah, yes, the forbidden fruit. So, where is she?"

Noah sobered. "That's the problem, and the reason I'm here. When I went back to scout the farm and figure how I'd take her, I found everything burned, most of the family slaughtered. The remains proved it was the work of raiding Indians, probably Delaware. I wondered if you know of any Delaware camped in this area recently, or if you've heard about any raiding last fall in the vicinity of Logstown or Fort Le Boeuf. I feel like I've been robbed of something that's mine, and I want her back."

Langlade chuckled deep in his throat, taking the cigar from his mouth. He put his feet down and leaned forward, his elbows on the desk. "You want to be first to break her, eh?"

Noah fought to mask his abhorrence of the man. "Something like that."

Langlade leaned back again. "I do not blame you for being upset, my friend." He smoked for a moment, apparently weighing his next words. "I have not heard of a white woman captive around here, Noah, but I believe the Delaware from up around the Ottawa

187

River near Montreal did some raiding in that area last summer and fall. Perhaps Father Piquet at La Présentation can help you."

Montreal! No wonder he'd found no clues. He'd gone in completely the wrong direction! He slowly nodded, feeling sick inside at the distance he'd have to travel and the precious time he'd lose making his way to Montreal in this weather. "Good advice. I'm grateful for it."

"Well, since I've heard of nothing like that here in Detroit, it is the only possibility I can think of. Of course, if some Delaware warrior has decided she belongs to him, you will not have an easy time winning her back."

"I'll find a way. If not, I figure he owes me something, at least a few damn good beaver pelts. She's worth that much and more."

Langlade laughed again. "I am wondering," he said, suddenly sober. He glared at Noah with the wild look that sometimes flashed in his eyes, a look that betrayed the madness that lay beneath the man's friendly attitude. "Since you were in the area of western Pennsylvania, did you not see or hear about a contingent of Englishmen in that area, led by a Major George Washington?"

Noah held the man's gaze steadily. If he looked away or acted one tiny bit uneasy, Langlade would read it. He couldn't help wondering how the man already knew about Washington's visit. Apparently, in the time it had taken Noah to look for Jess and find the mess at her farm, someone had made it up here to Detroit to tell Langlade about Washington.

"I saw no English in the area except for the few settlers there. What was an English major doing there?"

Langlade sighed, his demeanor again changing to friendly. "You know as well as I do that the bastard was probably spying. He visited Logstown, then Venango and Fort Le Boeuf. Do you want to know what he did there?"

Noah raised his eyebrows, as though curious. "I'm sure you're going to tell me."

Langlade's eyes literally darkened with the look he used for anyone he held in contempt. "The fool gave a letter to captains Joncaire and Saint-Pierre from a Governor Dinwiddie of Virginia, warning us, the French, to retreat from our forts there, claiming they were built on land belonging to England. They also warned we must not build any new forts, or the English will take offense and the peace between England and France will be broken."

Langlade suddenly broke into hardy laughter, as if enjoying a wonderful joke. Noah joined him, laughing mostly because he was relieved to finally have a possible lead on finding Jess.

"Imagine, the English warning the French to get out," Langlade spoke through his laughter. "We are ten times more fortified than they, and we have nearly the entire Iroquois Nation calling us friend and willing to fight with us!" He laughed more, his eyes literally tearing.

And then, in the manner common to the strangely emotional man, he suddenly stopped laughing, his eyes again gleaming with dark hatred. He banged his fist on the desk and rose. "If the English dare make one move upon a French fort, or dare to begin building forts anywhere near our own and making more threats that we should leave that country, they will be very, very sorry, I assure you." He glared at Noah. "I hope you feel the same."

Noah also rose, facing him squarely. "Of course I do."

Langlade slowly nodded. "I have eaten the heart of a Miami chief who once insulted me. But I have never eaten the heart of an Englishman. How do you think that would taste, Noah?"

Noah grinned. "Like tea, I imagine."

Langlade broke into ribald laughter again. "Tea! I like that, Noah! Tea!" He walked around his desk and put out his hand again. Noah shook the man's hand firmly.

"Noah, go and look for this English girl and bring her back here. I would like to see the young beauty that has you traveling around in one of the worst winters ever, just to find her. Maybe you will share her with me once you have the privilege of breaking her in, eh?"

Noah had to congratulate himself on his ability to hide his contempt for the man standing in front of him. "I'd be glad to share her with the man who helped me find her."

Again Langlade laughed so loudly Noah wondered if everyone outside could hear him. He smelled whiskey on the man's breath. Thank God he was just drunk enough to be in a good mood, but not so much that he angered too easily.

"You bring her back here, Noah, and let me have at her. And, my friend, perhaps you can also join me and my French soldiers in a march to the south, no? We will go and see if this George Washington makes good on his threat to stop us. I hope that he does! I will enjoy cutting him to pieces!"

Noah nodded. "I'll settle for his red coat and his white wig," he answered.

Langlade laughed once more, slapping him on the shoulder. "I sent the news on to Governor Duquesne about the English threat. I am sure that when you reach Montreal he will want to see you also. Perhaps by then he will have decided what to do about this George Washington and this silly warning. As always, you can be of great service to us. I have no doubt I will see you again, Noah, especially once you are done playing with the young English girl—unless some Iroquois warrior has you tortured and killed for trying to take her."

"I'll win her the proper way," Noah answered.

Langlade nodded. "You had better hope she has not been sold to some old Iroquois man who wants a new, young wife instead of just a slave. Then you will never get the enjoyment of being her first."

The thought of what the man was suggesting made

Noah feel sick inside. It was all too possible that was exactly what had happened to Jess. "There is only one way to find out," he answered. "And I intend to do just that."

"And I wish you luck, my friend. Perhaps in time to come we will again march together. We can watch Englishmen squirm under our knives and tomahawks, no?"

No, Noah thought. Torn as he'd been in his loyalties since his imprisonment, talking to Langlade only reinforced his desire to keep the French and leaders like Langlade away from English settlements. "Thanks for the good cigar, Lieutenant. There is still plenty of daylight left, and for once a little sunshine. I think I'll leave today for Montreal."

Langlade put a hand on Noah's shoulder as Noah headed out of the room. "It will not be an easy journey in this weather. Tell Governor Duquesne you have seen me and how I feel about the English threat. Tell him I am ready to go and fight any time he deems it necessary. I have already sent a few spies to the area. I have a feeling the English will try building a fort there. We will never let that happen."

Noah thought about young George Washington, so excited about building a fort at the forks of the Ohio, Allegheny and Monongahela rivers. He felt sorry for the major, who truly believed his letters would somehow deter the French. Washington just might be in for a hard lesson in frontier warfare. He wished he had time to warn him and Dinwiddie that not only were the French laughing at the English threat, but they were even planning to build more forts rather than close any of them. Dinwiddie and the others had taken too long to fortify the western frontier, and English settlers were bound to pay for it.

27

Mid-January 1754

Jess sat eyeing the women who surrounded her, speaking in their own tongue. By the way Thunder was greeted at this village, she guessed they had finally reached "home," wherever that was. They'd trudged for more endless miles and endless days to get here, and hope of being found was fast fading. Even Noah couldn't possibly find her now. He would have to always wonder what had happened to her, if indeed he'd even come looking for her. If he had, maybe he'd determined she'd been burned up in the fire. He would, after all, find four bodies, two of them women.

The reality of such hopelessness almost brought her to tears, but now she fought those tears for a different reason. If she was going to be stuck here, she'd better win the respect of all these people. Maybe then they wouldn't beat her or abuse her in some other way. She knew enough about the Iroquois to remember the women held high importance. If the women who discussed her now grew to like her, it could help her survive; and that was something she'd decided to do whether Noah came for her or not.

She was tired, hungry and sore, and had not yet been allowed to sleep or eat, but at least she was again inside someplace warm. She was sick to death of being constantly cold, constantly walking through deep snow and eating mostly raw meat. She'd lost so much weight she wondered that she could even get up and walk.

Upon arrival here, Thunder had handed her over to these women, the center of their attention. She wished she could understand them. She took hope only in the fact that Thunder apparently intended to save her for a wife, which meant they probably would not harm her; but then, she'd given up trying to figure out anything these people might do.

The circle of women, who numbered fifteen, were dressed in a fantastic mixture of Indian and white clothing. A couple of them actually wore English dresses, although they did not fit well and it was obvious they wore no undergarments. Some wore white-woman skirts but nothing else from the waist up but mounds of necklaces, mostly beads and quills. One sat nursing a baby, but she was the only one who appeared even close to Jess's age.

Others wore more traditional-looking Iroquois garb—deerskin tunics or deerskin skirts—but again, they, too, were naked from the waist up. Jess hoped she would not be expected to walk around naked when summer came, as she'd heard many Iroquois did, both men and women.

She braced herself when it appeared the women had finally made a decision. "What are you called?" one of them asked.

English! Another one who spoke English! "Jessica," she answered. "I am Jessica Matthews, and I want to go back to my own people. Why do you keep me here?"

The Iroquois woman, who was perhaps Jess's mother's age, was actually quite pretty, but she had a rather sour look about her. "Thunder say you know why. Someone already tell you that you are to be his wife. Until then, you will be slave to one of us. And if you do not behave, Thunder will sell you to an older warrior who would like a young wife." She shook a finger at Jess. "You are worth much wampum to Thunder. If you displease him, he will sell you."

Jess decided then and there to do whatever she was told and not complain. If she pleased Thunder and was going to be saved for him, it might give her time to escape or be rescued before he could make her his wife. Survival was all that mattered now.

"Just tell me what you want of me now," she answered the English-speaking woman. She sat straight, glaring right back at the woman. "I am tired and hungry, and I am sick of never knowing what is going to happen to me. Am I here to stay, or will Thunder take me on to yet another village?"

The woman seemed to soften just a little. "I am

called Josephine." She suddenly smiled proudly. "I took a white woman's name. Do you like it?"

"Yes. Josephine is a very nice name."

The woman held her chin proudly. "I took it because the white woman who had the name died honorably." A teasing look came into her eyes, and Jess suspected Josephine was trying to scare her. "When I cut off her ears," the woman continued, "she never made a sound. Nor did she scream when I pierced her heart with a burning stick. Then I cut out her heart and ate of it, taking her bravery into my bones and blood. Then I took her name." Josephine straightened in a way that reminded Jess of a proud warrior. "That was many seasons past, when our people helped attack the white settlement called Albany. We did it to teach them a lesson, but they still have not learned that lesson—that they must leave this land to the Iroquois and the French."

Albany. That was where Noah's wife, Mary, had been killed! After what she'd seen of Iroquois cruelty, Jess could better sympathize with what Noah must have suffered when he found his wife. He'd never gone into detail, but now Jess could imagine what had happened to the young woman. "Does one of these other women plan to take my name?" Jess asked boldly.

Josephine laughed, saying something to the others, who also laughed. Josephine shook her head. "No, Jessica, not if you are a good girl and a good wife to my son."

"Your son? You are Thunder's mother?"

Josephine nodded. "We will make you more beautiful for Thunder. It will be hard for him to wait more seasons to take you, but he is not yet thirty summers. Young warriors fight better when they do not have a woman at home to worry about. They spend the first part of their manhood willing to die for the Iroquois, and thus they should have no family to leave behind. Then they take a wife and produce more strong, young warriors. Thunder tells me you behaved bravely and never wept or fought him, nor did you ever hang your head. He thinks you are worth saving for himself. You have time to continue showing that worth. And while he waits, we will make you more beautiful."

Jess worried what that meant. "Doesn't he like me just the way I am?"

Josephine shook her head. "An Iroquois woman is always more beautiful wearing jewelry, and with her face painted. You are too thin. We will feed you well and fatten you up. A woman who is to bear children cannot be so thin. We will coat your skin with bear fat to keep it soft, and we will pierce your ears."

Jess drew in her breath. "No! I do not want my ears pierced!"

"You have no choice. It is the first thing we do to mark you as our own. Our duty here is to dress you and paint you properly, to pierce your ears and put in them special ornaments made of wampum that Thunder's father left to him. This will mark you as belonging to Thunder."

Jess cringed at the thought of being so marked. If her ears were pierced, could she ever reenter the English world and be accepted? Would Noah even still want her? Her heart fell at the thought. What did it matter? He would never find her now, and maybe he'd never even tried. She had to give up that hope.

Josephine told her to stand, and the women proceeded to strip her, as had happened at the last village, where they'd stopped for one night. They smeared her all over with bear fat, which Jess thought stank horribly; but the Iroquois women thought it was wonderful. Josephine emphasized how soft it would keep her skin, and that in the summer it would keep bugs from biting her. That was the only remote benefit Jess could imagine to such a smelly coating.

They smeared more of it into her hair, which they then smoothed straight back and tied with rawhide strips. Throughout the procedure, the women studied her, obvious admiration in their eyes. They sat her down and painted her arms and chest with some kind of purple dye. Jess couldn't help wondering if she would ever be able to wash it off. They applied red paint to her face and hair, and each woman then removed one of their beaded or shell necklaces from around their necks and hung them around Jess's. Jess sensed they considered the necklaces as welcome gifts, so she pretended gratefulness. By the time they finished, fifteen heavy necklaces decorated Jess's chest, and she realized they indeed intended she remain naked from the waist up. They made her stand

and wrapped a deerskin skirt around her waist, but that was all the clothing she was given before being ordered to sit again.

Anger and humiliation raged inside her, made worse then by Josephine's announcement. "Now we will pierce your ears and decorate them." The woman turned to take something out of a pouch nearby, then held up what looked like a thin piece of bone. "It only hurts for the first day," she told Jess, whose stomach turned at the realization the ugly-looking instrument would be used to puncture her earlobes.

"I do not want my ears pierced!" Jess insisted.

"To become a true Iroquois woman, it must be done," Josephine replied firmly.

One of the other women grasped hold of Jess's head. Jess tried to wrench herself away, but more of the women grasped her arms and held her fast. Josephine stretched out her right earlobe. Jess gritted her teeth, and then came the quick, ugly pain, in an act that would mark her for life as an Iroquois captive. For the first time since her abduction, tears slipped down Jess's cheeks, but she made no sound. She could only pray they would not also pierce her nose, or permanently mark her body with tattoos.

28

Early February 1754

Before leaving Fort Detroit, Noah used nearly all the money given him by Governor Dinwiddie before he left Virginia, buying an extra horse and stocking up on plenty of trade goods. If he had to buy Jess, the Delaware would expect plenty in trade. He left with supplies of beads, mirrors, jewelry, steel tomahawks, knives, three pistols, blankets and even some purple shells from quahog clams, valuable wampum to the Iroquois.

As he forged ahead through more bitter storms, he had plenty of time to wonder what might lie waiting for him and for those he cared about. His father needed him. The French probably thought *they* needed him. Governor Dinwiddie was probably wondering what had happened to him. George Washington was undoubtedly in for a hell of a fight if he did go back to build a fort on the Monongahela. He had no idea what had happened to little Billy, if the child was with Jess; and then there was Jess herself. God only knew where she might be by now, or if she was dead or alive. He'd damned well find out!

He'd literally ridden his horse across parts of frozen Lake St. Claire, never knowing when he might hit a soft spot and sink into a horrible, cold death. He'd taken every shortcut he could think of as he pressed on to Fort Oswego.

He was actually in English territory then, but he didn't dare stop at Fort Oswego for fear of some officer recognizing him and hailing him down, much as he would love to go inside and warm up and rest. Instead, he kept to the deeper woods surrounding the fort, his destination being La Présentation and the man who ran the settlement, Father Piquet. The useless priest knew everything that was going on in northern New York and among the Iroquois there, as well he should. The man had built the fort at La Présentation himself, not once but twice, not giving up after Indians burned it down the first time. He'd been in the area for years and had won the confidence of the Indians for miles around.

One would think the old priest was a dedicated Christian, but he cared more about impressing French aristocracy and getting gifts from them than he did about teaching the truth. Piquet had the Indians believing Jesus Christ had been a Frenchman crucified by the English. What a hideously ridiculous picture that was, but the Indians had no way of knowing otherwise. Maybe Piquet had had good intentions when first coming here. Maybe he thought since he was a Frenchman himself that by spreading such a lie he could keep the surrounding Iroquois friendly, and therefore keep his own throat from being slashed.

Where would all the lying and backstabbing end?

All of this came from greed—the French wanting all the trading rights; the English wanting all the land; the Iroquois figuring both belonged to them; the missionaries wanting to convert all the Indians; England jealous of France; France jealous of England . . . And who suffered the most? The colonists.

Noah's father's suggestion that some day the colonists just might decide to rule themselves and kick the king of England out of the picture was beginning to make a little more sense. Colonists would suffer because England was being too slow and too selfish to send in more troops and provide more money to protect them. If all this led to a bloody frontier, the colonists would not soon forget, or forgive.

Once he reached La Présentation, he would be much closer to Montreal and back in French territory. It was getting to the point where he had to force himself to remember which hat he was wearing, English or French. He once thought of himself only as Noah Wilde, a farmer from Albany who just happened to have both French and English blood in his veins. A lot had changed since Mary's awful death.

The smell of wood smoke told him he was finally nearing La Présentation. He'd been traveling a good six weeks, pushing himself with every bit of daylight he could savor and even sometimes traveling at night when the moon was bright on the snow. La Présentation was a combination of fort and mission. It was surrounded by various Iroquois clans, mostly bands of Oneida, Seneca and Onondaga, a few Mahican and even Delaware, although most Delaware had moved farther south, into parts of Pennsylvania, which would explain how Jess might have been taken by them. If a Delware war party from this area had gone south to visit relatives, they might have decided to raid English settlements on the way back north. Because of English and French settlement, the Iroquois were becoming more scattered now. All the common places they once had called home were changing. A man hardly knew where to find which tribes anymore, except that the Mohawk still lived mostly in New York and were one of the few Iroquois tribes who remained friendly to the English.

La Présentation finally came into sight, and Noah noticed the supposedly Christian mission now sported even higher walls, along which cannons had been positioned. Father Piquet's "church" now consisted of heavy palisades surrounded by block houses. Noah ignored the stares of others as he wondered at the growth of the place since he last visited. The once small village had grown immensely, and all around the area were barns and stables, storehouses, trading posts, a bakery; in the distance he could see a sawmill, lumber piled everywhere. All this was the fruit of Abbé Francois Piquet, the "humble" priest who'd come here to teach the Iroquois about God. That his version of Christ and the crucifixion only served to make the surrounding Iroquois swear their allegiance to France seemed to matter little to anyone, especially French leaders.

French soldiers eyed Noah now as he approached the massive doors that led inside the "mission." It was obvious the place had become a virtual fort that France could garrison and use in a war against England. Any fool could see that Piquet had both the Indians and the French in the palm of his hand, and Noah was well aware that the priest often taught the Indians that it was right in God's eyes if they arose and slaughtered the English wherever they found them.

Several Iroquois women ran to greet Noah before he entered the mission gates. Some of the younger ones ran their hands along his thighs, making an obvious offer of a pleasant time. A man bringing two extra horses loaded down with supplies was a man to befriend.

Noah ignored them and headed inside, toward where he knew Piquet usually stayed when not "serving" his "beloved Iroquois"; some even called the man the "Apostle to the Iroquois." Having to show any respect for him irked Noah, but Piquet was as clever as Langlade or Pontiac or any others loyal to the French. He would betray a man as readily as any heathen.

Always curious to know who was invading his territory, the balding, medium-built priest, dressed in his usual black robe, exited his sturdy log dwelling to greet Noah. Noah noticed he wore around his middle a fine leather belt greatly decorated with wampum, most likely a gift from some warrior.

"Noah Wilde!" the man greeted him. "I have not seen you for two, maybe three years."

Noah was a little surprised Piquet even remembered him. "Things have really grown around here," he told the priest as he dismounted. He grudgingly shook the priest's hand. "I'm not on any official business this time," he continued, speaking in French, aware Piquet preferred using his native tongue. "I'm just stopping for a short while to see if you might be able to give me some information about someone."

"Fine! Fine! Come inside, *mon ami!*" the priest told him. "It's much too cold to stay out here." He turned and ordered a young French boy to tend to Noah's horses. "You have quite a stash of supplies there," he noticed.

"I might need them this trip," Noah answered. "I have to say, in return, that's quite a belt of wampum you're wearing."

"Yes! It's a gift from an old Delaware chief who felt I had done much for his people."

Noah followed the man inside a comfortable cabin. An elegant, beautifully carved desk sat in one corner. Piquet motioned for Noah to be seated in a red velvet chair near the desk while the priest retrieved a bottle of wine and two gold-rimmed wineglasses from a shelf behind the desk. "You've done well since this place was burned down," Noah told the man.

Piquet chuckled, pouring Noah a full glass of dark wine. "Indeed. I stuck it out, my friend, in spite of the hardships and dangers. When one works for God, one must expect such things and be willing to face them."

Noah was glad he'd not sipped any of the wine yet. He might have choked on it. "God is lucky to have men like you who are willing to die for him," he answered.

Piquet held up his wineglass and Noah did the same, saluting each other before taking a drink. The wine was sweet and smooth, obviously a good grade, probably sent down from Montreal.

"So, why are you here?" Piquet asked.

"I've come from Detroit. I'm looking for a young English girl whom I suspect was taken captive by the Delaware who still live north of here. I spoke with Charles Langlade at Detroit. He thought you might have some knowledge of the English girl. She's nowhere around the Detroit area."

Piquet frowned, and Noah saw an odd flash in the man's eyes that said he knew something. "Where did she live when she was taken?" the priest asked.

"Western Pennsylvania. I think they might also have taken her little brother, about two years old. Do you have any knowledge of either captive?"

Piquet's eyebrows arched. "Now, why is it you care about English captives?" He drank more wine, studying Noah intently.

Noah grinned. "Because I saw her first. I'd intended to steal her away for my own pleasure, but some Delaware warrior got to her before I could."

The priest smiled. "I see. So, it's a matter of ownership." His belly moved as he laughed from somewhere deep inside. "Well, let's see," the man continued, a sly grin on his face. "Is my information worth anything to you?"

Damned if the man wasn't demanding money for his news! Noah wanted desperately to strangle him. "That depends on what you can tell me, Father."

The priest downed the rest of his wine, setting the glass on his desk with a little more force than was necessary. "I can tell you exactly where she is. I can even tell you where her brother is. How much is *that* worth to you?"

Noah thought a moment, gauging the man's haughty look. "Something tells me you're going to quote the price yourself."

Piquet chuckled. "You are a smart man, Noah, and a loyal Frenchman. And believe it or not, my price is not gold or wampum or any of the supplies you might be carrying with you."

Noah grew even more wary. "I can't imagine what I have that's worth more than anything I'm carrying," he answered.

Piquet rose. "You have a vast knowledge of the entire wilderness west of the Alleghenies." He began to pace while Noah sipped more of his own wine, dreading what was coming. "Word has come down to me from Montreal, my friend. Spies have told us that the English are planning construction of a fort at the forks of the Ohio, the Monongahela and the Allegheny. The French, as you know, have begun building a series of forts in the same area, and they do not intend to allow any forts to be built there by the English."

Piquet came to stand beside Noah, looking down at him with a glint of evil joy in his eyes. "I happen to know that Captain Saint-Pierre is ill and has been replaced by Captain Pierre de Contrecoeur. I also know that Governor Duquesne plans to send Contrecoeur south with over one thousand Canadian militia, both to build yet another fort and to move against those building the English fort. They will take that fort away and build their own there. Not only that, but they will move against a contingent of English soldiers and colonial militia who have fortified an area east of the new fort. I believe they are led by a young man called George Washington."

Noah had to hide his astonishment that Piquet knew so much about English movements. Part of him wished he had time to ride to Albany, not all that far away now, and tell Governor Clinton how much the French knew and the danger Washington was in. More than that, he wanted to warn George Washington. He drank down the rest of his wine. "And what does all of that have to do with what I owe you for information?" he asked, rising to face the priest. He towered over him, and Piquet moved back a little. Noah sensed that for a brief moment Piquet had lost his arrogance and realized it might not be wise to threaten Noah Wilde.

The priest turned and paced again. "Well, Noah, you know how important it is for me to continue in the good graces of men like Governor Duquesne. He'd be pleased to discover I have run into one of our most cherished scouts and convinced him to help lead our French soldiers south. All I want is your promise that if you find and win back this English girl you want to make your slave, you will report to Montreal and agree to accompany Contrecoeur south in a raid against Washington and his men."

Noah's heart suddenly felt heavy as a stone. Just as he'd been forced to make war against the unknowing English traders at Pickawillany, now he might end up having to do the same against George Washington, a man who'd become a good friend. How was he going to bear going through something like that again?

He wouldn't! This time, by God, he would manage to warn Washington and fight *with* him, not against him. For the moment he would do anything to find Jess, but he'd be damned if he'd again slaughter men who were supposed to be his friends.

"All right," he answered, glaring at Piquet. "You have my promise. How do you know I'll find her quickly enough to reach Montreal in time?"

"Because she is no more than another week's ride from here, at the Delaware camp of Tonnerre."

"Thunder?" Noah knew the young warrior, a fierce man eager to prove his worth. Jess would be quite a prize for him. It would not be easy bargaining to get her back. The only good news about this was that Thunder was young enough that he probably had not made a wife of her yet. He could only hope he hadn't traded her to some older Iroquois man.

"Now, was that information worth what I've asked of you?" Piquet asked.

Noah nodded. "Damn well worth it. What about the little boy?"

"He's right here!"

"Here?"

Piquet chuckled. "I figured someone might come along willing to bargain for him. I never expected *you,* however!"

"Where is he? Is he all right? How in hell did he end up here?"

Piquet smiled. "The boy is fine." The man literally glowed with pride at having the upper hand. "Some of Thunder's fellow warriors took him first to Fort Toronto to try to sell him. A childless white couple traded whiskey and guns for him. Then, I'm told by the trader who brought him here, the couple took a fine horse in trade for the boy, for whatever reason. The French trader brought him here to sell for beaver skins. An Iroquois woman who'd lost a child not long ago adopted him. However, I might be able to convince her to give the child over to you, since very recently another Iroquois woman died in childbirth and the baby was given to this very same woman. She is more involved now with tending the new baby and not so attached to the little white boy after all. What did you say his name was?"

"Billy."

Piquet nodded. "See? I've made your promise well worth it. If you wish, once you find the English girl, you can bring her here for safety while you go on south with the French soldiers."

"No! Where I go, she goes! I'll never let her out of my sight again!"

The priest's eyes widened in surprise. "You sound like you have *feelings* for her."

Noah realized he'd given too much away. He put on a look of threatening anger. "She's worth a lot to me in trade," he answered. "I might even be able to use her as some kind of ransom when we meet up with George Washington."

Piquet grinned then. "I see. Not a bad idea." He sighed and walked back to sit down behind his desk. "As you can see, I know just about everything that goes on in a very big area, *mon ami,* from Albany to Toronto to Montreal. Do not forget that I will also know if you do not show up at Montreal to report. I would have to consider you a traitor if you did not go there. I do not believe you would like then to have to answer to men like Pontiac or Charles Langlade."

There was the threat. It was getting so Noah hardly knew whom to hate the most—Dinwiddie, an Englishman? Langlade, a Frenchman? Pontiac, an Iroquois? This alleged priest, who was supposed to be a neutral holy man? And now there would be Thunder to deal with. The list was getting longer.

"Don't worry about me showing up at Montreal," he answered, his anger rising. "What about Billy?"

"You let me take care of the boy. It is best we do not go to the adoptive mother just yet. I will work on that for you. By the time you return here after getting his sister back and reporting at Montreal, I will have persuaded Billy's Iroquois mother to give him up. He will be waiting for you."

Noah decided the man had no reason to lie about Billy, although it irked him that Piquet had known about both captives and had done nothing to help them. So much for the man's Christian charity. "Fine," he answered. "If I went storming over there now and demanded the boy, I'd get nowhere. You just make sure he's ready and waiting for us when I return with Jess, which brings us to the original subject of my being here and agreeing to your terms for information. Where is Billy's sister?"

Piquet grinned with satisfaction. "It will be easy for a man like you to find her. Go directly north from here. Follow the trail through the old snow and you'll come to Thunder's camp within seven or eight days. After you retrieve the girl, you can report at Montreal and then come here and get the boy." He walked toward the door. "I wish you luck getting the woman away from Thunder, Noah. I am glad that I could be of service to you."

Of service? Noah questioned the man's true sense of duty. He felt the weight of more and more responsibility on his own shoulders. He'd likely pay a much higher price for Jess than he'd anticipated, thanks to having to promise to report at Montreal.

29

Mid-February 1754

Jess sat amid a group of women stitching beads to various belts, aprons, moccasins, tunics and sheaths. She'd quickly caught on to how to make moccasins, having made similar footwear for her own family for winter. This seemed to impress the women, but learning how to do fine beadwork was another matter. It was tedious and even painful work. Her fingers were sore and blistered from constantly trying to pierce a piece of thick hide with the heavy iron needle she'd been given, something no doubt purchased from French traders. She'd noticed these Indians used a good number of white man's goods, from iron pots to clothing.

Still, they insisted on beading just about everything, and Jess could not help being impressed with some of the spectacular designs the women could create, let alone the amazing speed with which they worked. She, on the other hand, had sore, blistered fingers, and it never seemed as though she could put the needle in the right place to make the bead stay where she wanted it.

For the most part, life was physically bearable. At least she sat in a warm longhouse with other women, most of whom were decent to her, though certainly not friendly or loving. Most of the affection she noticed was that of the women toward their babies.

Another form of affection, and one Jess considered most embarrassing, was the mating that went on between husbands and wives. Iroquois couples did not seem to be concerned about privacy. She'd seen and heard plenty, enough to know that not one Iroquois man, not even Thunder, was going to do that to her. She'd die first! Such things should be reserved for that one special man with whom a woman wanted to share her life, and whom she wanted to father her children.

With the right mate, surely there was something good and beautiful about the act of making love, if the Iroquois even thought of it that way. There was a time when she daydreamed about giving herself to Noah that way, but she realized now she might never know that kind of experience.

Emotionally, she'd grown numb. Sometimes she wondered if she would ever know true human feelings again. She felt like a totally different person than the one who'd kissed Noah Wilde good-bye that last night she saw him; from the daughter who'd cooked for her father; from the sister who'd helped mend her brother's clothes and feed her little brother; from the girl who'd fed the chickens and milked the cow and made butter and baked bread and pies. Sometimes she could smell that bread, hear her mother's voice, feel Sonny's arms around her, or little Billy resting in her lap.

She literally shook her head to get rid of the memories. Why did they keep sneaking up on her like that? It just wasn't permitted to think of such things anymore. Feelings, memories, love—all that was behind her, maybe forever. Once in a while Thunder would come to her with a dead rabbit or some deer meat, handing it over proudly, as though that would make her care about him. She supposed that was a way the Iroquois men had of impressing their women.

Another, even more shocking way, apparently, was to hand over scalps of the enemy. She'd seen plenty of dried-up scalps hanging around; some were even used to decorate clothing and belts. She'd noticed also that shells seemed to be of great importance to these people, especially purple ones. If she could understand their language, their beliefs, maybe it would help her gain some kind of perspective, some kind of understanding of these people, enough to bear life here until she could escape.

For now, she sat with her face and the part in her hair painted red, purple still on her arms and chest. Her pierced ears had given her considerable pain in the weeks following. Infection had made one ear swell, and both lobes were now scabbed over the rawhide loop that had been tied into them. She couldn't budge the rawhide at all, in spite of Josephine keeping some kind of ointment on the holes. Little pieces of tin dangled from the loop, and it was impossible to sleep well at night, since she couldn't stand to lie on either ear, let alone get comfortable on the reed mat she slept on.

At least she was allowed to keep her winter moc-casins, and she had two real wool blankets to cover herself with.

She slept with Josephine and the woman's daughter, Willow, who still nursed a small child. She'd learned that Thunder's father was dead, as was the father of Willow's baby. Thunder provided for both women, but slept with other young warriors who were not yet mar-ried.

Jess noticed most young men stayed away from the women, and she supposed it had something to do with making sure they concentrated on the warrior ways in their youth. Many of the young women appeared to belong to older warriors, as did older women, who were probably their first wives. Unmarried young women were kept separated from the men, most likely being saved for one of the warriors—just as she was being saved for Thunder.

She winced when yet again she poked a finger trying to shove her needle through the thick hide she worked on. She managed to pull the needle free just as a commotion arose outside. Dogs began barking, and someone shouted. The other women with Jess became alert, and Josephine barked some kind of order as she rose and walked to raise the bear-hide door cover to peek outside. She listened and watched for a moment, then turned to the others and spoke. Whatever she said, it caused the rest of the women to look in sur-prise at Jess.

Jess glanced up at Josephine in curiosity. Why was

she again suddenly the center of attention? The others whispered among themselves, then seemed to begin joking about something as they listened to what sounded like an argument outside. Jess listened herself, hearing a few yips and shouts, and the sound of two men speaking loudly to each other. She'd heard Thunder's voice often enough in those long weeks coming here to recognize it. The other voice was deeper, and somewhat familiar, but she couldn't quite place it with any of the men she'd met here.

Josephine suddenly walked over to Jess and jerked her to her feet. Alarmed, Jess dropped her sewing. Josephine grabbed her hooded fur cape, indicating Jess should put it on. Thunder barged inside then, before Jess had even finished tying the cape. He appeared to be alarmed and angry. He grabbed her wrist and jerked her outside into bright sunlight. The day had warmed enough that a lot of snow was melting, and the ground had turned to slop. Although it was still chilly, Thunder wore only leggings and moccasins, his chest bare. Jess slipped and slid trying to keep up with him as he hurriedly yanked her along. She looked down to watch for puddles and to keep her balance as they rounded another longhouse, where Thunder stopped.

Jess looked up, and there stood Noah Wilde!

30

Stunned, Jess's scrambled emotions left her speechless. Noah! There he stood in the middle of a pack of Delaware warriors who looked ready to kill him. How in God's name had he found her? And how was she supposed to react? Just as quickly as their eyes met, Noah glinted at her, actually looking angry, and he shook his head slightly.

Think quickly! He knew these Indians. He was an English spy in French territory, surrounded by Indians who considered themselves friend to the French. Confused, she looked away, never having to try so hard in her life to hide her emotions. Her heart beat so hard it hurt her chest, and at the moment Thunder gripped her wrist so tightly that it, too, hurt. She tried to pull away from him, but he yanked her closer. She wanted to cry, finally, from confusion, relief, love, pain, memories . . .

She blinked back tears as she stood there clinging to her fur cape, not wanting Noah to see that under it she was naked from the waist up. She waited for him to do the talking, unable to understand why he and Thunder were yelling at each other. Thunder finally let go of her wrist, and she gasped when Noah grabbed her by the hair and yanked her his way. She yelped at the pain of it, reaching up to grasp his wrist. He only twisted her hair and pulled harder. Why was he doing this? She thought about the way he'd fought the Ottawa the day he'd saved her; how he was a man who could be so gentle, yet just as vicious as the Delaware around her if need be.

My God! She thought. How must I look to him, with a painted face and pierced ears! What is he thinking about me? Does he think I've been soiled, that I've become a loose squaw?

Noah suddenly let go of her, actually shoving her slightly. He glared at Thunder, who stepped back and looked her over, then seemed to grudgingly agree to something. He spoke to Noah, who at the moment appeared so angry and threatening that Jess wondered if she should be afraid of him.

"You!" he said, making her literally jump. "Does anyone else here speak English?" he demanded.

Jess looked around, seeing only a large group of younger warriors. She was scared to death for Noah. She met his intense gaze. "No. As far as I know, only Thunder's mother does. She's called Josephine. She's at the longhouse in the distance."

Noah looked in that direction, then back at Jess. "Thunder has given me permission to speak to you alone," he told her, "to explain to you that I have laid claim to you and have come to take you as my captive."

"What—"

"Don't think for one minute that your fate with me will be any better than with Thunder," he interrupted, again glancing at the longhouse as though to be sure Josephine heard him. "Thunder says you are Iroquois now, and therefore he believes you should choose between us. Nod your agreement to him that you will speak with me."

Jess hesitated, not really sure what she was supposed to do. Obviously, she was to pretend she didn't know Noah, but his anger seemed so real she wasn't sure if she should pretend to be afraid, or if she really *should* be afraid. Living the way he did, maybe there was something about her being a captive that made Noah look at her differently now.

"Dammit, woman, tell the man you will speak with me! I saw you first and I'm by-God claiming you!" Noah barked the words so loudly that it was difficult for Jess not to think he truly would be vicious with her. She'd seen that side of him, and it had been so long . . .

She blinked back tears and turned to Thunder, nodding her approval. Thunder stepped back and pointed to a wigwam, and Noah grabbed Jess by the hair again and half dragged her to the hut. Jess decided it might be best to scream and fight all the way, and she did just that. It was not difficult, as Noah's grip on her hair was painful. Finally, he shoved her inside the wigwam and dropped the deer-hide flap that covered the door. For a moment they just stared at each other.

"Jess!" Noah groaned. "My God, I'm so sorry!"

Jess put a hand to her painted face, then to one of her ears, from which dangled a string of shells. She began to tremble with shame and doubt. "*Why,* Noah? If only you'd come back—"

"I couldn't. I was imprisoned. There's no time to explain it all now, Jess. I've been looking for you for months. When I found the cabin destroyed, found all those dead bodies—"

"Oh, Noah! Noah!" she wept, the reality of his being there washing over her. "It's really you!" She stepped closer, and instantly she was in his strong, sure, consoling arms. She wrapped her own arms around his waist, thinking how she never wanted to let go ever again. "How did you find me? How did you know I wasn't one of those bodies left at the farm?" she sobbed.

He rubbed his hands over her back, kissed her hair. "We can't talk about that now. There isn't time. I was arrested and imprisoned because of Pickawillany. They said I should have warned them."

"But you couldn't—"

"It's over now. It can't be changed."

A wave of memories and reality swept over Jess. Seeing Noah, hearing his voice, it brought back all of it, her family, that last night Sonny played the fiddle while she and Noah danced, little Billy jumping around with them, her parents watching, smiling . . .

"They're dead, Noah! They're all dead!" she wept. "All dead! It was horrible! Horrible! They chopped Sonny's head off and they burned—"

He held her so tightly she could barely breathe. "Don't talk about it, Jess. Not yet. Not now. You don't have to explain. I've seen Indian attacks. And I've seen what was left at the farm." He drew in his breath and sniffed, and Jess could feel him tremble with his own tears. "I never should have left, or I should have made your family come with me right then. If I just had stayed longer—"

"It wouldn't have mattered, Noah. There were too many of them. You would have been killed right along with Pa and Sonny." Jess sobbed against him, praying this was not all just a dream. He was really, really here. She could smell him, touch him. Here in his arms she was safe. It felt so good to be safe and protected and wanted and cared for.

Noah finally pried her away, forcing her to sit down on a mat. He sat down beside her and held her against his shoulder, placing a big hand at the side of her face and using his thumb to wipe at some of her tears.

"We've got to stop crying, Jess." He smiled a little, looking almost embarrassed as he wiped at his own tears. "I'm just so happy to find you alive. All I could envision was the way I found Mary." He breathed deeply. "There are things we have to decide quickly. Thunder isn't going to let us stay in here much longer. And when we leave, you have to seem like you're crying out of fear."

It felt so good to finally let the tears flow. Trying to stop made her head ache. "My God, how I must look to you," she lamented. "They pierced my ears, Noah!" She started crying again. "I'm marked for life! No one in English society will ever accept me now. And they—under this cape—"

"I know how captives are treated, Jess. You don't have to explain, and it doesn't matter, and it doesn't make a damn bit of difference to me. Just tell me they didn't force you to lay with some damn visiting trader or some old warrior."

The question embarrassed her, and she refused to look at him as she wiped at her tears again, noticing she was getting red paint on her hands. "No one has touched me that way," she answered, still shivering in sobs. "I was to be saved . . . for Thunder; but I'd already decided . . . I'd kill myself first!"

He stroked her hair. "Jess, my Jess. If my plan works, you won't have to be sorry about that."

Jess met his dark eyes—Noah's eyes. "What will you do? Noah, you know how the Iroquois can be! If you make them mad I'll end up watching them torture you! What can you possibly do to get me away from here?"

He took her face in his hands and gently kissed her forehead before answering. "I'm to the point where it doesn't matter if I die helping you. I'm so sorry about your family, Jess. And to think what you must have suffered, being dragged here by—" He stopped, just then noticing her neck. He closed his eyes. "My God," he murmured again.

Jess had not looked into a mirror since her abduction. Now she knew her neck must be scarred. Noah moved away, and she saw his hands ball into fists.

"It's a wonder you didn't freeze to death, or die of hunger, or strangulation," he growled.

"Noah, what are you going to do?"

He sighed and rose. "First I'll try to buy you," he answered, facing her. "I've spent nearly every last bit of money I had on gifts and wampum. I have to hope that what I've brought is enough. If it isn't—"

"Then what?" Dread filled Jess's heart.

"Then you have to tell me to interpret to Thunder that you've decided the only way to solve the problem is the better man gets you."

She frowned. "But you said Thunder told you I had a right to choose."

"He won't stick to that," he sighed. "I told Thunder I was looking for an English girl I intended to kidnap myself to sell into slavery. I told him I traced her here, and then they produced you. I said you belong to me, not him. That's the only story I could come up with to keep the doubt off me as a devout Frenchman. I couldn't very well tell the man I was in love with you and wanted to marry you and take you to Albany."

Jess managed a smile. "Is that still true?"

He lightly gripped her chin. "How can you doubt it, after what I've been through just to find you?"

Jess looked down. "But . . . the way I look now . . . my ears . . . my neck . . ."

"I knew how I'd find you if you were alive, and I've never seen a more beautiful sight in my life."

She met his gaze again. "Nor have I," she said softly.

224

Voices rose outside, bringing them back to their present dire situation. "You've got to tell Thunder you can't make up your mind, Jess."

She frowned. "You said that if I didn't choose, I would go to the better man." Their gazes held, and Jess began to shake her head. "Please don't tell me that means what I think it means."

"It's the only way to truly end it so they don't follow us."

"Noah!"

"I'll be all right."

"But they don't fight fair! The horrible things they can do . . ."

"Jess, I managed to kill five Ottawa the day they attacked you, remember?"

"And you almost died!"

"This is just one man."

"What about your shoulder? Your leg?"

"The leg is healed. The shoulder still gives me trouble, but not enough to stop me from doing what I have to do. And don't forget that I can be just as vicious as the worst of them if it's necessary. I'm not new to this, Jess."

She put a hand to her stomach, turning away. "And if you lose?"

He touched her shoulder. "I won't."

Jess faced him again. So sure. So confident. It was just another sign of how much he loved her. "Would it be a fight . . . to the death?"

"I don't know. It's their choice."

Jess rose, turning away again. "I know it sounds strange, after what they did to my family, but Thunder didn't do any of the killing. On the way here he was the only one who showed me one tiny hint of kindness. And I've come to know his mother well." She faced him. "Can you try not to kill him?"

Noah frowned, also getting to his feet. "What!"

"I just . . . maybe there would be less trouble with the rest of them if you didn't kill him."

"He'll most likely damn well try to kill *me!*"

She closed her eyes. "I know. And if there is no other way out, you will *have* to kill him. I just thought . . . if there is any other way to somehow dishonor him but not kill him . . . I don't know . . . where does it all stop, Noah? Where does all the killing stop?"

She tried to picture Noah as a young farmer with a young wife, dressed like any other white man—then finding his wife horribly murdered. "Killing changes people. Even just *watching* it changes people. I feel so different after all I've seen, and I know you aren't the same man you were all those years ago before your wife died."

"No, I'm not. And if I manage not to kill Thunder, it doesn't mean I won't kill again. I've paid yet another price for you, Jess."

"What do you mean?" she asked with a frown.

"The man who told me where you were is Father Piquet. In return for the information, he made me promise to stop at Montreal and offer my services to Governor Duquesne in a French movement against

English soldiers attempting to build a fort at the Monongahela."

"No! You could end up in the same situation you were involved in at Pickawillany!"

"I had no choice. But this time I intend to try to warn them. I intend to take you with me. I'll not leave you behind, no matter what! It means a lot of traveling, but at least you'll have a horse instead of traveling on foot. We'll be together. Can you do it?"

"I'll go wherever you take me. You know that. It's *you* I'm worried about!"

"If I get through what's waiting for me out there, I can handle the rest, especially with you along." He longed to tell her about Billy, but he didn't want to get her hopes up just yet. First they had to get out of their present situation.

Their gazes held for a long, quiet moment. "I love you, Noah," she said then. "No matter what happens, you're the only man I'll ever love."

He pulled her close. "And I love you. I never stopped thinking of you for one day or one night." He leaned down and kissed her again, and in that one kiss Jess understood the kind of love her parents must have shared, and what must be beautiful about mating. The kiss lingered, becoming deeper and more desperate out of sheer joy, terrible fear, intense desire. He finally released her.

"I'll try to buy you first. If it comes to a fight, I'll try to at least make Thunder promise you will never be touched by anyone but him. Once you're the wife of a warrior like Thunder, you will he greatly honored and well treated."

Jess shuddered. "Noah, don't even suggest it."

"I love you, Jess. I know that whatever happens, you'll be strong. You'll be all right. And when we go out there now, don't forget you're my captive. You've never met me before now. I'm sorry to bring you pain, but I have to make this look real. Are you ready?"

She studied the love in his dark eyes and nodded. "God be with you."

Noah kissed her lightly. "And with you." With that he grasped her hair and dragged her back out of the wigwam.

31

Noah yanked Jess in front of Thunder, his entire countenance again changed to one of anger and fierceness. He let go of her, and Jess stepped back, genuine fear in her eyes—fear that Noah would be killed before the day was over. Noah and Thunder conversed in Thunder's language. She knew Noah was telling Thunder that she could not decide, and suddenly Thunder grinned, looking proudly down his nose at Jess. Apparently he was pleased with her "difficult" choice. Jess could not help thinking that any Iroquois woman would probably be proud to marry a warrior like Thunder, who without the ring in his nose and all the paint would be a handsome Iroquois man. What she could not understand was how these people could think she could have feelings for the very people who'd mercilessly slaughtered her family.

Noah grasped her arm and yanked her closer, spouting something to Thunder. He turned to Jess then. "Don't move!" he ordered. He walked over to his packhorses and began untying blankets and leather bags. He carried armloads of gifts over and dropped them in front of Thunder. He spread out blankets, and on them he set a copper kettle, iron pots, mirrors and three large knives. He opened a leather pouch and reached inside, pulling out a handful of red, blue and yellow beads of all sizes and shapes.

Obvious pleasure shone in the eyes of the surrounding warriors. Thunder folded his arms and looked haughtily at Noah, saying something that Jess guessed was a remark that he'd need more in trade for her. Appearing even more angry, Noah took yet more supplies from his packhorses, this time coming over with a large pouch of tobacco. Thunder sniffed it, then grinned and smiled. He pointed to yet another bag Noah held. Noah rolled his eyes and reached inside, pulling out what looked like a brand-new pistol.

Ooh's and *aah's* came from the lips of the warriors as Noah handed the pistol over to Thunder, then reached inside and pulled out yet another pistol. Jess was flabbergasted at the realization at what it must have taken him to afford so many gifts. She felt flattered, but also sorry that Noah had to spend so much.

Thunder looked over one of the pistols, then the other, grinning and nodding. He bent down and laid them on the blanket, then studied the knives, getting a feel of them in his hand, touching the blades. He deliberately pricked his own finger with one of them to test its sharpness. He rose then, and with a haughty look in his dark eyes he reached out and pressed the bleeding finger against Noah's buckskin shirt. Noah wore no coat, and Jess thought how the day was becoming too warm for the fur cape she wore. She kept it on, however, embarrassed for Noah to see her wearing only Indian necklaces over her breasts.

Thunder sneered at Noah and seemed to be daring him. The look Noah returned intimidated even Jess. He was furious. Apparently, Thunder was saying that all these gifts still were not enough. Noah turned and took one more leather pouch from a packhorse. Both packhorses were now almost totally relieved of their supply packs. Noah brought over one of the horses and the leather pouch. He handed the horse's reins to Thunder, and Jess realized he was now giving the man the horse. It was a fine, healthy-looking mare, a wonderful gift. Then Noah opened the leather pouch and reached inside, taking out a fistful of purple clamshells.

Some of the warriors actually gasped. Jess had figured out enough about them by now to realize they treasured purple clam shells above just about anything. They called such things wampum. Some of the warriors wore belts or sashes with wampum sewn onto them. The shells were highly prized even by white men, because they were one of the best things to have on hand when dealing with the Iroquois. Such a gift could even save a white man's life.

Looking rather astounded, Thunder reached out and took a few of the shells, studying them a moment. He looked at Noah again, then down at all the gifts. Then he reached out and yanked the sack of shells from Noah, throwing it onto the blanket. He stepped back slightly, looking from Noah to Jess, then back to Noah. He barked something to Noah, who just stood there breathing heavily for a moment. Jess decided that if looks could kill, Thunder would be lying on the ground with his heart cut out. Noah finally turned to Jess.

"Apparently, all my gifts are not enough," he growled at her. "I think he's enjoying this damned game, trying to make an impression on the rest of the warriors. He still wants you to choose, says the gifts are his no matter what. If you choose me, he'll probably just have me hacked up by the rest of these warriors and keep you *and* the presents. There is only one way to solve this."

Jess breathed deeply for self-control. He was asking her to let him fight Thunder. She turned to Thunder, studying his native fierceness, his haughtiness, knowing the pleasure such Iroquois men took in torturing. She had no doubt that if he got the better of Noah, he would not kill him. Rather, he would wound him just enough to render him helpless. Then the rest of them would take their time finishing him off. Racked with fear and dread, she looked back at Noah. He'd told her what she must do.

"Tell Thunder that I will go with whoever is the better man and can prove it," she said firmly.

Noah interpreted for her, and the look of fierce pride and a thirst for blood radiated from Thunder's eyes. He was pleased with her answer.

32

The shouts of the warriors were so shrill they hurt Jess's ears. Nearly everyone in the village had gathered to watch the contest between Noah and Thunder. It seemed to Jess that any chance young Iroquois men had to fight and taste blood, they jumped at it, or they invented a reason to show off their prowess.

One of the warriors grabbed Jess about the waist and pulled her along as Noah and Thunder moved to a flatter piece of ground. Josephine had come to watch, and she and the other women cheered right along with the men.

Noah removed the quiver of arrows as well as the musket he'd carried over his shoulder, then pulled off his buckskin shirt. Jess noticed the lingering white scar on his shoulder from the wound he'd suffered from the Ottawa. That seemed a lifetime ago. She noticed his skin was not all that much lighter than Thunder's, and his powerful physique was just as intimidating. Still, this would be no simple fist-fight. If only fists were the only weapons they would use . . .

They all moved to a central fire, where, to Jess's wonder, two warriors put the barrels of their own muskets into the hot coals, apparently to deliberately heat them. She watched Noah, but he never looked at her. He kept his eyes on Thunder. He'd pulled his hair back and tied it with rawhide to keep it out of the way, and he stood watching boldly as one of the other Iroquois men walked up to Thunder.

Jess gasped when the man pressed the red-hot gun barrel against Thunder's chest. Thunder's skin literally sizzled, but Thunder stood rigid and silent. Jess realized they would do the same thing to Noah, and he most likely was also expected to make no sound. If he did, he would already have lost the contest.

Horrified, Jess turned her head away as the second warrior approached Noah. She could hear the sizzling sound, and she wanted to scream for him. Noah made no sound, and she felt sick for the pain he must have suffered—all for her.

There came more shouts as the entire swell of Delaware moved to yet another location, pushing Noah along with them and dragging Jess. Jess realized that pretending not to care what happened to Noah would be almost impossible. She realized she was being forced to watch so that she could determine who was the better man. Whatever Noah suffered, she would have to suffer it with him in her heart, but not let it show in her face.

Thunder kept raising his fists and screaming war cries, deliberately keeping the others worked up. He seemed totally unaware of the deep, red burn on his chest.

They came next to an area where in the distance a tree was marked with white paint. Thunder took hold of his tomahawk, and the others spread out as he took aim at the tree. He flung the tomahawk, and it landed smack in the center of the white mark. More cheers filled the air, and Thunder turned to Noah, gazing at him challengingly. Noah then took his own tomahawk from where it hung at his waist and stepped up, taking aim. Everyone quieted and waited. Noah flung the tomahawk, and it literally split the handle of Thunder's tomahawk, the iron blade clanging against Thunder's blade and falling to the ground.

The Indians quieted, and Thunder looked astounded—and angry. He turned to one of the others and shouted an order. The burn wounds on his and Noah's chests were now both bleeding and blistering. The warrior to whom Thunder shouted began rallying several others, appearing to be rounding them up for something. Several of the youngest men formed two long rows, facing each other, and then produced what looked like small whips. Others picked up rocks, while still others held arrows and clubs in their hands. Noah and Thunder took their places at one end of the line of warriors, while Jess was dragged to the other end.

She could see what was coming, and she did not want to watch. The warriors' screaming reverberated throughout the area, and Jess did not doubt they could be heard for a good mile, maybe farther. Josephine stood nearby, screaming for her son just as loudly as everyone else.

Thunder started through the two rows of warriors, and they whipped him, threw rocks at him and poked him with arrows. Some simply kicked him. They seemed to be sincere in trying to hurt him, but Jess had no doubt they would try a lot harder when Noah got his turn.

Thunder emerged a bruised, cut and bloody mess, but he straightened and looked haughtily at Jess, smiling and panting. He remained beside her as he waited for Noah to take his turn at the gauntlet. Jess dearly wanted to close her eyes, but she dared not this time. Noah began his charge through the line, and just as Jess had guessed, the Iroquois wreaked their havoc on him with even more severity than on Thunder. Someone tripped him, but he got up and kept going. He made no sound as whips and rocks rained down upon him, and arrows poked and pierced him, seeming to draw blood from every part of his body.

He finally emerged covered with blood and bruises, but still he did not look at Jessica. Panting and sweating, he glared at Thunder challengingly, as though to dare him to come up with something else by which to test his prowess. The others were screaming for blood, and Jess feared they would get so excited they would forget this was supposed to be a contest and would simply decide to attack Noah and hack him to death. Then Noah shouted something to Thunder, apparently suggesting his own form of test. Thunder glared at him, considering the challenge. Then he nodded.

The line of warriors broke apart, and again a circle was formed. Jess felt sick with worry over what would come next. Then one man stepped forward and tied Noah's and Thunder's left wrists together with a cord that looked about four feet long. Each man pulled his own knife, and they began circling each other. Jess watched with a pounding heart, aware that an ugly challenge was about to take place. Both men were already wounded and tired, more susceptible to failure.

Thunder slashed out, then Noah, each man able to jump out of the way or suck in his belly quickly enough to avoid being cut. For the first few minutes they seemed to be feeling each other out, testing, slashing, jumping, whirling. Now a cut appeared on Noah's right forearm, then one on Thunder's chest. The dodging and slashing continued for what seemed to Jess an eternity; several misses, several hits. Blood covered both men, and those around them reminded Jess of a pack of dogs circling their prey for the kill.

Thunder managed to slash Noah right through the burn on his chest. She saw Noah wince, but still he did not cry out. The look on his face was no different from that on Thunder's, a desire to kill, a taste for blood. For the moment he was one of them, just as he had been when he fought those who'd attacked her last summer.

Suddenly, Noah yanked Thunder toward him, then stuck out a foot and kicked him behind the knees, causing the man to fall. Moving like a panther, Noah struck, bending his knees and landing hard into Thunder's middle and causing the man to grunt as the air went out of him. Noah slashed at Thunder's right hand, and Thunder dropped his knife. It all happened in a matter of perhaps one or two seconds, and then Noah's knife was at Thunder's throat.

Everything quieted. Thunder lay there struggling for breath, his eyes wide as he waited for his throat to be slashed open. Then, even though his left wrist was tied to Thunder's, Noah managed to grasp Thunder by the scalp lock. He jerked the man's head sideways and deftly sliced his knife through the scalp lock. Cutting the cord that held them together, Noah stood up and raised the severed ponytail victoriously. Jess realized he meant to heed her request. He would not kill Thunder. He'd found a way to disgrace the man. For the Iroquois, that was worse than death.

Noah turned and shoved his bloody knife into its sheath, and in that moment Jess could see there was a very thin line between wild and tame in any man. For the moment Noah was the conqueror, and he was enjoying it as much as Thunder would have. He walked toward Jess as Thunder rolled to his knees. Thunder felt the back of his head and let out a wild howl, raising his knife as if to land it in Noah's back. Noah whirled, and at the same time Josephine barked something to her son. Panting, bleeding and covered with mud, Thunder stopped with his hand in midair. Josephine again shouted to him, as if scolding him. Thunder savagely tossed the knife so that it landed in the ground at Noah's feet, then turned and walked away.

Josephine turned to Noah. "Take the horse and the wampum," she told him in English. "My son has been defeated, but he is also disgraced, as am I—not because of his defeat, but because he meant to kill you after the defeat instead of acknowledging his defeat with honor."

Noah, practically every part of his body bruised and bleeding, answered her with short breaths. "I'll take the horse. The rest . . . can be divided among the others . . . for allowing a fair fight. The wampum . . . is yours."

Josephine's eyes lit up. "I am grateful." She glanced at Jess, then back to Noah. "This is more than just claiming a captive, is it not?"

Noah managed a bit of a grin. "No one has to know that."

Josephine nodded. "You came to claim her the honorable way, rather than to try stealing her. I will tell the others that the gifts are theirs to share. They will want to discuss how to divide them. That gives you time to get away with no more hard feelings. Take Jessica and go."

Noah wiped at blood that ran into his eyes. He gave Josephine a quick nod, then grabbed Jess's arm and walked with her quickly to one of the packhorses. He lifted her onto it, then handed her a blanket. "Put this around yourself for warmth. It will be colder when we get deeper into the woods."

Jess was speechless. She did as she was told. Noah walked over to where he'd left his shirt and, wincing, he managed to slide it back over his head. He picked up his musket and his quiver of arrows and walked over to hook the quiver and the gun case over the pommel of his saddle. He mounted, and, giving the others one last look, picked up the reins to Jess's horse, then ordered her to take hold of the reins of the third horse, which Josephine had brought to her. He headed out, away from the village.

Jess followed, still rather stunned at the turn of events. Not long ago she'd been sitting with other Iroquois women learning to bead and thinking she was doomed to such a life forever. Now she rode right out of their camp a free woman. Still, she was not really free at all. She belonged to Noah Wilde.

33

Noah rode ahead of Jess, and she noticed spots of blood showing through his buckskin shirt where he still bled from some of his wounds. Whenever he looked back at her, she saw the dried blood on his face. She remembered how he'd looked when angry, when facing Thunder. Yet he'd spared Thunder's life.

Why did she almost feel sorry for how Thunder had been shamed? Somehow she'd managed to gain an odd respect for the man and his people, perhaps because she'd seen love and concern in Josephine's eyes during Thunder's fight with Noah; because she'd seen women being loving toward their babies; or because Josephine seemed truly heartbroken that her son had suffered defeat, yet was fair about it with Noah.

Life in the wilderness changed men like Noah—and women like herself. She would never be the same. Nor would she have any doubt as to how much the man ahead of her loved her.

She followed him blindly, trusted him implicitly. The man could do whatever he wanted with her. Maybe there were even certain things he expected from her now, but that didn't frighten her. She'd seen all there was to see—nakedness, lust, blood and murder. She'd lost all that was dear to her, including her innocence of bloodletting and hatred. She'd seen the worst in man—and the best. Noah Wilde represented both, and now he'd become her whole world. He'd searched through the dead of winter to find her, fought a feared Iroquois warrior to get her back.

After they left Thunder's village, Noah led her through thick pine and deep woods, dead branches snapping under the horses' hooves as they plodded through cold slush to go wherever Noah led them. Noah had said nothing, and Jess suspected that after such a vicious fight and the beating he'd taken, he needed time to calm down and think clearly. She decided not to speak until spoken to. Occasionally she looked back, part of her fearing Thunder's warriors would come after them. She'd seen no signs of pursuit.

They moved down dangerously slippery hillsides, both concentrating only on properly guiding the horses over wet leaves and fallen branches. Jess said a quiet thank-you to God for her release from the Iroquois, and for the unusual and blessed warmth of the day. More cold weather was bound to hit them before spring truly awakened, but this was a nice hint of things to come. Here and there she spotted buds on trees and some underbrush actually beginning to green.

They came upon a creek and followed it most of the afternoon, its waters gushing over its banks, rushing so loudly that Jess determined she and Noah could not hear each other even if they did talk. After being freed from a life of dread, everything looked beautiful to Jess; the baby leaves on plants and underbrush; the smell of wet pine and wood; a family of robins; a baby bunny hopping alongside them for several feet; the sound of the creek waters that raged from spring thaw; the look of Noah, a big, sure man who sat on a horse as though he were part of it. She felt safe, loved, protected.

"We're stopping up ahead," he shouted to her, his first words in nearly three hours. As they continued on, the sound of the rushing waters grew louder, until a magnificent waterfall came into sight. It thundered over a rock ledge. Jess guessed that in late summer it was probably more of a trickle, but now it roared in splendid white foam as it hit rocks below. She followed Noah up a steep hill almost to the top of the falls and then to a cave at their edge. Clear, cold water poured over part of the cave entrance, but the rest of the long, narrow entrance was easily accessible.

Noah dismounted, then walked back to her and lifted her down. There was a look in his eyes that almost frightened her, yet made her blood rush in a strange, exciting way.

"I'll tether the horses," he told her. "Start unloading what's left of my supplies. At least I didn't have to give them my food." He turned away. "Take in as much as you can."

Jess obeyed, untying packs and making several trips to get most of them into the cave. There was just enough room to stand inside, but not enough that

Noah would be able to stand up straight. He tethered the horses and began gathering wood and stacking it toward the back of the cave.

"I've stayed here before," he told her. "Somewhere toward the back there is a draft that pulls smoke up with it. We can build a fire in here."

Jess marveled at how well he knew the land. She asked no questions as she unpacked supplies. Noah pulled at dry brush that had somehow grown inside the cave, seeming to sprout right out of rock. He used it for kindling as he struggled with a rock and damp flint to get a fire going, cursing a time or two until flames finally appeared. He blew on the kindling gently until the fire grew a little bigger, then placed some of the damper wood on top of it. The damp wood created steam and smoke, but just as Noah had told her, the smoke was sucked toward the back of the cave by the mysterious draft, then out through the hidden opening somewhere beyond the human eye.

"Make some coffee," Noah told her. He still seemed rather withdrawn and brooding. Jess knew he was not liking the idea of having to go on to Montreal, and surely he was still in pain from the wounds he'd suffered just this morning. She obeyed his request, thinking how good hot coffee would taste. She walked over to the waterfall to fill the pot, then carried it back to the fire. Noah removed his shirt and his weapons belt, and her heart ached at the sight of him, the ugly burn, the bruises and cuts.

"I'm sorry," she said, feeling responsible.

"Don't be," he answered. The look in his dark eyes reminded her of a proud warrior. He'd won the battle. He was still feeling it. Suddenly, Jess felt very small and helpless. She turned away and set up an iron tripod over the fire, then hung the pot of water over the flames. She searched through Noah's things for coffee beans, then ground some with stones and put the ground beans into the water.

When next she turned, Noah was standing outside under the waterfall. Jess was astonished that he could bear the cold water, but perhaps it helped ease the pain of his burn and cuts. She was even more astonished to realize he was naked. For a brief moment she drank in the sight of his muscled thighs and buttocks. She could not see that part of him that would embarrass her. She wondered at the fact that he could strip like that in front of her, but then, he was probably doing what was best for his wounds; and, after all, he was still feeling his wilder being.

She looked away so that he would not catch her watching him. She waited, still amazed at her changed world. She stared at the flames, thinking how a year ago she would have found this situation frightening and appalling.

Minutes later Noah was standing beside her. Bashfully, she turned her head to see his bare feet.

"It's your turn," he told her.

She looked at the fire again. Was he still totally naked? "Mine?"

"I'll lay out some blankets. We can curl up in them

244

by the fire until we're warm."

"What?"

"You know what I mean, Jess." He moved behind her and grasped her under the arms, pulling her to her feet. He turned her, and she faced his bare chest, the ugly burn. She touched it lightly.

"Noah. Poor Noah."

"Get undressed, Jess." He grasped her face and forced her to meet his eyes. His long, dark hair still dripped over his bruised shoulders as he held her gaze. "I will not take the risk of some heathen being your first man. It should be me. I've spent months searching for you, and I'll die before I risk losing you again. I want you, Jess Matthews. You're the strongest, bravest woman I've ever met, and as soon as we get the chance, we'll be married the proper way. Right now I'll marry you the Indian way. You're no little girl anymore. You're Noah Wilde's woman. I risked my life to win you. You belong to me."

Jess swallowed. "What if I said no?" she asked bashfully, rather astonished at the bold announcement, feeling more like a captive than the woman he loved.

"Do you *want* to say no?"

Jess studied him several long, quiet seconds, with only the sound of the roaring water behind them. "I want to say yes," she finally told him, her eyes tearing. "I love you, Noah. I think I would have killed myself if Thunder had won that fight, but. . . . right now I'm scared of you."

His gaze softened. He leaned close and kissed her mouth gently. "Don't ever be afraid of me," he answered, kissing her eyes. "Not ever." He moved his lips to her mouth again, kissing her forcefully yet gently as he reached down and untied her cape. He let it fall, then stepped back to remove the necklaces she wore. One by one they were tossed aside, until she stood before him with bared breasts. All the while she looked down, not sure what to do or say. He stooped down to untie the wrap skirt she wore, laying it aside. She wore nothing under it.

34

Noah gently caressed Jess's bare bottom and kissed her flat belly as he worked his way upward, kissing each breast, then her neck, her lips again, setting her on fire. He drew her close, crushing her breasts against him in spite of his burn and cuts. She felt that part of him that would make a woman of her swelling hard against her belly.

Then he stepped back and looked her over lovingly, before leaving her to rummage through one of his supply bags. He brought out a piece of lye soap and a towel, then turned and took hold of one of her wrists, placing the soap in her hand.

"Go and wash the paint and grease out of your hair and off your face," he told her. "I'll cut the cords in your ears and pull them out. The holes will grow back together."

Jess obeyed, deciding that with everything Noah Wilde knew and had done for her, she would not question anything he told her. Daring the freezing-cold water, she managed to wash and rinse her hair and face, as well as scrub the bear grease off her arms and body. She kept her back to Noah, shivering fiercely by the time she was done. She turned then to see him standing there holding an open blanket. He was smiling.

Jess backed into the blanket, and he wrapped it around her, then picked her up and carried her over to where he'd laid out another blanket. He set her on it and took a piece of wool cloth from his supplies, briskly rubbing her hair with it. He picked up his knife then, the same knife he'd used to slice off Thunder's scalp lock, and with which he'd undoubtedly killed many an enemy. She thought how afraid she'd been of a knife in the hands of an Iroquois, but in Noah's hand she felt only trust. He brought the knife close, then briskly cut through the leather cord in her left earlobe.

"Hold still," he told her. "It will only hurt for a second."

Jess remembered hearing those same words when Josephine first pierced her ears. She winced when Noah yanked out the cord, then fought tears when he did the same to her other ear. He picked up a small flask of whiskey and splashed some on each ear, and she could not help a small cry at the sting. Noah held a softer cloth to each ear for a minute or two until the bleeding slowed.

"I have a salve that will help keep your earlobes soft and help the holes grow back together," he told her. He kissed her forehead, then picked up a small, flat tin can, opening it and applying some of its contents to each earlobe. "Better?" he asked her.

Jess watched his eyes. All that anger and fierceness were gone. "Yes."

He smiled again. "I have a surprise for you."

"What is it?"

"After we stop at Montreal, we're going to La Présentation to pick up Billy."

Jess's heart filled with joy. "Billy! You've found Billy?"

He put a hand to her face. "Quite by accident. The man who runs the place, Father Piquet, he's the one who told me where you were. I had to lie to him about why I was looking for you, just as I've had to lie to everyone since getting into French Territory. Whenever we get to any of those places, you have to act like an unwilling captive."

She grasped his wrist and turned her face to kiss his palm. "I'll always be your captive, but never unwilling." She closed her eyes as more tears came. "How did Billy end up there? I was there myself. I only know because a woman there who spoke English told me they followed a man called Father Piquet." She stiffened and frowned. "He tells the Indians there that Christ was French and was crucified by the English!"

A hint of anger moved back into his eyes. "I'm well aware of the things he does. He's also the one who made me promise to report at Montreal before leaving Canada. He'll know it if I don't, so I have no choice."

Jess leaned forward and rested her head on his shoulder. "At least he told you where I was."

Noah ran his hands through her hair. "I happened to ask about Billy, and apparently a different group of Delaware took him to Fort Toronto and sold him. Then he was traded to a man who in turn took him to La Présentation and sold him to an Iroquois woman for beaver skins. The woman adopted him as her own. Father Piquet promised to see about getting him back from the Iroquois woman. He has a lot of influence among them. I'm sure he'll be successful, and that Billy has been treated well, Jess. We'll get your little brother back and then we'll go home." He kissed her hair. "We'll go home."

"Poor little Billy. He must have been so terrified."

"He's too little to remember much. He'll be all right. Children can be pretty resilient."

A lump rose in her throat. "Billy and I don't have a real home anymore. It's all gone, Noah. Everything I ever knew from birth to now is gone." She could not help more tears, and he let her cry for several minutes before wiping at her tears with his fingers.

"You have a home with me, Jess. You and Billy both. We'll go to Albany and live on my father's farm. We'll start a new family."

She kissed his fingers, turning her gaze to meet his

own. Through her tears his face was blurry, but she did not have to see it well to know how handsome that face was. "Are you sure those Delaware won't come after you?"

He shook his head. "They won't. We're safe here." He laid her back. "And after this night, you will always belong to Noah Wilde." He opened the blanket she'd kept around her, leaning down then to kiss her breasts.

Here was her whole world. Here was her hope. Here was her love. She breathed deeply, some of her remaining tears coming from sheer relief, abounding love, sweet joy and delicious freedom. This man had nearly died for her, not once but twice. She wanted to please him in every way. She wanted to belong to him.

She closed her eyes as his lips trailed over her breasts, and he opened the blanket fully, kissing her belly again, moving back to her breasts, then the scar at her neck.

"This will heal more," he whispered. "One day you'll barely be able to notice it."

He met her mouth with his own, while with one hand he explored places she'd never dreamed of allowing anyone to touch, not even a husband. He brought forth emotions and physical pleasure she never knew were possible, while his kisses grew deeper and his tongue searched her mouth. He seemed oblivious to his wounds as Jess reached around his neck and grasped his hair, coming alive with a womanly pleasure she could never have imagined before this man touched her.

She soon felt a wonderful rippling sensation deep in her belly, a feeling that made her wildly bold. She pushed against his hand, wanting something more. Part of her knew what it was she wanted. Part of her feared it. Noah moved on top of her, his kisses as wild and savage as this man could be, when necessary. He wanted to make her his woman, and she wanted the same.

She opened herself to him, then gasped with pain as he filled her with himself, tearing deep into her, moving then in wild rhythm. Hot fire seemed to tear through her insides in a pain that was oddly pleasurable. She closed her eyes and gripped his muscled arms as he thrust himself into her over and over, until she felt his life pulsing against her deepest being. He held himself there a moment, breathing deeply, then looked down at her with a fierce gaze of ownership.

Nothing needed to be said. She belonged to him now, and at last she understood the beauty and wonder and pleasure of mating. This was how it was supposed to be. If it had been any other way, with any other man, she would have wanted to die; but with this man it could not be more right.

He lay down beside her, moving one leg over hers and wrapping a blanket around both of them. "Are you all right?" he asked.

"I think so."

"The pain will go away." He pulled her close against him, stroking her back. "I love you, Jess."

She settled into his shoulder, and thought how being beside this man was probably the safest place in the whole world. Right here was where she always wanted to be. "What will happen when we get to Montreal?" she asked.

He kissed her hair. "Let's not talk about it. Let's just enjoy being here together."

Jess drifted off into sleep, able to truly relax for the first time in months. Somewhere in the night she was awakened to kisses, and in what seemed like a dream Noah Wilde was inside her again. Just like he'd promised, she didn't feel nearly as much pain, only extreme pleasure.

By morning the fire had died down, and the coffee had never been touched.

35

Early March 1754

Jess never thought she could travel through dense forest in unfamiliar territory with no fear. The likelihood of Indians skulking behind every tree did not intimidate her. If anyone would know there were Indians or a dangerous animal about, Noah would. She still could not imagine how the Delaware had known how to get to wherever it was she'd been taken; nor did she understand how Noah in turn seemed to know exactly where he was going. She surmised that if she were to travel in this country for years, she would still be constantly lost.

When they made camp at night, she slept in the safety of Noah's arms, unconcerned over what she once would have considered terrifying sounds coming from the darkness. Noah knew which creatures made which sounds, and his musket, pistol and tomahawk were always right next to him.

They made love often, and always with just as much hunger and eagerness as the time before. When she was giving herself to Noah, she heard none of the night sounds. She heard only her own whimpers of wonderful fulfillment, and Noah's groans of satisfaction. She'd had no idea that pleasing a man could be quite so fulfilling.

A landscape that once seemed intimidating was beautiful. She loved the sounds of birds, the bubbling waters of creeks and the louder, rushing waters of the Ottawa River, swollen from spring melt. They followed it for most of their journey to Montreal. At some places the water fell over rocks in ways that reminded her of the waterfall that partially hid the cave where she and Noah first consummated their love.

She would never forget that place, that moment. Never. She hadn't wanted to leave. When they had, she felt as though she had left behind the girl Jess, as though she could turn around and wave good-bye to her. The woman, Jessica, rode away.

They had stayed at the cave for three nights, long enough to talk about many things; about Noah's imprisonment and his mother's death; about Jess's family, her losses; about Mary; and how Jess and Noah would settle and build their own family. They were there long enough for Jess to cry again, letting go of the awful hurt, the terrible longing to see her mother again, her father, Sonny, even old Gabe and the family cabin. She knew she could never have truly given in to the sorrow without having Noah to hold her and feed his strength to her. He'd suffered his own losses, and he knew firsthand the savagery of the Iroquois. He understood. When she cried, he simply held her, and she found strength in his arms.

For days, from dawn to dusk, they traveled, stopping only to rest the horses. Noah had brought with him several simple dresses of wool and homespun cloth, and she loved him more for remembering she would need something decent to wear once he found her. He'd even brought underclothing, and she was surprised he'd come so close to guessing the right size. She still wore the otter-fur hooded cape and the warm winter moccasins Thunder had given her; certainly not because of any good memories, but only because they were both so warm and practical. The nights were still very cold, but the days were warm enough to be pleasant, and often she rode without the cape.

On their journey they passed another Delaware village, and Noah visited with the Indians there as easily as if they were English colonists, giving them gifts for the food they offered. Jess realized this way of life was as familiar to him now as breathing. It seemed strange to ride right into the camp of these fierce-looking, painted Iroquois and not be afraid. She'd learned that for the most part, Noah did not hate these natives. It was the French he hated, for instigating the natives into cruel attacks like at Pickawillany and years before at Albany. He had no doubt it was French soldiers who'd raped his wife.

Now, finally, after ferry rides across two branches of the St. Lawrence River, they reached Montreal. It was the middle of March, and although Jess wished Noah did not have to come here, she could not help being excited about all the new country she was seeing. For a young girl who just a year ago was wondering if she would ever see anything more than ten or twenty miles beyond the little cabin where she lived, to realize she was deep into Canada, deep in the land of the "enemy," a former Indian captive and now the woman of a French trader who was really an English spy, seemed unreal.

She followed Noah into the biggest settlement she'd ever seen. The streets were full of wagons, horses, carriages, people crossing, women lifting their skirts to avoid mud and horse dung. All sorts of buildings and establishments lined the streets, mostly stores, but also several taverns and rooming houses. On the second-floor balcony of one house she saw women whose faces were heavily painted, the bodices of their dresses cut so low it looked as though their breasts might fall out of them. One of them shouted something down to Noah in French. He looked up at her and smiled, and Jess felt a sudden, painful jealousy. As little as she knew about this unfamiliar world, she needed only instinct to realize what those painted ladies were.

"You know her?" Jess yelled out to him.

He looked back at her with a half smile. "It was a long time ago, way before I knew you existed," he answered. He winked, and she wanted to hit him.

"Hey, you are a lucky woman, no?" the woman shouted at Jess.

Jess looked up at her with a scowl, and the woman and her friends all laughed. Noah slowed his horse and waited for her to ride up beside him.

"Don't let those women get to you. It's just their way of being friendly and kidding with you."

Jess reminded herself she was a woman now, not a pouting child. "I don't ever want you to be with anyone but me," she said.

He leaned closer. "You are all I want and all I need," he answered. "You should know that by now." He straightened. "We're going to see the most important man in all of New France now, so remember, you are my captive and you're supposed to hate me and want to get away. Don't give any hint you're anything more than a captive, or I'll be in a damn lot of trouble."

Jess's jealousy was replaced by worry. "Do you really have to do this?"

He sighed as he kicked his horse in motion again. "I

really do." He headed up the street, at the end of which Jess could see a fine-looking brick building with a veranda supported by white pillars. She had no doubt it was the home of Governor Marquis Duquesne. Her stomach tightened as she followed Noah.

36

"Well, well, well. It has been a long time since I have seen you, Monsieur Wilde." Governor Duquesne stood near a marble fireplace in his sitting room, a room that seemed too grand for the wild country out-side. He smiled as he greeted Noah in French. "I believe it has been over a year since you wintered here after Pickawillany. Where did you spend the ensuing summer and winter?" He waved his hand toward a chair. "Sit down, Noah."

Noah walked to a velvet settee and took a seat. "You know men like me," he answered, sticking to the man's preferred French. "We're wanderers. When we feel like scouting, we scout. When we feel like hunting, we hunt. And when we feel like doing nothing, we do nothing."

Duquesne laughed and sat down opposite him. He picked up a glass decanter of wine from a tray that sat on a glass table between them. He poured some of the wine into two glasses. "Well, *mon ami,* you could not have picked a better time to show up." He offered Noah the glass of wine and kept one for himself. "I hope it is to tell me you are willing to scout for us again." He leaned back and sipped his wine.

Noah had been hoping he was too late for whatever the French were up to, but already he could tell that was not the case. "Maybe," he answered. He sipped some of his own wine and held up the glass. "Thank you," he said. "Actually," he continued, "I had planned to settle someplace west of Fort Detroit with a certain English captive I have with me, maybe sell her to the Indians there once I'm tired of her."

Duquesne, who Noah guessed was perhaps in his forties, raised bushy eyebrows. "So you *have* been hunting, even in winter." He chuckled. "Tell me, is your game tame, or wild?"

"She *was* wild. I tamed her."

Duquesne laughed again, putting his feet up on the table. His black boots were shined to a gleam, and Noah noticed the several obviously expensive rings the man wore on his hand as Duquesne twirled his wineglass, staring at it as he spoke. "I have always liked you, Noah. And I have always trusted you." He set his gaze on Noah again. "And I am told you are a very skilled man when it comes to the fight."

Noah smiled. "I'm flattered," he answered. "But I only came to say hello and see how things are going, not to offer my services," he finished, still hoping he could get out of whatever French campaign was coming next.

"Why, Noah, you seem to think I want something of you!" Duquesne chuckled again.

"You're the one who just said you hoped I was ready to serve as a scout again."

"Ah, yes." Duquesne put his feet down and leaned forward. He took another sip of wine, then rested his elbows on his knees. "Noah, I do not think you will want to pass up this opportunity. In only two days, eleven hundred of our best will be marching south, to be followed by more within a month!" His eyes shined with eagerness and anticipation. "The English have done little to fortify the frontier, and it is a perfect time for us to do just that and close the entire Ohio Valley and all areas west of the Alleghenies to the English. We will have every bit of the trade from here all the way south to Louisiana! It is a great opportunity for France, for New France and for traders like yourself. We are planning to build forts all the way along the Allegheny and Monongahela. We may even attack Fort Oswego eventually and rid ourselves of the only English outpost built illegally in French territory! In the meantime, word has it that a young captain named George Washington is making his way to the forks of the Allegheny and Monongahela to build an English fort there, but we will beat him to it. If he has already started such a fort, it will not stand long!" He grinned and slapped his knee. "How say you, Noah? Wouldn't you like to be a part of this mission?"

Noah thought how he needed to get this information to Washington. What better way to find out everything he needed to know than to march with the French army? "I have business at La Présentation," he answered. "Will we stop there?"

"Of course! And at Frontenac and Toronto. A ship will take the troops south from there across the western end of Lake Ontario to Fort Niagara. We will march south from there. Some of the men will station themselves just south of Venango, where a new fort will be built. The rest will go even farther south and see what the English are up to at the confluence of the Ohio, the Allegheny and the Monongahela. There the English will learn the might of the French army, and that it is time for them to stay to the east. I hope to chase them all the way to the Susquehanna River!"

Noah wondered if young Washington, or Governor Dinwiddie or Clinton, had any inkling of France's determination to shut them out of the west. English trade was in dire danger, as well as every English settlement along the entire frontier, from Fort Oswego all the way south to the Shenandoah in Virginia. He suspected Dinwiddie and others still had done little about the situation. Perhaps this latest French effort would wake them up. Either way, he somehow had to get word to Washington. He and Jess could travel safely with the French army all the way to Venango. Perhaps there he could find a way to escape and contact Washington. It would be risky, but it had to be done. He would consider it his last mission before going home and getting out of this mess.

He remained relaxed, sipping his wine calmly.

"Sounds exciting, Governor. I'd like to offer my services."

"I knew you would!"

"On one condition. I'd like to take my English captive with me. For one thing, I'm not ready to give her up. She's finally become more submissive. Besides that, we could perhaps use her as some kind of ransom, if things come to that; let alone the fact that if she sees what is happening and is ever returned to her own family, she'll have plenty to tell them about what she's seen of French strength. Maybe then the English will think twice about trying to build any more forts in French territory."

Duquesne nodded, eyeing Noah intensely. "I see." He thought a moment. "Of course you can take her. After all, some wives travel with the soldiers, let alone the whores who follow the camps." He leaned back again, laughing. "I see nothing wrong with you having your own whore along, no?"

"Nothing at all," Noah answered, secretly hating to drag poor Jess along. She'd been through enough. Still, for now it was a safe way to travel south, and a sure way to get Billy back. Once Piquet saw him show up at La Présentation with so many French soldiers, he'd have no trouble making the man stick to his promise to hand Billy over. His explanation to the commander of the French soldiers would be that Billy, too, could be used for ransom. What better way to show the English the danger they were in if they did not move out of the frontier area than to show them a woman and child captive? "Who is in charge of the soldiers?" he asked Duquesne.

"Ah! My own aide-de-camp, Captain Pierre de Contrecoeur." He rose, holding his chin proudly. "Part of the men will be left in the area of Venango, as I told you, where they will build a strong fortification they are to name Fort Machault, after our own French statesman, Jean Baptiste Machault D'Arnouville. And south of there, in the very area where the English propose to build their own fort, we will instead build one of our strongest posts, which will be named after me, Fort Duquesne!" He slugged down the rest of his wine.

Noah also rose, thinking if the tall, confident Governor Duquesne held his chin any higher, he would himself find it impossible not to slit the man's throat. "Congratulations, Governor. Maybe once we get the frontier fully fortified and win every last native to our side, there will be no more problems."

Duquesne's dark eyes narrowed. "Perhaps," he answered, "unless, of course, we decide to continue eastward and push the English all the way to the ocean. It's such a pleasant thought, don't you agree?"

Noah held his gaze boldly, slowly nodding. "I agree." He finished his own wine. "I appreciate the offer, Governor. I'll find a place to stay the next couple of nights with Jess, the girl I have with me. I left her outside under the guard of one of your men."

"Well, if she tried to run, she wouldn't get far in Montreal, now would she?" the governor said as he followed Noah to the door.

Noah stopped and faced him. "Where and when do I report, sir?"

"Right here. The troops will march off from here with my blessings, day after tomorrow. Good luck, Noah. I can't wait to hear from you when all of this is over."

Noah nodded. "*Merci,* Governor. I'll be sure to give you every detail of our victory." He turned and left. *I'll never see you again, you bastard,* he thought, glad to leave the man's presence.

Damned if he'd not ended up in the man's service again. His timing of arrival couldn't have been worse. Still, if it meant finding a way to warn George Washington and others of just how grim the French threat was, it would all be worth it.

37

Unaccustomed to the sounds of a settlement as large as Montreal, Jess could not sleep. She'd grown used to the sounds of the forest at night. Those sounds were almost soothing compared with the noise in the street outside the room Noah had rented for them at a boardinghouse. It was really nothing more than an extended cabin with rooms that contained homemade log beds and one small table with a pitcher and bowl and a bucket of water for washing. Still, compared with the way she'd lived for so long now, the room seemed luxurious.

She pulled back a thin white curtain to look outside. Lanterns cast just enough light that she could see people still walking about. Men on horses trampled by, then a horse-drawn wagon. She was surprised at so much movement this time of night. What on earth did people do here so late? She'd grown up going to bed with the setting sun and rising when the roosters crowed.

She could hear the laughter of both men and women, and she wondered how women like those painted ladies she'd seen could live that way, touched constantly by strangers. To think of Noah with women like that made her furiously jealous. He'd already told her that such women often followed soldiers when they left for war, that some would probably be along when they rode out with the French soldiers day after tomorrow. She would have to ignore them, if possible, and not act jealous if they came around trying to seduce him.

Damned if she'd be able to do such a thing! It made her shiver. She hoped Albany was not like this. She decided she'd rather live in the wilds again than to live with this kind of noise at night and knowing such lurid women hung about offering themselves to any man who came along with a few shillings or francs in his pocket.

"Jess?"

She turned from the window, looking at Noah by the

dim light of a lantern she'd kept lit. "I can't sleep. It's too noisy. Is Albany like this?"

Noah opened the covers, offering a warm place beside him. She never tired of looking at him now, all of him. Because they were safely roomed, and in a normal bed, Noah slept naked. The burn on his chest had healed to a puckered pink scar that would eventually fade, and all the other cuts and bruises were mostly healed. She walked over and lay down beside him.

"Albany is much nicer than this, more civilized," he told her. "There are even brick streets in the main area, shops, places for ladies like yourself to buy dresses and shoes and hats. There are churches and schools. Of course, we'd be at my father's farm most of the time, which is away from town, so you won't hear this kind of noise."

Jess sighed, wiggling against him and putting an arm around his neck. She kissed his throat. "Are there painted ladies there?"

He laughed lightly. "There are painted ladies everywhere. Don't worry about it."

She kissed his chin. "Do you enjoy me better than women like that?"

"You shouldn't even need to ask a question like that." He met her mouth in a deep kiss and moved on top of her.

"I don't like having to pretend I don't care once we leave here."

"Jess, look at me."

She met his gaze, seeing the love there. "Do you want to get through this with as little trouble as possible?" he asked.

"You know I do."

"Then there are certain things you will have to put up with. For one thing, don't worry about the whores. That's all they are, and with you along I doubt any will even give me the time of day. If any of them do, I will set them straight and that will be the end of it. As far as the rest of it, you've survived this long, Jess, and I'm damn proud of you. You just have to remember that if you want *me* to stay safe, you have to go along with everything I tell you to do, which means I won't treat you very nice when we're in the sight of others." He kissed her eyes. "It will hurt me much more than it will hurt you, I assure you. And we have to think of Billy once we get him."

"I know." She traced a finger over his lips. "Make love to me, Noah. I'm scared something will happen to you."

He smiled. "Nothing will happen, but I'll take any excuse you want to give for making love."

She felt better, and she laughed. "Neither of us will need excuses. It's just something we have to do," she answered, leaning up to catch his lips with her own before he could say another word.

It never took long to become lost in the man, in his prowess, his command of her, body and soul. So many changes. So much adventure. If not for the loss of her family, she would have found all of this wonderfully exciting. She surmised she'd never truly lived until meeting Noah Wilde.

His kisses deepened as he shoved her nightgown to her waist and moved his big hands under her hips. He trailed his lips over her throat, and she pulled open the buttons of her gown at the neck and pulled one side of it away so that he could linger for a moment at her breast. The feel of his gentle pull at her nipple created a sweet ecstasy that made her open herself to him, and in a moment he entered her with thrusts that made her insides feel on fire. For several delicious minutes he moved in an exhilarating rhythm that brought forth the exotic climax she'd discovered she could experience only when this man touched her or rubbed against her in magic places.

Her insides pulled at him on their own as she arched to meet his manhood, wanting him to go deeper and fill her with his life, life she hoped one day soon would take hold so she could give this man the children he so needed and wanted. She could see him as a father, a loving, protective father who would always provide well for his family.

It seemed every part of her ached for him constantly. She would never get enough of him. She ran her hands over the hard muscles of his arms and shoulders as he took her with the same passion with which he fought, loved her with the same passion he hated his enemies. He made her feel like one of those wanton, painted ladies, and she wanted to please him more than any of them ever had. She wanted to make up for the love he'd lost when Mary died. She wanted to melt into his very soul. And more than anything, she wanted this night to never end, so that they would never have to travel with French soldiers and more Iroquois Indians. She wanted both of them to at last be free of the dangers it seemed they constantly faced.

Again his life spilled into her, and after several minutes of lying quietly together, the reality she always hated to face returned. They had one more day and night in Montreal, and then the long march would begin.

38

Third Week of March 1754

Jess recognized La Présentation. How strange it seemed to be here again, this time with Noah instead of with Thunder. She even recognized some of the Indian women who came to greet the soldiers. She searched desperately for Billy, but did not see him.

Several Indians greeted Noah, some of them pointing to Jess. Noah spoke to them in their own tongue, and Jess recognized the name Tonnerre. One woman who recognized Jess put a hand over her mouth in surprise and whispered something to several others. The women all looked admiringly at Noah. Jess suspected they found him an attractive white man, more admirable because he'd won Jess from

Thunder, a formidable warrior.

The French soldiers with whom Jess and Noah traveled made camp. The first few days, several of them had offered Noah money to share Jess for a night, thinking she was just a slave with whom Noah could do as he wanted. Noah set them straight immediately, telling them he had no intentions of sharing her "yet," and warning them to stay away. To Jess's relief he was not a man others cared to cross.

Noah, however, was in turn so mean to her in front of the soldiers that she sometimes felt angry with him, even though she understood why he behaved so. Still, she knew Noah did not trust any of the soldiers. He kept a tight watch on her.

As predicted, several whores had followed the huge contingent of Frenchmen. They were kept quite busy at night by a certain few men whose wives had refused to travel with their husbands, and even by a few whose wives accompanied them! Jess actually came to be glad for the presence of both the wives and the whores. It helped keep the men's interest away from her; but none of the women along would have anything to do with her. She was English, and in their eyes probably somehow even more "soiled" than the whores.

Noah dismounted and tied the horses, then lifted her down. "Let's go see Piquet," he told her. He tied a leather strap to her wrist and then to his weapons belt, then led her toward the center of the imposing establishment that was obviously built to have the defenses of a fort rather than as a simple church and school for Indians. She had to walk quickly to keep up with Noah, who pretended not to care if she fell and had to be dragged. They approached a large, log establishment, and a balding man wearing a black robe was walking toward Noah with a grin on his face. He spoke to Noah in French, and when Noah explained who Jess was, he smiled, but looked her over rather scathingly.

Noah turned and with the sweep of one arm indicated the French soldiers who were making camp next to the settlement. Jess knew he was only proving to Piquet that he had indeed stopped at Montreal as promised and now was a part of this great effort by Governor Duquesne to rule all of the wilderness west of the Appalachians. The priest appeared pleased, and he and Noah spoke awhile longer. But then the priest lost his smile, and Jess noticed a change in Noah. He glanced at her with great concern in his eyes, then spoke more with Father Piquet. He seemed angry. The priest threw up his hands and motioned for Noah to follow him.

"Where are we going?" Jess asked as she hurried behind Noah's long strides. "Is he taking us to Billy?"

"Just wait," Noah told her. "I'll explain."

"Is Billy here? Is he all right?"

"Shut up, Jess!" He suddenly turned as the priest kept walking. He grasped Jess's arms and shook her slightly. "The man understands English," he said quietly. "Don't forget that." He closed his eyes and sighed. "Damn it all!" he seethed in a whisper. "Jess, I can't show you any kindness until we're alone." His eyes teared and he quickly shook his head as though to toss them away. "He says Billy is dead. We're going to see his grave."

Jess drew in her breath. "No! He's lying! He's lying!"

Noah grasped her chin. "Don't let him hear you say that. Do you understand?"

Jess pressed her lips together tightly as tears began streaming down her cheeks. She managed a nod in spite of his tight grip. "I'm sorry, Jess."

"Talk to the woman who had him. Make sure it's true. Will you do that?" she asked before gasping in a bitter sob.

"I will. Stay strong, Jess." He turned and began hurrying to catch up with the priest, and Jess had to run to keep up.

Billy! She'd thought she had at least that much left of her family. It would have helped so much. "How did . . . he die?" she sobbed, beginning to lose her breath because of her tears and from half running.

"Consumption, they think. He got very sick—fevered. He was having trouble breathing, had a deep cough."

"Oh, poor Billy! My poor little brother," she cried. "My poor little brother! He died without being able to be with me or his mama." Jess could hardly even see where she was going anymore. She was only aware they had walked out of the fort and around to one side and up a hill to a burial ground. Father Piquet led them to a small grave with a wooden cross pounded into the ground at its head. It bore an inscription in French that Jess did not understand. Grass had just begun growing from the dirt over the grave.

The priest turned to Noah and spoke. They exchanged a few more words, and the priest pointed to a longhouse in the distance. Then he made the sign of the cross and left them. Jess fell to the grave and wept bitterly.

"Goddamn it, Jess, I can't let you stay here long," Noah told her. "It would look like I care."

She couldn't answer at first, too consumed with grief. "I hate them!" she finally managed to say. "I hate all of them, the French, the Indians, the stupid English who have no idea . . . what life is like out here. And I hate the fighting . . . the awful . . . ugly fighting!" She looked up at him. "If anything happens to you now I'll kill myself!"

"Stop it!" Noah jerked her up. "I'm so goddamn sorry, Jess," he told her. He looked around before continuing. "If I'd had any idea this would happen when I came through the first time, I would have found a way to take Billy then; but I knew, or thought, he'd be safe here until we could come for him. I couldn't take a child like that with me on the journey to find you."

She shook her head. "Are you blaming yourself?"

He closed his eyes and breathed deeply.

"Noah, it's not your fault. It's theirs! It's the fault of all this hideous fighting, all this selfish desire for land

and riches! Billy's death isn't your fault, Noah, nor are you responsible for the death of my family. You warned them, but my father insisted on staying another summer. You did all you could, Noah."

"It wasn't enough!" he said angrily. He blinked back his own tears. "Come on!"

He left the grave, and Jess had no choice but to follow. She glanced back at her brother's grave, feeling sick to her stomach. "Are we going to see the woman who adopted Billy?" she asked.

"Yes. Then we'll leave out in the morning with the soldiers." He stopped and whirled. "And if we're damn lucky," he added in a near whisper, "I'll find a way to betray the bastards!"

He turned and kept walking, and Jess hurried behind him, the grief over losing her family consuming her all over again. He took her to the French camp and untied the leather cord that kept her attached to him, then unloaded their supplies and ordered her to put up their tent. She did as he told her, and when the tent was finished, Noah shoved her inside. To the hoots and hollers of some of the soldiers, he ducked in behind her and closed the entrance flap.

"We'll find the Indian woman later," he told her, sitting down and pulling her into his lap. "I'm so damn sorry, Jess. So damn sorry."

She collapsed against his shoulder. He'd realized she needed this privacy, needed to cry, needed to be held. Noah Wilde was truly all she had left. She felt his own tears against her cheek.

"What did . . . the inscription on the cross say?" she sobbed.

Noah sighed. "It just said, 'Little White Boy Captive.'"

Jess cried harder. Yes, she thought, poor little white boy captive.

39

After a long march from La Présentation to Fort Toronto, from where they sailed across Lake Erie to Fort Niagara, the French troops marched south, arriving at Fort Presque Isle in mid-April. Only the officers rode horses, and Jess was surprised at the stamina of the infantry and the speed with which such a large force could travel. Those on foot carried huge canoes over their heads, which would be used to float soldiers along the Allegheny to the Monongahela for an attack on whatever English forces might be present. The canoes would also carry French cannon currently being hauled on special small-wheeled carriages pulled by horses.

Jess had seen few Indians, mostly Ottawa scouts. This was a purely French undertaking; Governor Duquesne was determined to show the might of his well-trained soldiers. Noah warned there were plenty more Iroquois following them out of curiosity, watching from behind every tree. The Iroquois intended to witness whatever confrontations might take place, interested, Noah explained, in learning which force was, in their eyes, the strongest.

Several times Noah spotted Indians lurking in the trees and underbrush along the crude, stump-filled roads the soldiers used. Every time Jess looked, she saw nothing. Jess could only shake her head at his ability to detect the silent stalkers. Now she understood how the Delaware had been able to sneak up on her family so easily. Like wild animals, the Iroquois seemed to have a way of melting into the landscape.

Once they reached Venango they would be only about fifty miles from the farm her father had so loved, and roughly forty miles from the confluence of the Allegheny and Monongahela, the very area where she and her family used to meet once-friendly Indians and traders for the annual gathering each fall. She refused to think about the condition the bodies of her loved ones must be in by now. She could only hope settlers had found them and had managed to bury the remains. To think that any other settlers would stay after finding the horrors there was amazing, but French traders at Presque Isle verified that the whole frontier was "infested" with English colonists.

Considering what she witnessed now, and knowing most Iroquois and other tribes were loyal to the French, Jess could hardly bear to think of what might lie ahead for those still occupying the frontier, most of whom probably thought they were perfectly safe.

From Presque Isle they marched to Fort Le Boeuf, and Jess felt an anxious excitement at knowing how close she and Noah were to truly being free. If only Billy were with them. Her heart went out to Noah, who still blamed himself. He wished he'd never even told her about Billy until he was sure they would find the boy. They had met the Iroquois woman who'd adopted Billy, and she verified Billy's death, although she did not seem overly concerned. Jess could hardly bear the thought of the fears and loneliness her little brother must have suffered, let alone being sick, with no loved ones to comfort him.

The French soldiers finally reached Venango, where they made camp and immediately began construction of Fort Machault just across the river from the older French establishment, which was still occupied by a Captain Daniel Joncaire. Most of the whores had long ago given up following. They and several of the wives had remained behind when the men sailed from Toronto. It was difficult, too, for Jess to keep up, but knowing she and Noah would soon be free gave her the strength to keep going.

To her great relief, for the last three days she and Noah had been able to rest. Today Contrecoeur had summoned Noah for new orders, and Jess waited anxiously for his return. She and Noah were camped some distance from the soldiers, as usual, so they would be able to speak without being heard.

Noah finally returned from his meeting. Knowing others could be watching, Jess pretended unconcern as he sat down near where she stirred a pot of boiled potatoes.

"Contrecoeur is leaving tomorrow with about seven hundred men and at least twelve to fifteen cannons," Noah told her quietly. "They'll canoe down the Allegheny to wherever it is the Indian scouts say an English fort is being built. The scouts say there aren't many men there. I don't know what the hell the English are thinking, but they don't have a force in the area that can even compare to this French attachment. Damn fools!"

Jess moved away from the fire and sat down across from him, looking at her lap. "Will we go with them?"

"Yes, mainly because Contrecoeur thinks you might come in handy as a way to bribe the English to surrender. My thinking is that getting them to surrender won't be any trouble at all. The Iroquois scouts say there are only about fifty men there, and they look half starved. They haven't made much progress on the fort. It isn't even half finished. I'm not worried about warning them because Contrecoeur seems the gentlemanly sort. He claims he'll allow them to surrender formally. No shots will be fired, unless they shoot first. I don't think this will be anything like what happened at Pickawillany, but it's our chance, Jess."

She couldn't help raising her eyes to meet his gaze then. "Really?"

Noah straightened and looked around, then took a cigar from a pocket inside his buckskin shirt. He reached out and held one end of it in the fire, then quickly put it to his lips to puff on it and keep it burning. He rested his elbows on his knees as he continued, looking around first.

"If this works out right, I may be able to convince Contrecoeur to let me take you east to see if I can trade you back to the English. I've already planted the idea in his head—told him I'm tired of you, and taking you back would give me an excuse to spy on Washington's forces farther east and see what he's up to. He knows I can speak good English and pass myself off as an English trader rather than French. Once we hook up with George Washington and whatever forces he has with him, I'll warn Washington what he's up against and then we'll be on our way."

Jess fought to hide her joy. "You make it sound so easy."

"It *will* be. Both sides trust me. We can do this, Jess. If I don't return but happen to run into any French leader later on who knows me, I'll just tell him Washington made a prisoner of me and I couldn't get back."

"You won't run into any French leaders, because we'll go to Albany and you'll be done with all this."

Noah just kept smoking and watching the woods around them. Finally he met her gaze. "We're almost home, Jess." His eyes sparkled with his own happiness.

Jess looked down again to hide her smile.

40

From what Noah could see of the pitiful-looking, half-finished fort the English were building, it was obvious that in spite of the excitement George Washington must have expressed over building a fort here, English authorities had most likely not voted for enough money, men or supplies to build the thing right.

Hundreds of blue-coated French soldiers disembarked from their canoes and hauled out fifteen cannons, while Noah and Jess and some of the officers who'd followed along the river on horseback met up with them. Noah was certain that whatever English were fortifying the meager excuse of a fort could see the French coming, yet there was no gunfire.

"They know they are already defeated," he told Captain Contrecoeur.

The man smiled with a pompous air. "Of course they do. As soon as we position the cannons, the place will be ours."

Noah turned to Jess. "Stay well behind until I return."

Within twenty minutes the cannons were well placed, and soldiers marched in formation toward the makeshift fort. Contrecoeur led the "attack" on a white horse, Noah riding beside him to act as interpreter. Noah spotted a few men, none in any particular uniform, positioning themselves along the half-built walls of their fortification, and when they drew closer, Contrecoeur ordered Noah to announce in English their presence and their intentions.

"Find out how many there are and who leads them," he said.

Noah was certain Washington was not here, or he would already be walking out of the fort to meet Contrecoeur face-to-face. He worried how he would explain himself if that happened, praying Washington would realize the bind he was in.

"Hello in there!" Noah shouted. "I am Noah Wilde, and the man beside me is Captain Pierre de Contrecoeur, aide-de-camp to none other than Governor Marquis Duquesne of New France. He has been sent here to warn all Englishmen to retreat from this location, as this is the property of New France. We have seven hundred men with us, and fifteen cannons. Who is in charge?"

One man slowly emerged from behind the flimsy-looking wall, a white handkerchief tied to his musket. "I am!" he answered. "Ensign Edward Ward!"

Noah frowned. "You are the highest-ranking officer?"

The man looked around and came a little closer. "The man in charge is Captain William Trent. He left with some of our men to go to Redstone Creek for food. If there is none there, he will go all the way back to Will's Creek. Our men are starving, and there are few of us. I would ask that you please not fire upon us."

Noah felt sorry for the young man. "Where is Major George Washington?" he asked. "Is he not the leader of your expedition?"

The man swallowed, obviously nervous. "Yes, sir. He is at Great Meadows waiting for reinforcements. He is no longer a major. He is a lieutenant colonel. His senior officer is Colonel Joshua Fry."

Noah was amazed and angered at how handily the young man gave out the information. He was even more amazed that young Washington had already been boosted to lieutenant colonel! He explained the situation to Contrecoeur, who simply shook his head and laughed.

"Tell them to surrender, or we will blow them and their pitiful fort to bits," the man told Noah.

Noah delivered the message. Ensign Ward walked back inside the fort, and within minutes approximately forty weary and hungry-looking men exited the establishment and lay down their arms in front of them. Contrecoeur looked at Noah. "This is apparently going to turn out to be a very boring day, my friend."

Secretly relieved, Noah agreed.

"Tell them to leave forthwith," the captain told him. "We will take no prisoners, as long as they head east and keep going."

Noah delivered the message, and some of the men half ran as they left, obviously glad to get out without being massacred. Noah decided that if he made it home, he would deliver a raging speech to Governors Clinton and Dinwiddie about their despicable foolishness, reminding them how utterly stupid the English looked this day, and how freely Ensign Ward gave out valuable information. If any Iroquois were watching, which undoubtedly they were, their minds would be made up after such a display. They would now consider the French formidable warriors, and they would consider Iroquois women more fierce and braver than any Englishman.

Contrecoeur ordered his men to move in and destroy the partially built English fort. Noah sat and watched, remembering Washington's excitement at building a fort here. Someone was going to be properly embarrassed for this. He would see to it!

"Have you thought about my suggestion that I take Jess to the English forces so I can see what they are up to?" he asked Captain Contrecoeur.

The captain turned to him. "You are one man. Don't you fear being shot for having an English captive, especially a woman?"

"Not if you let me leave now by horseback and get there ahead of the men you just let go. I can tell them their men are surrounded by seven hundred French soldiers and will be slaughtered if I don't return. It will give me enough time to see how many men Washington has and what they are up to. The men you just released are too weak to get very far today. By horseback I can get there by nightfall."

Contrecoeur sighed, frowning. "You're a brave man to go alone, Noah, but skilled at dealing with such situations. I suppose if you warn them about our forces here, that might protect you. However, I plan to send out a detachment of my own tomorrow morning, perhaps thirty or so men, to spy on Washington for me, just in case you don't make it back."

A detachment of spies! This was valuable information. "Sir, if I need to plan an escape, where will these men be?" Noah asked. "They might be able to help me and maybe even spring an attack on anyone following me."

Contrecouer brightened. "Good idea! Go to the same creek you showed me on the map yesterday, the one you said would be a good place for men to hide if I sent them to spy at Will's Creek or Great Meadows. The men will be there."

Noah nodded, remaining casual. "Thank you, sir." Inside he felt incredibly elated at being given so much information that Washington himself could use. Maybe there was hope after all of the English recovering at least a little bit of their pride over this matter.

"I'd better go right away," he told the captain. "There is plenty of daylight left, and I know this country well. I can make good time."

Contrecoeur nodded. "As long as your wench can keep up."

"She'll keep up if I have to drape her over her horse and hog-tie her."

Contrecoeur chuckled. "I can't imagine wanting to get rid of her, but it does give you a good excuse to go there," he answered. "Be gone with you, then. Matters here are obviously well taken care of."

"Yes, sir." Noah turned his horse and rode back to where he'd told Jess to wait for him. He reached her in less than five minutes and grabbed the reins of the extra packhorse. "Let's go," he told her.

"Is everything all right, Noah?"

"There wasn't even a shot fired. You and I have to take off right away. Be ready to ride hard."

"Whatever it takes," she answered, her eyes shining with hope.

Noah smiled. "You're the strongest woman I've ever known, Jess Matthews, and the bravest." He turned his horse and galloped off, heading east.

41

Noah charged toward the encampment at Great Meadows, freshly thawed sod spewing from the hooves of his three horses. Jess, sore and tired from the hard ride with only one three-hour stop for rest, felt elated. At last, after all these months, she would be surrounded by men and women who spoke English. At last, she and Noah could go home and start their new life together!

She heard men shouting to one another as they

approached. They were watched closely, and Jess did not doubt that consideration was given to shooting them. Noah had assured her that would not happen, since there were only two of them, and one was a woman. He turned out to be right, as a few men even seemed to recognize Noah now and greeted him by name with welcome looks on their faces.

"Is Lieutenant Colonel Washington here?" Noah called out when he came closer.

One of the men pointed to a spot in the distance where it looked as though a log wall was being erected. In spite of her inexperience in these things, Jess had seen enough up to this point to realize that here, too, the English were nowhere near as prepared for a fight as were the French, nor did they have enough men to even think about facing the French army she and Noah had just left behind.

She remembered Noah telling her that Captain Contrecoeur expected many more reinforcements to join him at Fort Duquesne, most likely already under construction. With seven hundred soldiers already there, four hundred more coming soon from Fort Machault, and hundreds more expected to be dispatched from Montreal, the whole area would soon be filled with thousands of French soldiers. Besides that, they would be joined by perhaps as many Iroquois, ready and thirsty for a good fight. She was glad Noah would not be involved in any of it.

They reached the group of men, who were huddled over a map. One of them, wearing an officer's red coat and a white wig, turned to greet Noah.

"I don't believe it!" he said, smiling.

Jess was surprised to see George Washington could not be much older than she. She'd been unable to picture such a young man as a high-ranking officer until now. He looked up at her as Noah dismounted almost before his horse even came to a complete halt. The animal snorted and shook its mane, sweat flying from its neck. Its breathing came in loud, wild pants.

"By God, you found her!" Washington practically yelled, putting out his hand. "I'm glad for you, my friend."

Noah shook his hand. "*Merci,*" he answered. "It took a while, but I did find her, and I found much more than the woman I was looking for, sir." He released his hold on Washington's hand. "And by the way, congratulations on your promotion to lieutenant colonel."

Washington grinned proudly. "I became quite the sensation when I returned from that first excursion. Dinwiddie put me in charge of this campaign—well, almost. I am working under Colonel Joshua Fry. We decided some of the more experienced men might not be too fond of answering to someone my age, but I'm learning, Noah, I'm learning."

Noah walked back to lift Jess down from her horse. "You're going to learn a lot faster when you hear what I have to tell you," Noah answered. "First, I'd like one of your men to show Jess the best place to make camp for the night."

"I want to stay with you," Jess told him. "I can wait."

Washington grinned and looked her over, then lost his smile when he noticed the scar at her neck. It was unusually warm, and she wore no outer cloak. "My dear young woman, what have you been through?"

Jess put a hand to the scar. Noah put a reassuring arm around her before continuing. "It's a long story," he told Washington. "Right now you need to know that there are French forces at the confluence of the Monongahela and Allegheny, the very place where you intended to build an English fort."

Washington sobered, motioning for Noah to walk with him away from the other men. Noah gave Jess a light hug before letting go of her and walking a few feet away with the lieutenant colonel. Jess followed, leading the sweating, panting horses.

"I left men there to start that fort," Washington told Noah.

"The French have already taken it and sent those men back east," Noah informed him. "They should arrive tonight or tomorrow. It was no contest, sir. They didn't have a chance and they knew it. I was glad to see they had sense enough to surrender."

Washington's face fell. "I see." He closed his eyes and swore. "Damn!" He turned to face the west. "It's that bad, is it?"

"There are upwards of a thousand French soldiers ready to march against you, and probably as many Indians. I can assure you, any Indians who witnessed what happened back there are going to join with the French. The Iroquois love a good fight, and they don't like losing. They'll figure that can't happen if they are with the French. It's getting bad, sir. Is this all the men and fortifications you have?" Noah looked around the camp, which was spread out in the meadows, wide open to attack.

"There are more coming from Will's Creek. Colonel Fry is there training Virginia volunteers. We'll have plenty of men soon."

"Maybe not soon enough, and maybe not enough men at that. Let me guess—the House of Burgesses refused to permit the money and men Dinwiddie asked for."

Washington nodded with a sigh. "More will come than we'd hoped for, Noah. I have to believe that." He faced Noah. "How soon will the French come?"

"Within two weeks, I suspect. Maybe sooner. I have a plan, however, that could delay them for a while, as well as help you make up for losing the fort site at the Allegheny."

Washington stuck his thumbs into the pockets of the satin vest he wore under his red coat. "And what is that?"

"They are under a Captain Contrecoeur, to whom I was able to get close. He told me his plans. He's sending about thirty men this way to spy on you and see just what the situation is here. I know exactly where they will camp. I can lead some of your own men there for an attack."

"Noah!" Jess spoke up. "Don't get involved in more of this! You said we'd go home."

"I know what I said, and I meant it," Noah answered, still looking at Washington. "But something has to be done to deter the French troops. I'm the only one who knows where the soldiers are who will come into this area to spy. We need to take men there and wipe them out. When they don't return, Contrecoeur just might think twice about attacking, thinking maybe your forces here are stronger than he thought. It could buy you some time. Believe me, if more men don't arrive soon, you'd be better off marching back to Will's Creek than staying here, sir."

Washington rubbed his chin and turned to pace for a moment, thinking. "I suppose the way of the frontier is to simply go in there and kill every Frenchman and every Indian with them?" he asked, facing Noah again.

"It's the only way to send the right message," Noah answered. "Are there many Indians here to help?"

Washington smiled again but looked worried. "Your Seneca friend Chief Monakaduto is here with about fifty warriors. We have at least *some* help from the Indians."

"Good. I'll take Monakaduto and some of his men with me, and you, of course, should go. This is your battle, Lieutenant Colonel, a chance to make up for the disgrace that just took place this morning!"

Jess could hardly believe her ears.

"How many of my own men should go?" Washington asked.

"I would take roughly forty men, if you can spare them. French forces won't be coming here anytime soon, so the rest would be safe, and I'll leave Jess here."

"Noah!" He seemed to pay no attention to her.

"Contrecoeur will wait for this spy party to return, and for more men to arrive from Montreal, so you have a good two weeks. Maybe by then your enforcements at Will's Creek will arrive. In the meantime, you have to dig in and be ready. Right now you have no real defensive shelter."

"Yes, well, I will take care of that when we return. When should we leave out?"

"Tomorrow. They will be there by then, and we can sneak up on them at night."

Washington grinned, some of his confidence obviously returning. "Good idea. I'll go speak with the others about it." He put out his hand again. "It's good to see you, Noah. I'm glad you've made it back unharmed, and with the woman you were looking for. You're a good man to have around. I will be sure to tell that to Governor Dinwiddie, and rightfully scold him for having you imprisoned last summer."

Noah shook his hand. "I would most certainly appreciate that."

Washington left them, and Jess fought tears. "Why are you doing this!" she asked. "We can just keep riding, Noah! Why do you have to turn right around and risk your life again after all we've been through?"

He faced her. "Because the English can't let the disaster back there get out of hand. Something has to be done, or the next thing you know the French army will march the colonists all the way to the sea and back to England!"

"That could never happen!"

"Couldn't it? Don't be as blind as the rest of them, Jess. You've already seen what's happening. People have to wake up!"

She turned away. "My God, you're just like the rest of them."

"What do you mean by that?"

She wiped at angry tears. "You're no different from the French or the English or even the Iroquois. You've smelled blood. The fever of the fight is in you. You have a score to settle." She faced him. "One side wins, then the other, and the fighting and hatred go on and on. Pride and winning and showing who is the strongest take precedence over everything, even happiness!"

"Jess—"

"I'm tired of all of it!" She clenched her fists, wanting to hit him.

"It isn't for pride or a desire for battle, Jess. It's for what's *right!*" he answered, anger coming into his own voice. "You know as well as I do that if this isn't stopped, what happened to your family and to

Mary will happen to hundreds of others, including women and children. The English have to act soon or they are going to face disaster. We are headed for all-out war, and you know how hideous that will get with practically the entire Iroquois Nation on the side of the French. It's imperative that the English send a message to the French that this can't continue, and they have to show the Iroquois some strength or the natives will run over us like wolves after rabbits!"

Jess studied him, almost wishing he were not quite so noble. "You can't solve the problem all by yourself, Noah."

"I know that. But, Jess, I have to do this one last thing." He grasped her arms. "I've already promised Washington I would lead him to the right place. Monakaduto and his Seneca will be with us, and a good forty Englishmen. This will be a surprise attack. I'll be fine. I promise, when I get back we'll head out the very next day and that will be the end of it. In the meantime, I want you to stay with the few women who are here. They'll look after you and let you rest. Promise me in return that you *will* rest, Jess."

She nodded her head, wiping at tears. "Sometimes it frightens me when I see the thirst for a fight in your eyes; yet God knows if you weren't the way you are, I might not even be standing here safe right now. It's just that it seems like the fighting will never end." She looked up at him. "Tell me it will end, Noah, at least for you."

He leaned down and kissed her forehead, her eyes. "It will end." He studied her lovingly. "There is usually a chaplain accompanying troops like this. If there is one here, we'll get married today. If not, there's sure to be one at Will's Creek. We'll stop there and marry. That's a promise."

"First you have to come back," she answered.

"I came back, and found you against a lot of odds, didn't I? And before that I fought five Ottawa to keep you alive. I'll come back this time, too, Jess. I haven't broken one promise to you yet, and I won't break this one."

"No one can control their own destiny," she warned.

"No, but they can at least try to do something about it, maybe more about the destiny of others than their own. And after what happened to you and your family, you should want this as much as I do, Jess."

She watched him sadly. "Oh, I do; but you've done your share, my darling Noah. It's time for you to go home and be a husband and a father and have some peace."

"And I'll do just that, as soon as I take care of this one last matter." He leaned down and kissed her forehead. "We'll have that peace, Jess."

He turned to go and talk to Washington again, and Jess watched with an aching heart. "Will we, Noah?" she asked softly.

42

Jess sat listening to the downpour. The torrential rain only added to her concerns. Noah, Monakaduto and his Seneca, Washington and the men with him were out in this miserable weather getting soaked, while at the same time making their way in the dark to wherever it was the French soldiers were most likely camped.

She'd learned enough in traveling with Noah and with the soldiers that rain meant damp gunpowder and useless weapons. If their muskets and pistols would not work, that meant using knives and hatchets, which the Indians who'd accompanied them would probably do, anyway. All of that meant more blood.

She shivered into a blanket. The rain made it seem colder than it really was; but she knew it wasn't the weather that made her tremble. It was just plain worry.

There was no chaplain in camp. She and Noah would have to wait until they reached Will's Creek to marry, but first he had to survive this last battle.

Thunder rumbled in the distance, and the rain poured down even harder. Some of it began to leak right through the tent, and she moved to avoid the drips.

What was he doing now? Had they reached the French soldiers? Was Noah this moment fighting them? They had all left this morning, Noah and Monakaduto in the lead, Monakaduto and his men painted for war. Even Noah had applied black paint under his eyes. With his long hair and buckskins, he hardly looked different from the rest of the Indians. The plan was to ride hard and reach their location by nightfall, then leave the horses at a distance so the French would not hear them coming. Jess thought how ironic it would be if Noah were killed now, after all they had been through. If that happened, the faith in God she'd clung to through all of this would be destroyed.

The rain finally let up for a while, and it felt a little warmer. She lay down on the blanket-covered straw Noah had carried into the tent and heaped up for her so she would have a bed softer than the hard ground. She rested her head on a bedroll and listened to the night sounds—crickets, an owl, the sound of men talking in the distance. She heard a woman's voice. The few women who were here had been kind to her, but she saw how some of them noticed her neck and seemed curious. She could just imagine what they were thinking. She'd kept her hair down straight, hoping to hide her ears until they were thoroughly healed.

How could these women understand what she'd been through? It was impossible to explain. They only knew her family had been killed by Indians and she'd been a captive; but they didn't know the true horror of what she'd witnessed, nor could they imagine the gut fear she'd experienced when dragged away. Unless they went through something like that themselves, they could not, in their wildest imaginations, understand how bad it really was.

She supposed that was why these women and most of the men here and everyone who lived in places like Albany and Alexandria could not possibly understand the French threat. They were living perfectly peaceful, comfortable lives, with no inkling of life on the frontier. Much as she hated to admit it, Noah was right in saying they had to be *made* to understand, and that all the eastern colonies had to band together and donate money, men, horses, wagons and weapons to fortify the frontier.

What a strange turn her life had taken from a year ago. The ache in her heart from losing her beloved mother and loving father and big brother, and her sweet little Billy, the good life they'd shared for twelve years in the wilderness—that ache would never leave her. She vowed that when they reached Albany she would write about it, do what she could to enlighten eastern settlers about the perils and bravery of the frontier pilgrims.

She ached from sheer worry mixed with anger at men and war and Indians and wilderness. She tried to concentrate on the night sounds, thinking that if there was any fighting going on, maybe she would hear gunshots. It always seemed that sound carried farther at night; but then, they were probably much too far away. It was silly to think she could hear anything.

Listen and wait. Listen and wait. That was all she could do. The rain came down now in a soft drizzle that was almost soothing. She felt tired from the inside out, and her weariness caught up with her, sending her into a deep sleep from which she did not awaken until the faint light of dawn.

She jumped awake, the quick memory of where Noah had gone the night before hitting her with cruel reality. She rose and went out, having never undressed the night before. The rain was over and the sun was rising in a clear sky. She would be glad when it rose high enough to dry things out, as most of the tents sagged from a soaking, and the high grass was still very wet.

She still wore the winter moccasins Thunder had given her because they were so comfortable. On chilly, wet mornings they were perfect for walking in high grass. She thought how one day she would tell her grandchildren about her capture. She would show them her Delaware moccasins.

She rinsed her face from a bucket of water and smoothed her fingers through her hair to straighten it, thinking how wonderful it was going to be to live in a real house again and dress normally; most of all, to be clean and be able to wash her hair. She could only hope the scar at her neck would keep fading. Until then she would have to wear high-necked dresses.

Noah understood. In his arms she felt beautiful. What would she ever do without him? Again anxiety made her chest tighten painfully. She headed for one of the several privies built in the distance, then joined the four other women present in helping make something to eat for the remaining men camped there. Two of the women wore the same worried look that Jess did. Their husbands were with those who'd gone to attack the French spies.

"I'm sure they will be fine," one woman spoke up. Her husband was here in camp. The comment opened a conversation that lasted throughout the preparation of breakfast, such as it was. There was little meat left, with more supplies to come from Will's Creek, along with the promised reinforcements. Jess was beginning to wonder if that would ever happen, but she kept that worry to herself. To think of what this camp would face if a large French army attacked was too horrible to consider. Her biggest worry was that Noah would realize that also and decide to stay and help Washington.

When would all this end? She ate little, helped with cleanup, then sat and chatted with the worried women, who formed a sewing circle to mend shirts and pants and the like while they waited . . . and waited.

It was early evening when the attack party finally appeared on the horizon. Men scrambled for their muskets, taking positions behind what Jess considered poorly built wooden barricades. They had to first be sure the right men were coming, as even from the distance they could see blue-and-white French uniforms. The women gathered together behind a barricade and watched as more men appeared. Jess spotted Washington's red coat, then several men dressed in an array of normal wear and carrying muskets.

"It's Washington!" she shouted. "They must be bringing back prisoners!"

They all began moving out of their hiding places, still cautious. Now they could see the French soldiers were walking, but the men behind them rode horses. Of course! They were prisoners. The attack had been successful!

Jess noticed two of the Frenchmen carried a stretcher. Someone was wounded. *Please don't let it be Noah,* she prayed. She began running, searching. Several others ran with her, and several of the men surrounded the French prisoners, some of whom Jess recognized. Still she did not see Noah.

Then came the Seneca. They began yipping and shouting to announce a victory, and as they came closer she recognized Monakaduto, who held up a fresh scalp. She no longer needed to imagine what had taken place. She knew from experience. Most likely the muskets had failed because of the rain. Monakaduto and his warriors had likely moved in with their tomahawks and wreaked havoc on the camp. The sight of the warriors, still painted and celebrating, brought back painful memories.

Finally, Noah's horse appeared. Jess breathed a sigh of relief, but when he came closer she saw blood on his face. When he reached her she could see it was from a deep cut on his right cheek, from the side of his nose all the way down to his jawbone. It was scabbed now, but she could tell it was deep enough that it would leave a scar on his handsome face.

He halted his horse and just looked at her for a moment, then slowly dismounted.

"Are you hurt anyplace else?" she asked.

"No." He put an arm around her and walked with her, leading his horse by the reins. "Nine of them were killed," he told her, "a few with musket fire, but most of the gunpowder was too damp to do much good. It was the same for the French."

"I thought of that. I was worried about fighting with knives and tomahawks." She stopped and turned to hug him. "Thank God you're back."

He dropped the reins to his horse and put his arms around her. "Two got away, Jess, and of course there are these prisoners here, all of whom know now that I'm an English spy. Word will get back to Chief Pontiac, Charles Langlade, Governor Duquesne, all of them. I won't dare set foot in French territory again. If I'm caught I'll be hung, or turned over to the Iroquois to die slowly."

"Then let's get out of here, Noah." She looked up at him. "Let's go home and be done with the fighting."

He looked at her strangely. "Do you realize what is going to happen to Washington and the men here once those forces back at Fort Duquesne realize what has happened?"

"Maybe they will figure the forces here are stronger than they thought and they won't come."

He sighed. "They'll come, all right. They'll come. And it won't stop here." He leaned down and kissed her hair. "At least we've sent a message. We are not going to sit back and let the French run over us."

The terms "we" and "us" worried her. She met his gaze. "Tell me we're leaving now, Noah."

He sighed, looking around the camp.

"Noah?"

He studied her a moment. "Yes, we'll leave today. I made you a promise. The first thing we will do is find a preacher to marry us. One thing I have to do when we reach Virginia is tell Governor Dinwiddie what is going on here and see if he can send out more men and supplies. I have to at least do that much, Jess."

"Of course." She smiled through tears. "I love you, Noah Wilde. We're free now. We can finally live a normal life."

He smiled almost sadly, touching her face lovingly. "Let's hope so," he answered. "We'll give it a damn good try." He leaned closer and met her lips in a gentle kiss, then kissed her eyes. Then he surprised her by suddenly picking her up and swinging her around before setting her on his horse. He leaped up behind her and kicked the horse into a gentle lope. "Let's go pack our things and go home."

Jess leaned against his chest, enjoying the sound of the words. She wanted to hope that Noah Wilde was done with fighting; but this war was just beginning, and Noah Wilde was a man of honor, a man who took too many responsibilities upon himself. She decided that, after all she'd been through, she could now only take life a day at a time, and enjoy the days like this one, the days when she could feel safe in Noah Wilde's arms.

Center Point Publishing
600 Brooks Road ● PO Box 1
Thorndike ME 04986-0001 USA

(207) 568-3717

US & Canada:
1 800 929-9108